THE GRACELAND CONSPIRACY

PHILIP SHIRLEY

For Louella,
From one thriller lover
to another!
Enjoy!.

Philip Shirley

MINDBRIDGE PRESS

ISBN 978-1-7322707-1-8
LCCN 2019934565

Book Cover by James Harwell
Book Interior Design by Felicia Kahn
Author Photo by Virginia Shirley

Printed in United States of America
Published in Florence, Alabama

First Edition

Dedication

This book is dedicated to the King of Rock and Roll for the 50th Anniversary of his Comeback Special.

And to Mozelle Purvis Shirley whose countless hours reading to me at a very young age imprinted on my soul the value of the written word.

Praise for *The Graceland Conspiracy*

"Philip Shirley's latest page-turner is preposterously entertaining…and Hollywood-ready. From Texas pool halls to Alabama hide-outs to Mexico, Munich, and Venice, this couple-on-the-run tale of government heavies and Elvis intrigues takes more turns than a Hound Dog 45 rpm from 1956. You'll be tempted to pick up the phone and spoil the last-page surprise for your reading pals…but don't be cruel."

Charles McNair, author of *The Epicureans*

"Prodigal son meets government deception meets murder mystery in Philip Shirley's latest. Chock full of dead bodies, men in suits, and a grainy film that just might lead to one of the biggest conspiracies of a generation, *The Graceland Conspiracy* is crazy good fun, a pacey, globe-trotting thriller with a Southern twist."

Michelle Richmond,
New York Times Bestselling
author of *The Marriage Pact*

"Elvis has left the building…or not. Philip Shirley's Graceland Conspiracy is a genre-busting novel full of unexpected twists, tension, and fascinating characters."

Reed Farrel Coleman,
New York Times Bestselling
author of Robert B. Parker's *Colorblind*

"Philip Shirley is a terrific writer, better with each new book."

Tom Franklin,
New York Times Bestselling
author of *Crooked Letter, Crooked Letter*

"An ingenious mystery…fans of thrillers and Elvis alike can have reason to believe their expectations will be well-received in *The Graceland Conspiracy.*"

Kirk Curnutt,
award-winning
author of *Raising Aphrodite*

"The greatest thing a human soul ever does in this world is to *see* something, and tell what it *saw* in a plain way."

John Ruskin, 1843
Modern Painters

part I

NORTH AMERICA
1999

chapter 1

Before the fight started, I'd been working the back pool table for an hour in a dive east of San Antonio, hustling this burly guy who thought he was a hot stick. I'd take a game, let him take one or two. Patience was a friend as I waited for the right moment to take his money, though when the time came the outcome wasn't exactly what I'd hoped.

I'd learned strategy for money games reading a paperback on how to make money at blackjack someone had left in a fleabag motel room. Blackjack and pool and just about any other betting game has one foundation—making money isn't about the number of bets you win. A fat wallet is directly proportional to your nerve to raise the stakes when the time is right.

I found the bar by accident in Sequin, a few miles from my apartment, as I rode along the Guadalupe River that twisted through the county and split the town in two with a well-kept grassy park hugging the river banks. The place was known mostly for a big pecan festival. Cruising through on a bike I'd custom-built, I saw the sign just ahead of the traffic light that stopped me. Clouds were beginning to reflect the orange sunset, so I knew most of the guys in the saloon would be on round two or three. Time to play. A few chopped Harleys lined the front of the bar. I figured it was worth checking out. They had to have a ten-dollar pool game.

The red neon sign said Red's Bar.

Waiting for the light to change, I wondered about the story of this place. It didn't take a genius to see what had happened. Up and coming developers had moved out here on the edge of town in the sixties, always just ahead of the urban sprawl even this little town of twenty-five thousand couldn't resist. The dreamers had thrown up shoddy little shopping strips of six or eight stores at a time with big glass fronts and cheap metal awnings anchored by a backlit sign on a big white pole with auspicious names like Miracle Strip Shopping. Weeds and trash now lined the thin asphalt parking lots.

I scanned the historical marker at the corner, which indicated an "Indian fighter" lived in a clapboard house that once stood on this site. They still boasted that Texas Ranger Jack Hays had lived here when he ran the Comanches out of this part of Texas, long before he left for the California gold rush and helped found Oakland.

Half a block down I turned into the lot. Red's was a typical Texas bar scene. Guys in jeans and scuffed cowboy boots perched on a few wobbly mix-and-match wooden bar stools with half the arms torn off. Lone Star and Dixie beer neon glowed in every window. Car tags covered the bathroom doors from places as far away as Alaska and Maine. Window air conditioning units wedged into holes cut through the walls blasted a steady stream of cold air.

Peanut shells crunched as I walked to the far end of the bar near the pool games. Only a few black and white linoleum tiles held on, leaving bare concrete slab in places. Eight or ten bras—none dainty—hung from tacks above two televisions behind the bar. A juke box blared non-stop with a mix of Texas bands from Bob Wills to ZZ Top. One TV showed President Clinton—still trying to make the most of his second term—shaking hands with a small

Asian man, but there was no sound and I would guess no one but the bartender ever even glanced at the screen. The Yankees were playing someone on the other TV. Joe Torre was shaking his head, mouth open, saying nothing as he stared down at a short squat ump from two feet. Blue smoke swirled below the black-painted ceiling, reminding me of the storm clouds you could see coming for miles out there where it's so flat. Too bad I'm not that good at predicting the weather.

I took a high stool near the back table, ordered a beer, and waited. A wet-dog smell hung in the air. Several guys stood around watching or waiting their turn to play the five-dollar game, but the same guy seemed to win them all. I was a few beers down the road when the last loser threw another five on the table and wandered off to the bar shaking his head. The winner looked around for another game. No one stepped up. There were rules in places like this, so I waited, knowing I needed to be invited. I shrugged when our eyes met and said I'd give it a try if he'd spot me the break on the first game. Five bucks he said. The first few games were back and forth as I tried to see if he was a hustler or just spent too much time in bars. He was good, but he didn't seem to be holding anything back. Even after four or five beers I could take him.

Watching hundreds of pool games and making all sorts of wagers taught me one thing. When people get greedy—and that's most of the time—you can use it against them. I knew right off this guy would get greedy, so I thought I'd prime his pump. I was down ten and figured he had been counting, too. "Double it up?" I asked.

He nodded, holding back a smile as he cut his eyes over to his friends, but I saw it. Just the tiniest hint he thought he had me. He'd heard those words before.

He took the first game after I intentionally hung a seven in the pocket with the eight and nine in perfect position. Then I won back-to-back ten-dollar games that were oh-so-close and made him think he should have won every game, even though we were even on the money. His buddies were snickering in the background and talking in low voices. That did the trick.

He leaned on his stick, thinking. He was feeling it. The odds were in his favor. I couldn't take three in a row just on luck.

"Screw this small-time crap. Make it a hunnert," he said, just loud enough for his buddies to hear.

The din seemed to diminish a bit.

"That's a little out of my league."

"Come on cowboy. Don't be a pussy. One game."

Now his friends were laughing at me. His ego and his testosterone both spiked. Perfect.

I shrugged. "It's only money I guess."

I let him win the lag since I hadn't seen him run a table but once in two hours. He broke and sank the two ball, then made the one, three, four, and five before he lipped the six on a nice try at a cross-bank shot. I tapped in the six and ran the seven through nine and stood there leaning on my stick, shaking my head like I'd had a very lucky break. I waited for burly boy to fork over the hundred bucks. He stared at me, not moving. The wheels in his head were spinning. Finally he slid his hands into his tight front jeans pocket and removed a wad of twenties, which he held up and waved in front of a big fake smile as he stared at me. But he didn't hand them over. Just what I feared, but I wasn't that surprised.

He laughed and waved the clenched fist full of bills under my nose as he leaned across the pool table, close enough for his beer and cigarette breath to roll toward me like a dust cloud. "Listen Shithead, you think you can come in here and hustle us? If you want this money all you got to do is come over here and take it."

Behind him his buzz-cut friend laughed and crossed his arms, waiting to see if I tried anything. He was tall enough that even at six-one I had to look up at him, so I figured he'd go six-four or five. But too much meth had him thinned down to about 170 dressed and in his boots. His leather vest hung straight down like it was on a wire hanger. Without a gun, he wouldn't be much trouble. I'd scanned the room for obvious guns and had seen none so far.

My big boy pool competitor tilted his head back, shook long, greasy red hair out of his face, and began to drain a full Lone Star beer as if he'd won the game.

One of the things I know about money pool is that if you want the money, you live with a few difficulties in collecting a bet now and again. I'd bet right, and the odds had been in my favor to win. But the odds of collecting were different, and the rules—how should I say this?—the rules were that if you couldn't win by the rules then you had to change them.

Every town big and small that I've ever been through has at least one hall with a money game, but often the guys who hang there treat outsiders like, well, outsiders. And Texas seems to have more of these little bars and pool halls than most places I've lived. Winning was the easy part. Getting your money and your ass out the door in one piece, now that's another issue.

I glanced over to make sure the back door was unlocked while I decided what to do to get the hundred bucks I'd won. One guy wasn't much of a worry. Two made it more than interesting. I figured it was grab and run, now or never. Part of me knew I should walk away.

On one of my dad's few sober days during my teens, he taught me something that had saved my ass more than a few times. I guess I was about twelve at the time. It was the mid-eighties and, if you recall, our political correctness suggested that boys shouldn't be boys anymore and fighting wasn't accepted as just a part of growing up. "I don't want you fighting," he told me. "There's no shame in walking away. But if you ever see a time it can't be avoided, forget all that macho fair fight crap. Get in the first punch and make it a good one."

His voice had trailed off, and his eyes got a faraway look in them when he said, "That'll win most fights."

Now, fifteen years later, his words came back to me. This was one of those times a fair fight wasn't an option, and my first lick was one Dad would approve.

When the butt of my pool cue landed square on the fingers of the big guy's thick hand, the longneck bottle he held exploded in his face like a glass grenade. His other hand released the five twenties. For a moment, it was like time stood still. Movement stopped as everyone seemed to turn their heads toward us. The entire bar grew silent as the bills floated onto the table covered in glass shrapnel, beer foam, and blood. That was the first step of my plan, if you could call it one.

Burly Boy wouldn't be swinging at me with that hand, or even taking a piss with it for a long time. When he bent over screaming and put the bloody hand between his knees, I brought the cue down on the back of his thick neck. Not hard enough to kill him, but hard enough to even the two-on-one fight a little. All that time I spent lifting weights hadn't been wasted.

He slumped like a sack of potatoes dumped in the floor and then rolled onto his side and moaned.

From the bar stools, someone yelled, "Son of a bitch!"

I swept up the twenties and stuffed them into my jeans pocket as I spun around swinging my cue at whatever drunk might be joining this fight.

I almost waited too long. His lanky buddy cranked a homerun swing at my head with his own cue. I ducked and turned my head sideways, a fraction late. He didn't crush my skull, but it was a good try.

"How's that feel?" he yelled, drawing back his leg to kick me. "You still want that money?"

Later I'd find the cut wasn't that bad, but right then I expected to feel skin folded down over my ear as I reached up, stumbling forward off balance toward the guy and the boot I knew was coming fast.

I dropped to my knees, but I managed to swing my stick toward his right kneecap with one hand. I didn't have the strength for a hard lick, but made contact and slowed him down enough so the kick meant for my ribs just shoved me. I rolled under the pool table and came up on the other side next to where Burly Boy was on his knees trying to stand up.

My ear ached as I scanned the back of the room for anything that might be between me and the exit. Warm blood ran inside my left ear. This was a fight I couldn't win if reinforcements joined, first lick or not. These two didn't scare me so much, but the guys in sleeveless blue jean shirts at the bar had all turned around and stopped laughing as they waited to see if the two guys needed help. Not a good sign.

My homerun hitter was one of those skinny guys made of tanned leather cut at odd angles. On each of his huge forearms that seemed out of place on the meth-thin body, he sported a rattlesnake tattoo. He limped around the pool table and broke the pool cue over his knee. I guess the knee didn't hurt that much after all, and perhaps I had underestimated him. He clutched two sharp stakes that could skewer a pig.

I saw movement in the shadow beside the juke box. A tall, crew-cut, white-haired man in a dark suit stepped up ghost-like, grabbed a ball from a side pocket, and slammed Rattlesnake Man's forehead. His eyes rolled up in his head, and he dropped forward face first. Two teeth rolled across the floor like bloody dice.

The Suit was muscled up. Even in street clothes I could tell he was a gym rat. His shoulders were broad, and he had the neck of a linebacker. There was no fold below his chiseled chin. I raised my fist as Suit stepped toward me. He looked me in the eye and said, "Well, we'd better go." His tone was urgent but not panicked. It almost seemed he was holding back a laugh.

I wasn't sure what was happening and hesitated, thinking of just running, but it seemed obvious he was on my side.

"Let's go. Neither of us is welcome here," he said, more urgently this time, as he took my arm and pushed toward the back door, not even looking to be sure the guy stayed down. Clearly, he wasn't just some old guy in his Sunday best. White hair or not, he gripped my arm like a vise. I couldn't see why I should argue with someone who'd just saved me from an ass whipping, so I ran alongside him across the parking lot. My old friend Bugs loved to say never kick a gift horse in the mouth, so I opted to ride the horse.

"There," he said, pointing toward a black Crowne Vic as he

pulled out the remote door opener. As the lights blinked, I saw the car was closer than my bike, which was near the front door. The decision to make it for his car was easy after four or five guys flooded out the door as angry as whitewater. We sprinted the last twenty yards across the gravel. He waved me to the passenger side, and we both slammed our doors as we flopped into the front seats.

I yelled at Suit. "Get the hell out of here."

"Don't be in such a rush."

The guy just looked in the rearview mirror and watched as guys spread out and started to inch toward the car. They were hunched over staring through the back window, arms spread, looking from side to side at each other like something was wrong. Or maybe they were worried about a gun.

"Go, dammit," I yelled again.

"Not just yet."

He said it kind of gently and matter of fact, in a way that was oddly reassuring, considering we were about to get our butts kicked if he didn't make the right move.

"I don't like to speed," he told me, like that explained everything.

Suit put the car in reverse and spun the tires. We rocketed backwards toward the men behind us. They dove to the side in the gravel. The car slammed into the row of Harleys parked in front of the bar, smashing them into a pile of scrap metal against the side of the cinder block building.

I yelled at him to stop. Too late of course.

"One of those bikes was mine!"

He never even looked at me as he pitched the car in drive and shot a stream of gravel rocks out behind us all the way across the lot. The tires screamed when they bit pavement at the blacktop.

Only then did he look over at me and ask, "Would you rather I left you there?"

He drove toward McQueeny and on through the little pickup-truck towns of Marion, Cibolo, and Schertz. No one followed us. He eased back on the gas as soon as we hit sixty-five and just held it there, slowing to forty-five inside the small towns.

He was taking a familiar route toward Universal City where I lived just outside San Antonio. My head pounded like a diesel engine. The blood in my hair was beginning to dry. My shirt smelled like stale beer from rolling on the bar floor. I didn't know what was happening, but I knew if he wanted to hurt me, all he'd needed to do was nothing.

Half an hour after we left the bar, he steered the big car into my apartment parking lot and backed into a space near the back where he could still see the entrance. Suit hadn't said much since we left the bar parking lot, despite me peppering him with questions about who he was and what was going on. He'd handed me a handkerchief from his coat pocket, and I still held it against my head to make sure I stopped the bleeding. He put a small white card about the size of a business card on the seat between us. A phone number was written on it. No name.

Then came the stunner. "You need to call home."

I told him thanks for the help back at the bar. But who was he? And why was he helping me?

He said none of that was important, just call home.

I told him he had me mixed up with somebody else, that I didn't even have a home to call.

I remember exactly what he said next. One of those mind photos that sticks there like it's burned into your brain. "Your name is

Matthew Boykin. Marshall Boykin, retired from the National Security Enforcement Office, is your father. You left home seven years ago and have never been back. You're twenty-seven, six-one, and weigh somewhere around a hundred ninety-five pounds. You live in apartment 171 B. You've been arrested five times in three states since you turned twenty-one, but have no felonies. You've ridden with at least two biker clubs but never affiliated, and for some reason you don't have a known tattoo. That phone number is your parents' home in Birmingham, Alabama. Now get your bleeding ass off my seat and call home. Your father's been in a serious wreck."

chapter 2

When I sobered up the morning after the bar fight, I sat in my boxers at the kitchen table in my apartment near San Antonio, drinking milk from a quart carton and trying to figure out who in the hell was the man in the suit. My head had a hot poker sticking in the side of it from the whiskey shots I'd drunk the night before to go to sleep, and my hair was matted with dried blood on one side. Staring out the back door that I'd apparently left wide open, I tried to understand what had happened in the bar. I hadn't used my real name in four years, yet the Suit knew it. He knew too much. Way too damn much.

I found the aspirin next to the sink and downed four or five, sticking my mouth under the sink faucet to help me swallow. The little white card he'd given me lay on the table between a plate smeared with catsup and a crumpled beer can. I again read the number written on it in black ink, though I didn't need to. The number hadn't changed in the years since I left home.

Technically you can't call what I did running away from home. After all, I was twenty, in college, and of legal age in Alabama, but that's what my leaving amounted to. I simply couldn't deal with my Dad any longer, and the way Mom defended him turned me a little bitter toward her, too. I couldn't understand how she could defend his worthless ass and frequent drinking until he passed out.

I couldn't stand to be yelled at to get out of the house. I couldn't stand to see him yell at Mom and her simply walk away and let him get away with that kind of abuse.

One day in the middle of a class at UAB, I just left. I walked out of a math exam that made me feel wholly unprepared for college, got on my Honda 305 Superhawk, and drove away. The bike was one of the last Superhawks they made before the last one in 1967 but was still in great shape. A guy on our block had bought it new. He kept it garaged for twenty years, and I hardly ever saw him ride. He later restored it completely. When he died from a heart attack, I bought it from his widow cheap, and she let me pay a little along.

I stopped by the house just long enough to grab four hundred in cash I'd saved from mowing lawns and to write a short message to Mom, but I honestly can't even remember what I said except I was leaving. Didn't stop until I arrived in San Francisco after five days, one flat tire, a broken chain, a couple of cheap roadside motel rooms, and half of my four hundred in savings gone.

I meant only to disappear for a couple of weeks, to get away, maybe to send a signal or something that I couldn't stand what was happening at home. I honestly can't describe it. But once I left, it was like I was just drifting free on ocean currents. When the mystery man saved my butt and told me to call home, I hadn't talked to my parents for nearly eight years. I'd written my girlfriend Kristine a few times, but she never answered. Three or four times I'd mailed a post card to my father's friend David Collier, telling him things were okay and to please tell Mom. I couldn't recall when I'd written last, but I remembered why. It'd been one of those moments when I'd seen some couple that reminded me of how happy my parents had been back before the whiskey ruined everything.

Now here I was, staring at my old phone number, given to me by a man I'd never seen before and who had no obvious way of knowing me. I wasn't using my real name because of what happened out in California, but that's not a part of this story. A stranger in a business suit saving me in a bar fight and telling me to contact home made no sense. I'll never forget the man's eyes when he handed me the card. They flashed pure cold steel, but it was a look of strength, not anger or meanness. Something friendly behind the look made me think I should listen. I picked up the phone and dialed. The phone rang four or five times at the other end. Halfway glad no one picked up, I was about to hang up when I heard, "Hello, this is the Boykin residence."

Despite the years I'd been away, I recognized the soft voice immediately. Soft, yet confident. Very proper. Each word enunciated with emphasis on the right syllable, despite the heavy Greek accent. Mr. Costeridies. From across the street. A small man who couldn't be more than five feet four in his thick-soled black Sunday shoes. Even when I was a child, he seemed like an old man, but now he sounded like he was a hundred. I struggled with a simple answer.

I'm sure he could hear me breathing hard. "Hello, hello? Who is there? Is someone there?"

Finally, I swallowed hard and answered, "Mr. Costeridies, this is Matt."

"Matthew, hello. Your mother needs you here now," he said, without explanation or even a howdy-do. His voice was like that of most men his age who have learned that what you've got is what you're going to get and have accepted it. Nothing much knocks them off course any more. They seem to know that all of us muddle through just fine and then fake it when we have to or we're not sure what to do. "Do you know about your father's wreck?"

"Someone told me he had one. How is he?"

"He's stable. I'm just over at their house now trying to do what little I can to help out," Mr. Costeridies said. "My Martha died two years ago, and your parents have been so good to me. Please come home. Janice needs you here."

I said, "I'm sorry to hear about Mrs. Costeridies. What happened with my Dad?"

"Thank you, Matthew. Your father left to go to the store and never returned. They found him around midnight when someone called in to say they saw car lights down a ravine near Parker's Bridge," he said.

"Was he drunk?" I asked.

"You know your father, but I'm not sure this time that he was." He paused and then went on. "I shall tell you this. Lately I noticed when I saw him that he hadn't been drinking. It seemed like he really was trying to stop after all these years. In fact, I haven't seen him drunk in several months. That's why I was so surprised when I heard of the wreck."

"What hospital is he in?" I asked.

"He's at University. Critical Care Unit," he said. "Shall I tell Janice you will be coming home?"

"Yes, I guess so. Tell her I don't know about flights, but I'll get there as soon as I can," I said.

"Matthew, one more thing . . ." he hesitated.

"Yes sir?"

"I don't know what happened to make you leave home and I won't ask," he said. "But I'm old enough to say what I want, and I want to make sure you know something. I'm not preaching, I just want to tell you something. Are you listening?"

"Yes, Sir, I'm listening," I answered, but my throat felt like it was closing. Things I'd refused for years to think about—my parents and friends and the life I left behind—became just scenes of my past flashing around inside my head like reflected light. I pictured him standing in Mom's kitchen at the end of the white Formica counter where the phone hung on the wall beneath a calendar.

His voice grew a little softer. "Your mother is a saint. She put up with your dad all these years and never spoke a word against him. It broke her heart for you to be gone. For a year or two, she hardly left the house. Then one day I saw her outside when Martha and I were walking. She told us they knew where you were in California and that you were fine. Now listen, Matthew. Do not come here and break her heart again. Do you understand me?"

That conversation left me speechless, like one of those times when you know you've just learned something important and dangerous, but you're not sure what the information means.

Little alarms were blaring in the back of my brain. I found myself slumping to the floor, my eyes closed, a sound like the hooves of horses pounding in my ears as all that past came rushing back. I remember everything he said after that, but something didn't fit about my Dad.

How could Dad have tracked me? Was there something about him I knew but refused to admit to myself? I listened as Mr. Costeridies began to fill in some of my parents' lives from my years away.

I listened, wondering if the little black bow tie Mr. Costeridies was certain to be wearing was the same one he'd worn when I was a child. He never dressed without it. Even now the image was fresh of him mowing his front lawn with an electric mower, his short sleeved white shirt neatly tucked in and him wearing a black bow tie. It didn't seem like he even sweated.

"I didn't ask how Janice knew," Mr. Costeridies said, "because I could tell from the way she talked that they had not heard directly from you, but after that she was better. She went back to tending her rose garden. And her smile returned, that wonderful smile, Matt."

There was a pause and a weak cough on the line. "She cared for your father when everyone else had given up. She is a saint I tell you, and now it's time someone looked after her. That's all I have to say."

I mumbled something about understanding. I heard him place the phone down softly to disconnect the call as I stood there with the phone pressed to my ear.

chapter **3**

Going back to Birmingham was always in my head, especially when I'd moved to Texas from California, halfway home. The call a few minutes earlier with Mr. Costeridies sealed it. I'd thought of fifty scenarios of how it would happen, but now it was happening with no warning, no plan, no real purpose other than doing what people do when someone is hurt or dying. And now my dad was hurt and maybe dying.

Packing was easy. Hearing of the terrible time my mother had after I left was not easy. Looking around my crummy little apartment at the stacks of old *Rolling Stone* magazines, cinder block and two-by-four shelves, and music festival posters tacked on the walls for art, nothing there felt significant enough to take. For a moment I was ashamed.

The only valuable thing I owned had been the Harley. None of the furniture was mine, and few personal items decorated the place. I'd read every paperback in three tall stacks by the mattress at least twice, and I had no use for the half-a-dozen Budweiser, Harley Davidson, and Spiderman mirrors won throwing darts at the state fair in Austin. I stuffed some jeans, a few shirts, and my ditty bag into a duffle.

Using the back of an envelope, I wrote a note to Mike, the landlord who looked after this place for the owner. Mike was a friend, so I told him if I wasn't back in two weeks he could keep anything he wanted, burn the other stuff, and rent the place. I'd already paid rent through the end of the month. I left a full quart of George Dickel on top of the note.

I took one last look around each of the two rooms and felt like I was seeing the place for the first time. I noticed the light fixture hanging crooked and the ceiling plaster crumbling from a leak I'd never given a moment's thought. The carpet had pulled loose along one wall and the sink dripped non-stop. Why had I never paid attention to any of that? I had an odd moment of clarity.

With a couple of photos, half a bottle of aspirin, and my stash of two grand in emergency cash stuffed into a backpack, I walked out without looking back. I had no reason to care about the latest rat hole I stayed in, just one in a long line of cheap one-bedroom apartments I'd lived in over the past few years. Something in the back of my mind told me I'd never see the place again.

Without checking for flight times, I grabbed the first taxi I could flag down to the airport. I got lucky with a standby flight to Dallas, then a direct flight that landed me in Birmingham around five in the afternoon. During the flight, I dozed and dreamed of horses bunched around me, stomping and frightened, nostrils flared. The horses were familiar, and the hot dusty field was one I'd visited many times in these dreams, staggering in the soft sand as horses jostled me and I struggled to stay on my feet.

Upon arrival, the sky was the first thing I noticed. The orange tint in the clouds from the steel mills was gone. A Yellow cab delivered me to the edge of the University Hospital complex. I wandered around for half an hour before I found the right building.

I felt like a tourist in New York for the first time and had to force myself not to look up with my mouth open. I couldn't believe how many red brick buildings with white concrete columns had been built since I left. The place was huge, and the University of Alabama in Birmingham and the University's medical college had grown like crazy. Streets had been closed to create pedestrian walkways. New landscaping of thick, yellow flowers and well-manicured boxwoods stationed at each corner created a look saying the place offered a real college experience, instead of the way it looked years earlier when I took a few classes here—a series of plain buildings that could have just as easily been government offices. I could smell pizza baking somewhere close by as I reached the front door. The directory listed the CCU on the third floor, so I figured that was the place.

The elevator opened, and I rode up alone. Walking the white tile hallways, I felt that dazed feeling hospitals always give me, that sort of low-pitched humming noise of fluorescent lights and distinct hospital smell, a mixture of cleaning products, floor wax, flowers, and decay.

I didn't know what to expect or what to say. For years I'd imagined the moment when I would see my parents again and had practiced a thousand funny first lines. Now not one of them came to mind.

Rounding a corner, I almost ran right into my mom. She glanced up but didn't recognize me. I just stood there. Then tears appeared in her eyes, and she reached out to hug me. I took her in my arms and held her that way for a long time. I swallowed hard. She felt smaller in my arms than I remembered.

Finally, she stepped away to look up at me, wiping her eyes on her sleeve. She placed her hands on my shoulders and held me at arm's length. Her eyes narrowed as she tilted her head.

"Matt, they tried to kill your father," she choked up and couldn't even finish a sentence. I felt like I was in a movie. A bad movie. I held her tight until she seemed in control.

"No, Mom. Mr. Costeridies told me about it. Dad had a wreck and was probably drunk, as usual," I said.

As soon as I said it, I wished I could take back the words. I mean, here's your Mom that you've not seen in eight years, and you sound like some cynical college kid.

I'd spent those years, well let's just say, hanging with people who said whatever they felt like at the time. I suppose I'd lost a little of my Southern politeness that makes us hold our words just a second longer to make sure we don't offend anyone. I'd really never even spoken to my mother as an adult. I was still a student the last time I had seen her and couldn't recall a single adult-style conversation we'd ever had.

I'm sure all of us have that "aha" moment when one day we realize we can relate to our parents not just as a son or a daughter but as another adult, full of our own views of the world and our own prejudices and preferences. So here I was, automatically questioning my mother, not accepting that she was a woman of experience and years, an adult with a perspective I should respect. I was back again as an 18-year-old who knew everything and thought she knew nothing. I kicked myself and tried to listen.

"No," she said eyeing me with a look of iron I didn't remember. There were no tears now. "He wasn't. He hadn't had a drink in a long time. Not for five months. He was finally turning things around and was beginning to be like his old self from twenty years ago. That's why they did this to him."

She was very stern, almost pleading, but whispering. I had to fight the feeling that maybe Mom had cracked under the stress or something. I did my best to put those thoughts aside and really consider what would make her feel this way. I still didn't believe her, but I wanted to understand her.

I said, "What are you talking about? Who did this? Why would anyone want to do anything to Dad?"

"There's so much you don't know," she said, cutting her eyes around as she did. She took my hand, turned, and opened the door to a patient room. I followed her in and saw my Dad. His head and face were swollen and purple. What seemed like a dozen tubes fed into his arms and chest with various clear drips and fluids.

"Is he awake at all?" I asked her.

"Not really. Mostly he's just like this. He's moved some and seems to slip in and out of a light coma. They said he might wake up in a day or a week or longer. They just don't know."

I touched his hand and began talking to him. "Dad, I'm here. If you can hear me, I'm here to take care of Mom." At that moment, his fingers began moving. His eyes opened, and he looked at us both.

My Mom smiled but said nothing. She gripped my upper arm as she leaned her head on my shoulder. Dad tried to speak but no sound came out.

"That's about all he can do," she whispered. "Just open his eyes once in a while, like he's trying to wake up. He's said a few words, but then he seems to just fade away again."

Mom turned to Dad and put her hand on his arm. "Matthew's here, Honey. You just rest now," she said to him.

I told him, "I'll be here, and there's plenty of time to talk later."

Dad closed his eyes.

Mom spoke in a hushed tone. "I know you don't remember much about him before he started the drinking, but he was a great and gentle man. He did some important things for our country," she said, the pride in her voice obvious, "Things you should know one day that will make you very proud."

I left Mom holding Dad's hand and walked down the hallway to look for coffee. But what I wanted was just to get out of there for a minute to regroup. My head was spinning again. What had Dad done for the country that would make me proud? Obviously, I had no idea who he was. As I turned toward the nurses' station, I recognized one of the three men standing down the hallway as my father's close friend Jim Robinson. Jim recognized me and turned away from the other two men to walk toward me.

"Matt, it's nice to see you. It's Jim Robinson," he said as he stepped forward and held out his open hand. "You've been away for a long time."

"Yes sir, I have. Good to see you, too, Mr. Robinson."

"Jim, just Jim, Matt. I'm sorry, I didn't recognize you when you walked by me earlier, Matt. How long has it been? Five, six years?"

"More like seven or eight I think." His handshake felt like I'd caught my hand in the car door. Little about his look had changed other than some gray sprinkled in his otherwise jet-black hair. I remembered him mostly as someone Dad fished with and who was always at the office cookouts, where the adults drank beer and the kids wandered the neighborhood.

"You're what, twenty-six, now?"

"Twenty-seven."

"Well, I'm very sorry about Marshall, but it's nice to see you. Is there any change? Is he awake? I'd sure like to talk with him."

"He's sort of in and out. Mostly out. He's not talking yet."

The two men hovered down the hall away from us. Jim waved toward them and said, "I'll call you later." One of the men turned his head and nodded slightly to acknowledge. They walked toward the elevators without speaking.

"Just a couple of guys who knew your father," Jim said, seeing the question in my eyes. "Word gets around pretty fast, you know. I'm sorry, guess I should've introduced you. So, what've you been up to all this time, Matt?"

"Oh, nothing much worth talking about," I told him. "Just worked some in California on a gas pipeline. Spent the past couple of years working the oil fields in Texas and Oklahoma." It wasn't the whole story, but it wasn't a lie, and something I could talk about if pressed. I'd spent time as a welder for natural gas and oil production companies.

My mother walked out of Dad's room. When she saw us, she turned the other way and walked down the hall and out of sight around a corner.

"How does it look for Marshall waking up soon?" Jim asked.

"I'm not sure. I haven't talked to his docs yet. Mom says they don't know if it'll be a day or a week or what. He seems to be trying to wake up and say something, but I just got here, so I don't really know much."

He just nodded.

"Listen, Mr. Robinson. Jim. Do you know why my Mom would think someone tried to hurt Dad? She seems to think someone did this on purpose. It sounds crazy to me, but something made her think that."

I thought I glimpsed just the slightest bit of a shadow pass over him before he smiled and responded.

"No, of course not. Is that what she thinks? Matt, it's probably just the stress, and I bet she hasn't slept well for the last couple of days. I wouldn't think anything of it."

"Yeah, I'm sure you're right," I said.

"Look Matt, I'm off today so thought I'd just sit in the waiting room a little to see if anything changed in your Dad's condition." He tilted his head and motioned with his left hand toward a row of blue vinyl chairs in front of a small television, indicating where he'd be sitting.

"I'm sure he'd appreciate that," I said.

I excused myself to find coffee and get back to Dad's room. The smell of rubbing alcohol and floor wax filled the hallway. As I walked over the gleaming tile floor, the thought crossed my mind that I really had no idea what Robinson and my father did together at work.

I sat in the corner chair of Dad's room and gripped a Styrofoam cup of steaming coffee, my hand resting on the arm of the chair. With my feet stretched in front of me, I leaned my head back and fell asleep. Soon I was chasing wild horses, the same ones I'd tried to catch my entire life. I had them boxed in at the end of a familiar-looking canyon. The horses milled about, watching me, snorting and swishing their tails, but before I could move, a nurse woke me up as she pulled the curtain around Dad's bed to give him a sponge bath. For the second time that day, I wouldn't touch even one of the horses, as I sometimes did when the dream didn't scare me.

chapter 4

For days I sat around the various waiting rooms of the hospital, learning that many of the same soap opera stars I left behind years before were still in the same marriage difficulties and hiding the same secret affairs. I marveled at how Erica Kane's face was unchanged, though her neck showed a few tiny wrinkles. Between shows I paced back and forth to the coffee stand in the corner of the cafeteria. I counted a hundred and seventeen steps to the coffee if I took the stairs.

One morning while standing at the window of Dad's room, I noticed a tall man standing in the small entry garden of the building across the street from the hospital entrance. He seemed oddly familiar, standing perfectly erect and still between rows of blooming white crepe myrtles, hands behind his back as he appeared to stare across the street. I wanted to know who he was. But with his dark sunglasses and me looking down from above him, I couldn't see his face well, though he appeared recognizable. By the time I made it down the elevator and out the front door, he was gone.

Despite the days dragging on into a week, the smell of decay in the hospital never faded, but I got used to it. I couldn't get Mom to leave Dad's side very often, especially after he began saying a word or two now and then. When I couldn't stay awake any longer and

Mom said she was fine to sit with Dad, I drove to my parents' house and tried to sleep two or three hours at a time. During one of those nap trips, I noticed a photo high up on a shelf in Dad's office. I'd been wandering from room to room, just looking, noticing how much remained the same and finding only a few surprises here and there to update me on my years away. One five-by-seven photo in a simple black frame startled me, but gave me a clue about how I'd gotten home. The picture included a group of men talking at what looked like a backyard barbeque. Suit, the man from the bar fight, was standing next to Dad. He wasn't one of the group of my father's friends that I had gotten to know as a kid. I didn't recall ever seeing this photo or remember him at all from my years growing up. His hair was dark, but he sported the same crew cut in Texas. He was wearing a T-shirt in the shot, so I could see his thick biceps and realized his weight lifting was a lifelong habit.

A few days later when I returned from a nap at home, Mom said, "Eleanor Masters called to check on your father."

Eleanor Masters had been some kind of assistant or secretary or something in Dad's office, but I never really knew what she did. I just knew she was raising her daughter Kristine by herself after being divorced for a long time and never remarrying. Apparently her ex died in a car wreck in Atlanta just after the divorce. Kristine once told me she never had met her father. He had left her mother before Kristine was born.

Eleanor was usually around when Dad or Jim had people over. She usually brought Kristine, who became one of my best friends growing up. Kristine and I were the same age, so we hung around whenever the parents from Dad's office got together to grill hamburgers or play Canasta or something. As we got older, the friendship evolved, and she became my steady girlfriend.

I tried my best to react normally to the news of Eleanor calling. Mom was watching for my reaction. "How is Mrs. Masters?"

"She's fine," she said, smiling a little. She didn't volunteer any more information, so I had to ask, "Did she mention Kristine?"

"She just said Kristine's fine. Working for a lawyer, I think. You should look her up."

I could feel my heart speed up a little. "Is she here in town?"

"I think so," she said, looking away. Then sort of wistfully, "But there's so much we should talk about sometime."

I'd thought often of Kristine in the past few days since I returned to Birmingham but had not been ready to track her down yet. Or maybe I was just plain scared. As I said, Kristine had been my best friend growing up, and when it gradually progressed into a boyfriend-girlfriend relationship, I never dated another person in high school.

I was about to ask what Mom meant when Jim Robinson peeked around the half-open door, lightly knocking as he did so. "Good morning. How's our man doing today?"

I would have to wait to learn more about Kristine.

"He's moving around more and trying to say a few words. The nurse said that's a good sign," I told him.

Jim Robinson seemed to be around every time I looked up, always in a dark suit with yet another conservative striped tie, always with blue, red, or yellow. I thought little of him being there so much, except to realize he and Dad must have been better friends than I knew. Looking back on it now, I realize that almost every one of Dad's close friends except one neighbor was from his office. They must have been a close group.

I walked into the hallway with Jim, and we chatted about nothing much. I wanted to ask him about the photo I had seen of the men that included Suit with Jim, Dad, and others. "Jim, I'm curious. The tall guy with the crew cut in a photo of you guys at some kind of cookout. Who is that? Dad had the picture in his study."

"Big strong guy, slim waist, but with a big chest?"

"Yeah, that sounds like him."

"Mark Pugh. He's been early retired for years. Moved up north to some little town up in the Michigan peninsula right on the water, I think. No one has heard much from him since. Why do you ask?"

Something told me not to say anything about Suit or the bar. I don't know what I felt at that point, but I just had a feeling. "No reason, I just saw the photo and didn't know who he was."

Jim looked at me for a second, his forehead wrinkling like he had a question, but then he smiled and relaxed. "Your dad is well liked and always made friends easily. Mark was one of a lot of friends he had from the agency."

I let it drop. Despite the bad feelings I'd had about Dad that made me leave home, I appreciated someone like Jim caring so much that he would come day after day to check on him, even if I myself had turned my back years before. I knew now that I had always wanted to come back, wanted my family again.

Dad's other two friends in their own dark suits stopped by a couple of times, though I never seemed to get a chance to speak to them other than a basic hello. It was only later I realized how odd that none of them ever went into Dad's room but seemed just to sit in the lobby at the far end of the hall and talk to Jim whenever he came out of Dad's room.

I didn't get a chance that day to ask Mom what she meant about Kristine. There always seemed to be someone around.

That evening, Dad's close friend David Collier walked in. I knew it was David, although his dark hair in my mental picture of him from years ago was now mostly white. He had been a neighbor growing up and maybe Dad's real best friend, but he had recently moved out of state. I'd called him Uncle Dave as a child, and he was the only person from home I contacted during my seven years away.

Dad was improving. We were sitting in his room, and he finally managed to swallow a couple of bites of Jell-O when someone knocked. I opened the door, and there was David, holding flowers.

Mom rushed across the room as I stood up. "Oh, David, thanks for coming. Marshall will be so glad to see you."

"I came as fast as I could, Janice. I'm sorry I couldn't get here earlier," he said, looking over and recognizing me behind Mom. "Matt, you're looking fit. Nice to see you."

"Isn't it great to see him?" Mom said, hooking her elbow around my arm and patting the side of my shoulder with her other hand. "I'm so happy to have you both back here. Marshall will be so pleased."

David shook my hand, then walked over to Dad. Dad's eyes came open when David put his hand on Dad's arm. A smile spread across Dad's face. He seemed to be nodding his approval.

We spent the evening remembering good times, left around midnight, and were back in the hospital at six the next morning. David had slept in the guest room, and I was back in my old bedroom, which hadn't changed much.

While we sat with Dad, I talked about my life for the past seven years, with an unspoken agreement to ignore the fact that I'd disappeared suddenly, abandoning my family and friends. It was as if I had merely finished school and moved away to take a job. I told them about driving my motorcycle to California. I told them of the string of jobs I'd taken when I first got there, starting with being a housing construction crew "board toter" as they called me, then working my way up and learning carpentry. Later I got work on a pipeline construction project as a carpenter and made friends with a guy who taught me welding. That job paid a lot more, so I eventually traded my saw for a torch. During that time, I found myself burning up the roads every spare moment and needing something bigger to ride.

My welding skills paid off in building a good bike. I'd trade welding to guys in exchange for parts or a little cash, and pretty soon had a really nice bike pieced together.

I never joined a motorcycle club, but sometimes my lifestyle felt like I had. Certain clubs would let you ride with them if you had a good friend inside. Yes, there were fights and too much booze, though I skipped that part for Mom's sake when I told them of my travels and how I made a living for the past years. Yes, there was a string of jobs and women and long nights in smoky bars playing pool for twenty-five or a hundred or even two hundred bucks a game. I left out that part, too. For some reason I had a knack for pool. I won and lost thousands of dollars playing, but mostly I made money. During the good times when I wasn't drinking too much, I really didn't need to work a regular full-time job because I could make a few hundred dollars a week playing pool, and Uncle Sam didn't get to take half of it off the top.

I'm not proud of any of that. I mention it only because I don't want that stuff to be hidden and come out later as a way to discredit this story. I did what I did. I can't take it back. I'll say one thing that some people will want to know—I never hurt anyone (okay, bar fights with a broken nose or two, a few teeth loose, and a few knots on the side of a head excepted). I never robbed anyone or stole anything or sold drugs. And that's all I'll say about those years. They're behind me.

But there were lots of good things to tell my Dad and the others. I told them of driving my Harley from L.A. all the way to Olympia, Washington, the incredible beauty of the red-brown cliffs at the edge of the ocean, and the whale pods playing along the coast.

I told them of my older friend Jack, the guy who took me under his wing and taught me welding and who, despite the age difference, became my best friend of my entire life. About how Jack once saved my life by running through a fire that started when a spark from my torch set off an explosion in the pre-fabrication building and knocked me silly. I told of watching Jack die of pancreatic cancer, but of how he worked those brief last months right until the end "because that's all I know to do," he said. Jack told me I reminded him of his son. He said his son had been stationed in San Diego in the Navy and had died in a car crash while driving home on a weekend.

I told Dad of the many times I wanted to call home. Of how I missed him and Mom and my girlfriend Kristine that I lost touch with, but by the time I realized what I had done I just felt so cut off that I didn't know how to get back to them. Of how I had called home so many times just to hear a voice but hung up before I said anything.

After I brought them into the present, I told my parents and

David I was sorry. I'm not sure why after all the years away I had suddenly decided to return to the fold, whether it was the shock of Dad's injuries and possible death or if I was just tired of running. I really don't understand what happened to me so quickly as to want to put those years behind me, to be back with my family, but it happened just that fast after the Suit, Mark Pugh, had me call home and start the process. Mom seemed to accept me being home as natural with nothing to forgive or get over.

I don't know if Dad heard many of my stories as he dozed off and on. Mom said little. David had to leave after dinner to drive back to Mississippi.

Three days later, Dad seemed more alert, and his eyes were wide open during the afternoon. The docs said they thought he was most likely out of the coma for good, but that didn't mean he couldn't slip back into it. They poked and prodded him for nearly an hour, but he never spoke more than a whispered word or two at a time. He could sort of nod and squeeze their hands to let the docs know he was awake and alert.

Finally, Mom and I were alone with Dad, and we knew he could hear us, though he couldn't really speak well. I told him I was happy to be home. Mom said she knew we could be a family again. I noticed tears in Dad's eyes, and I had to look away.

Mom said she wanted to call some friends to tell them Dad was out of the coma, so she left the room to walk down the hall to use the phone in private. When she left, Dad sort of motioned me close with his hand. He was trying to speak.

I leaned closer to his ear to listen, but he was having a lot of trouble speaking loud enough.

"Loooo a high frizer," he said. "Looooooooo, looooooooo."

"Dad, I'm sorry, what are you saying? I don't understand."

Suddenly he reached up and grabbed the front of my shirt. I was stunned by his strength. He pulled himself up, with his face mere inches from mine. He swallowed hard and looked right into my eyes. He spoke slowly and obviously with great effort. "Loooooooooooo, looooooook behind the refrigerator."

With that he smiled. I saw his eyes roll up into his head as he fell back completely limp. A light began flashing and a beeping sound began on the heart monitor beside his bed. Two nurses ran into the room within seconds as I was just standing there trying to understand what was happening.

One nurse pressed buttons on the machine while the other leaned in close. She opened Dad's eyelids with a thumb and finger. The male nurse ran to the door and yelled to someone outside in the hall, "Crash cart, stat!"

Three or four people crowded into the room. Someone pushed me out the door just as Mom was coming in. I grabbed her and held her outside the door. We listened to the chaos behind the door of squeaking shoes, furniture banging the walls, and several people talking at once. Gradually it grew quiet in the room.

I was still standing in the same place ten minutes later, holding Mom as she stood there stoically, saying nothing, when the door slowly opened. White coats from the room floated down the hall. Dad's doctor walked out last. During the rush of white coats, I hadn't even seen him come in. I knew his words before he spoke them.

chapter 5

Two days after Dad died, we held a funeral at Southside Methodist Church where my mother sometimes attended services off and on when I was young. The morning was hot, the sun high overhead in a cloudless light gray summer sky. We walked up the front steps, through the heavy wooden double doors and into the cool hushed sanctuary. They took us around a side hallway until everyone was seated, and then the funeral guys in their black suits walked us to the front row. The pews were covered in a long purple cushion that ran the length of the seats.

They rolled in the casket, covered with the largest blanket of yellow roses I had ever seen, and the preacher walked up in front of the casket and smiled out at the folks seated in the sanctuary. "Please join me in prayer."

He prayed for what seemed like ten minutes, his words more like a sermon than a prayer to me. His words were admonitions directed at us sitting there and not prayers to God. We sang a couple of hymns. "Rock of Ages" was one I remember. I just stared at the words in the hymn book as Mom held onto my arm. Then the pastor talked about not worrying about Dad because he was in a better place, and maybe we should all be sure our relationship with God was as certain as Marshall's had been. Another ten minutes at least.

Some woman I didn't know—I guess someone from Mom's church—sang "Closer Walk with Thee." I say Mom's church because Dad was Episcopal, but he never went to church except once in a while here with Mom or on Easter or at Christmas to Christ Episcopal.

When we left the church, Mom and I rode in a big black SUV to the cemetery with the funeral director driving. A string of cars filed into Elmwood Cemetery behind us, but I recognized few of the people, mostly the men in dark suits. I wondered who all those other people could be.

They seated us under a little green tent on metal folding chairs with slip covers over the backs, advertising the funeral home name. The pastor prayed again. I think that was the third or fourth time. He nodded to Jim Robinson, who came up and talked about Dad for a couple of minutes. Mom had asked him to say something, but the person he described as "brave in the face of adversity, heroic under fire, and a real patriot" sounded like someone I'd never known. His words had no relationship to the father I knew.

Then a young Episcopal priest I didn't know—he looked about fifteen to me—read scripture as the green funeral tent became an oven. Then he added his prayer, which was full of formal language and sounded more like something from an old English book with all its Thees and Thous.

The director thanked everyone for coming and handed Mom a rose and an American flag from the top of the casket. He shook my hand and stepped back, signaling to lower the casket. Then dozens of men in black suits and women in black dresses filed past, bending to hug Mom. She sat with red but dry eyes, neither smiling nor frowning, her hands folded and resting on the triangle of flag in her lap. I knew almost none of them, though I had seen one or two somewhere before. A childhood friend we called Bugs came by and shook my hand, which surprised me a little, but in a line like this, he only said a few things before moving on. He'd grown up a couple houses down, but I had hardly thought of him in years. A bit later when I looked up, he stood back behind the crowd. Then I realized the woman standing next to him was Kristine.

Before I could go to them, the crowd suddenly parted. I recognized from TV Charles Ryan Leopold, head of the NSEO. He removed his dark sunglasses and bent down in front of Mom, taking her hand while men who looked as if they even slept in their dark glasses stood erect on either side of him, the coiled wires to their radio earpieces clearly visible. Cameras loved him with his tailored dark blue suits, perfect haircut, and closely shaved chiseled chin. He had made it clear that with him as the new head, the NSEO would take a more visible role in addressing national security issues. His face had appeared everywhere on the news a few months back.

"I'm deeply sorry about Marshall. I've always been fond of him."

Mom nodded and held a handkerchief to her eyes.

He shook my hand. "Your father was a good man. He handled some important work for the country. You should be proud."

Before I could ask what he meant, he turned and was gone, along with the two dark suits flanking him on either side. When I looked back over the crowd for Kristine and Bugs, they were gone, too.

That was the day things began to come together in my mind, and I considered that maybe my Dad had not been merely an accountant as I always believed but had been active in something larger in the NSEO. What I didn't know was why it had been a secret. And I wanted to know.

———

We rode back home in the back seat of Mr. Costeridies' big Oldsmobile. When we arrived, the house was filled with women in Sunday dresses, loading the dining room table with casseroles, big bowls of peas and mashed potatoes, and large platters of ham and fried chicken. Several men stood in the front yard, some of them smoking cigarettes.

I took Mom to her room.

"Do you want anything to eat?" I asked.

She wanted to get in bed and hardly spoke as we passed through the small crowd. I came back out to the kitchen to get a glass of water and thanked the women for the food but thought it rude to tell them we were not hungry. I went to my room, lay across the bed with my clothes on, and dozed off.

An hour or so later, I came out again and everything had been cleaned up. No one was there. The refrigerator was filled with glass casserole dishes covered in aluminum foil. Two pecan pies sealed in plastic wrap and a chocolate cake in a crystal cake stand sat on the counter.

———

I called the doc early the next morning after Mom spent the entire afternoon and night in her bed, sobbing off and on, repeating, "they killed him, they killed him." I tried to talk her down, but nothing she said made sense. She went on and on about Dad being killed and how no one would believe her and that Dad only wanted to do the right thing.

Doc gave her something from his bag, and then he handed me a prescription for her. He said I needed to fill it during the day and make sure she took another pill before evening.

After getting Mom into bed, I thought she should try to eat before she took a pill.

"Mom, the fridge is full of ham and casseroles," I told her, but she didn't want any of it.

After much coaxing, she told me the kind of cooked chicken and bread she preferred to buy for sandwiches.

I took the phone off the hook and drove her car across Southside to Western Supermarket. I waited while they filled her prescription, bought a few groceries, and was back at the house in about an hour.

Mom's bedroom door was closed and all was quiet when I returned, so I put the groceries away and sat down to watch television with the volume very low. Finally, she can get some rest, I thought.

I sat there remembering being a kid and how Mom, Dad, and I rolled around wrestling on the floor every night in front of the little black and white TV, a square of foil like a shiny silver flag on the rabbit ears to bring in one of the three local channels. Dad tickled me until I couldn't breathe and I screamed for him to stop. When he did stop, I jumped on top, laughing as if life were perfect. If that didn't work to make me laugh enough, he held the nub of a finger he'd somehow lost up to his ear or his nose, as if the finger were jammed all the way inside his head.

After the news, which was mostly the latest thing President Reagan said about the Russians, came *Happy Days* or *The Jeffersons*. Or if Dad wasn't in one of his rages, I could watch *Magnum P.I.*

Our little neighborhood is known as English Village, just up the hill from the Birmingham Zoo where we visited so often I gave the monkeys names. Everyone called our street Diaper Row because of all the families living here with kids.

The sun was down when I decided to check on Mom. I had made her a sandwich and poured a small glass of milk. I knew she'd had nothing but coffee and half a piece of toast that morning.

I eased her door open a few inches, not looking in.

"Mom?" No answer. "Mom?"

I opened the door and was surprised to see no one in the bed. I walked across to her bathroom door.

"Mom, you in there? You okay?"

The door was open, so I peeked in. A bloody razor blade lay next to the tub.

I remember yelling "Oh God oh God oh God" over and over as I saw her there in the tub with her nightgown still on, hands crossed in front of her, her face completely gray, the water stained crimson red. I reached to pull her up and check her pulse, but I knew I was far too late. I put my fingertips against her still warm neck. For what must have been half an hour, I kneeled next to the tub while holding Mom's head. I told her over and over that I loved her. But inside I was telling myself this was somehow my fault.

chapter 6

For two hours I sat in a large stuffed chair answering questions, watching police and medical people file reports. After the police left, I asked Mr. Costeridies to help with Mom's funeral. He had been sitting across from me without speaking for nearly an hour. He told me to let him do all the arrangements, so I asked him to work with the funeral home to bury her beside Dad. No church service. He argued with me that she deserved better. After a few minutes of back and forth, I agreed to have her pastor at the graveside, and he could do whatever he wanted.

Then I drove Mom's car to the ABC liquor store. Although I had the money and enjoy good bourbon, taste was unimportant right then. I grabbed five fifths of Jim Beam, tossed a hundred on the counter, and walked out without waiting for change.

Two days later, I finished the third one just before going to Mom's funeral and was still numb hours later as they lowered the casket into a hole next to a large pile of red dirt partially covered by a green cloth. Two funerals in three days for my parents I hadn't spoken with in years until only days ago.

There was nothing to say, nothing I wanted. Food had no appeal, and if I felt hunger I don't remember it. I just shook my head and turned away when people tried to talk to me. I hated everything but mostly myself.

How could I fail to see in her eyes the kind of desperation that causes someone to take her own life? I'd seen nothing to even be concerned about. Was I so out of touch with people that I could let this happen and do nothing?

At some point well after the funeral, which had been attended by maybe a third of the hundred or so people who had gathered two days earlier in this same location, Mr. Costeridies took me by the arm as I sat on a tombstone a few feet from my parents' graves. I allowed him to walk me to his car to drive me to my parents' house. I looked back at the two mounds of fresh earth side by side, out of place among hundreds of granite stones and marble crosses. Only then did I realize everyone else was gone now, even the funeral director and his men who had shoveled the earth onto the casket.

Mr. Costeridies motioned for me to get in. "Let me take you home."

I think I just nodded.

"Matt, there are no words I can say that will help. But what can we do but go on?" he said as he turned the key in the ignition. "I've had a cleaning service over, and the house is ready for you. Your folks had always left a key with me for emergencies."

It had not crossed my mind until that moment that there would be blood stains all over the bathroom. If I said anything, I sure don't remember what. And I don't remember who else was there that day. I hardly looked up during the funeral.

———

Back at my parents' house, I closed the door quietly behind Mr. Costeridies after telling him I would be fine. I walked to the couch and opened another bottle of whiskey, pouring it straight into a tumbler, not bothering with ice or water. I sat there for hours and vaguely remember the sky growing lighter.

I must have finished the bottle and passed out. When I awoke, the sky through the front windows signaled the sun was going down, with hints of pink and purple reflecting on the undersides of clouds gathered on the horizon.

I sat up and realized I'd not eaten for two days and my head was being crushed under a loaded dump truck tire. Staggering around the house, I began searching for aspirin. Hesitantly, and after searching everywhere else, I entered my mother's bathroom to look in her medicine cabinet. The tiny white tiles on the floor and beside the tub were stark and icy with the shower curtain, bath mat, and towels removed. Even the soaps and shampoos were gone. The room sparkled as if no one had ever lived here.

Swinging open the mirrored door of the cabinet above the sink, I saw the Bayer Aspirin. As I reached for the bottle, I noticed it sat next to a full bottle of sleeping pills. I swallowed four or five aspirin and lay across my Mom's bed, staring up at the ceiling.

After forty-five minutes the pain in my head began to ease up, and I thought food might help. I remembered the chicken and bread I had bought for Mom.

As I reached for the bread Mom asked me to buy, it hit me how precise she'd been about the type of sliced chicken and the brand of bread she preferred. For her, not me. I wondered why someone about to kill herself would be so specific about her food, if sending me to the store was just a way to get me out of the house. Maybe she had not yet decided to kill herself when I left? But could a person decide and then do something like that in an hour?

I made a sandwich and walked into the living room, choking down the food but not really caring about the taste. As I walked by a floor lamp, I reached to turn the switch. Nothing happened. I felt for the bulb to check if it was screwed in tight. No bulb was there.

I flipped the overhead light switch before I sat down to finish eating the chicken sandwich. Just as I sat down, I suddenly came fully awake with a rush like when someone startles you from behind. I sat forward on the edge of the chair. Where was that light bulb? I thought back to when I had used that lamp earlier. I was certain the lamp worked two days ago. When had Mom had time to take a bulb out if it blew? When was I not around?

I thought again about the food Mom had asked for, and the hair stood up on my arms. The sleeping pills! Now I knew what bothered me about seeing them. Why would she slit her wrists if she had sleeping pills that could do the job with no pain and no mess?

I found myself standing in the middle of the room, looking around as I turned in circles, my arms horizontal with fingers extended, as if feeling something so wrong it hung in the air like mist. I dropped the half sandwich that was left as a feeling came over me that lifted the fog. Small things were not right. Too many. The chair normally behind the desk was now pushed all the way up. And what is different about that desk? As I looked at it, I noticed that the indentations in the carpet did not perfectly match the placement of the legs. The desk had been moved an inch to the side. Hold on, I told myself, Mr. Costeridies had a cleaning crew here. That was it. They had moved a few things. They had taken out the bulb when it blew.

Still, what about the sleeping pills? As I continued looking around the room, I noticed something that made me catch my breath. The photo of Dad and three of his friends standing beside a big marlin they had caught on a trip to Cabo had always stood on the shelf behind the desk but was now missing. I'd noticed the picture before Dad's funeral because the two men I'd seen in the hallway at the hospital were in the shot, along with Dad and Jim Robinson. Then I realized the photo of the barbeque was missing, too. Where were the photos?

I called Mr. Costeridies. He picked up on the first ring. Two minutes later I knew something was wrong. He said he was very specific about only cleaning the bathroom. And it wasn't even a normal house cleaning service, but one that specialized in environmental contamination and crime scene cleanup.

A thousand questions ran through my mind. At that moment, my Dad's last words came back to me. "Look behind the refrigerator."

I felt a little foolish walking into that kitchen. Well, honestly, a lot foolish. Am I paranoid? All those little things can be explained.

I grabbed the sides of the large black refrigerator and pulled. I was able to slowly roll it out about three feet so I could squeeze behind it. I found nothing. I looked at the wall, just a normal wall with an electric outlet in it. I found a small screwdriver in a kitchen drawer and looked behind the outlet cover. Nothing unusual. I turned and looked at the back of the refrigerator itself. Nothing.

You've lost it, I told myself. *Look at you. You're standing behind a refrigerator because you want someone to blame for what happened.* I started getting mad at myself. Well, in truth, I lost it. At long last I had tears big as teaspoons. I hit the wall with my fist. I pounded on that wall four or five times, not an action totally foreign to me, I admit.

As I slammed the wall, one small area caved in a little. Sheetrock tape rippled as a section about a foot and a half square gave way under my fist. Something wasn't right. I ripped off the tape and pulled the sheetrock loose. The wall had been cut out, repaired, and repainted between the wall studs. A damn professional job, too.

As I jerked away the little square of sheetrock, banded stacks of hundred-dollar bills fell from the wall and lay in a pile at my feet. I looked inside the wall and found more cash, removing it and stacking piles on the nearby counter.

Picking through the cash on the floor, I found an envelope addressed to me. I ripped off the end of the envelope. Inside was a letter, a baseball card, and a weird key unlike any key I'd ever seen. The typewritten letter was dated three months earlier and had my father's signature.

Dear Matt,

If you are reading this letter, it is likely I have failed in my efforts to right some of the wrongs of my past, but that's not important now. I'm probably dead if you find this, and I have to assume your life and your mother's life could be in jeopardy. Please do exactly what I ask, as I believe this will be your safest option. You probably know by now that I had an NSEO friend who had the agency resources to follow your travels and keep up with your life once in a while as long as you weren't really trying to hide. Another friend may be the one who helped you find this letter, or perhaps you figured it out for yourself. If you did, that makes me feel even better that you are up to the task ahead. Forgive me for spying on you, but I wanted your mother to know you were doing fine and we both felt that you would make it home one day. Our fear was that if we reached out you might disappear and really be gone. David told us you said you loved us, so we always had that. I know that you have grown into a very capable man, and one who is not, I am proud to learn, afraid to act when you need to. I now have to trust you will use your wits to keep you and your mother safe.

The letter punched me in the gut harder than any burly guy could ever do. I had failed to listen to my father, so I failed to figure out what was going on. And worse, I hadn't done that one important thing he would ever ask of me, which was to keep Mom safe. A lifetime of running away had left me empty. The one thing I owned was failure.

Let me assure you how much I love you and your mother. I know I didn't show it well. I only hope that someday you can understand the guilt I have felt for so long over my drinking and the way I allowed it to destroy our family.

Again, son, I'm sorry we secretly checked on you, but we both loved you so much we had to know if you were okay. As you read this letter, you'll understand some of why I felt I had to keep your mother from contacting you. I'm so sorry I could never tell you about my real work, which was with a very small unit of the National Security Enforcement Office, and I won't go into great detail here. I've left this $400,000 in cash for you to use in taking care of your mother and yourself in the event *something happens to me. There's also plenty of insurance, pension, and retirement money, so your mother should be fine. This money is mine and it's legal, and you shouldn't hesitate to use it. But you must tell no one. I kept it in cash in case I had to go into hiding quickly to protect your mother. By now you must be wondering what in hell is this about, but for your own sake I won't tell that, yet. It's far too late to make excuses now or try to make you understand, but my work for the government gave me some difficult assignments, which I completed without questioning. People of my era did that, but I believe your generation has learned that it is healthy to question authority sometimes. I believe my work was important for our country. But there was one operation my team completed that I couldn't live with after I learned of the real reason behind the mission. Ultimately, I didn't know how to cope with what I'd done, and I turned to the bottle like so many other fools. I know how lame that sounds, and I admit it was a coward's way out. Recently I'd decided to right that wrong, or at least expose it, but the fact you're reading this tells me I may not have done so. Revealing any more could put you even more in harm's way, so I won't say anything else in case this letter is found by the wrong people.*

The punches to my stomach became blows to my head, and the voices I heard were shouting at me. The murders were real. My mom had been right. Why didn't I listen? Now, my father was telling me I'd been separated from my family for all the wrong reasons. I knew as I stood there reading these final words of direction from my father that my life was about to change again in radical ways I couldn't yet imagine, but there was no going back.

> *Please believe me when I say you could be in real danger if anyone learns of this letter. I had asked a friend to contact you in the event of my death to answer any questions about my past and to make sure you found this money and information. There are only two people I completely trust, and I believe they will find you. For your protection and theirs, I cannot name them here so they will be safer and able to help.*
>
> *As for what is going on, Mr. Mack can help explain. I hope you'll remember all the good times we had when you were young. I still remember the great time we had when you turned seven and we went out for your first "men's day." Do you remember that? Those memories are the way I hope you'll remember me. I love you Matt. Please take care of your mother.*
>
> *With much love,*
>
> *Marshall*

All of this was confusing as hell, and I wondered who I should tell or who I should report the letter to. I was uncertain about what was going on, uncertain about what I knew or thought I knew. But I did know one thing for sure. Someone had to answer for murdering my parents.

chapter 7

Sitting in a high-back kitchen chair, slumped over the table on my elbows, I reread the letter. The baseball card lay on the polished maple table in front of me. The letter didn't make any more sense than it had before. What was the funny key with little dots and no normal teeth? And who the hell was Mr. Mack? I sat up well into the night thinking and fell asleep gripping the letter, walking among horses in my dreams, patting their firm flanks, and feeling the rippling muscles under their sweaty shoulders.

I woke and saw the baseball card, a 1958 Mickey Mantle Topps card, the year he'd led the league with forty-eight homers. This was the card I most treasured as a kid. Since Mantle went into the Hall of Fame in 1974, the year I was born, I always thought it gave me a special tie to Mantle. Of the hundreds of cards I had collected, this was my favorite. Not to mention priceless. I'd often wondered what happened to this card when I left home. Leaving it for me was Dad's way of saying he loved me since he'd kept the card all this time and knew what it meant to me. He'd given me the card on my ninth birthday, at the bowling alley, on another Men's Day Out as he called it. That was a precious memory for me, coming about the time things turned ugly and left us with little we wanted to remember.

As I thought back on that day, I realized who he meant by Mr.

Mack, though it seemed improbable and odd. Mac worked at the bowling alley when I was a child. Mac wasn't his real name, but everyone called him that. I think it was McWilliams, maybe. Although I had to wonder if this was some weird paranoia of my Dad, I had to admit that something more than suspicion was going on. And his note about "Mr. Mack" would be a good way to hide his identity from someone, since they would find no Mack in the phone book or even a family phone address book. And I doubted his name had ever come up in a conversation Dad had with anyone at work. Regardless of whether or not the threat was real, using the name Mr. Mack had been a safe way to tell me something, though I didn't yet know what.

Mac was a twenty-something year-old but with the mind of a ten-year old. He could find your shoes in the right size by memory, or bring your order of hamburgers and fries, and he kept the bowling alley spotless. I don't remember ever going there and him not being around, busy, polishing every surface, dressed in his short-sleeved plaid shirts buttoned to the top, red high-top Converse sneakers and a ragged Yankee baseball cap as he constantly moved around the room, cleaning counters and wiping down seats. When asked, he knew all about the Yankees and could recite stats about Mantle and Maris until your head would spin. Everyone loved him and called him Mac, or Mister Mac, if you were a really small child. He remembered everyone's name and always seemed so pleased to see you. I never saw Mac when he wasn't smiling and hustling around that place on some errand or chore.

The message was clear that the bowling alley had something to do with this. I had to find out. I found a large canvas bag with a zipper top and stuffed Dad's cash inside. I threw the letter in with it. After stashing the cash in the trunk of Mom's car, I backed down the drive and started toward the bowling alley. A dark Lincoln Towncar parked two blocks down the street caught my eye. I suppose I had reason to be paranoid, so I watched the car as I passed by and noticed two men inside, not something terribly usual in this neighborhood. I took the Highway 280 onramp toward downtown Birmingham but slowed as much as the traffic would allow. Before I'd gone a mile, I saw the dark Towncar behind me. I exited the freeway and drove toward the AmSouth Plaza parking lot. The bank complex covered the entire block, with multiple exits. If someone wanted to follow me, they'd have to come inside the parking deck, which had several entrances that led to the retail shops in the building. As soon as I was inside, I wheeled the car around and backed into a slot reserved for parking attendants and slid down low in the seat.

A minute later the Towncar entered the lot and began winding up toward the second level. Same car, same two guys with identical short haircuts. In that moment, I knew Mom hadn't been crazy, and I knew someone really had murdered my parents. I pounded on the steering wheel, yelling, mad at myself. I was ready to hurt someone.

I entered the exit lane and was back on the street before they ever realized I was not in the garage. A reservoir of guilt was building pressure in my head, and my jaw clenched so tight my teeth hurt.

———

This time of day only a handful of cars sat in the parking lot of Hoover Lanes, with just a few old timers here for the eleven o'clock Early Bird Special Two-for-One Bowling advertised on the marquee out front, so I found a space behind the building and parked Mom's car. I brushed back my hair and wiped my eyes, confident I had control again. I was not unlike my Dad, I guess, in keeping most of my feelings to myself.

The smell of furniture oil and popcorn brought me back to my childhood as I walked through the double glass doors into the lobby. The carpet was new, and the game room and snack bar had been updated, but the twenty-four bowling lanes were just as I'd pictured them from childhood.

The sound of balls sliding down the polished lanes and the distinctive clack of pins toppling in every direction, along with the muted lighting, had a soothing effect, not unlike the hushed, cool sanctuary of church. I stood just inside the front doors feeling the chilly air that always blew here like wind, looking around and taking in the changes, uncertain of what to do next. I half expected Mac to still be here, ready to run up to me as he'd done many times in my childhood to say *Hey Matt, let me get some shoes for you. Size seven. Ten-and-a-half's for Mr. Boykin?* Then he would lope off without waiting for an answer, swinging his arms and bobbing his head to music only he could hear.

The guy at the counter certainly wasn't Mac. He had large gold rings in both ears and three tiny loops at the corner of his left eyebrow. A tattoo of what could pass for Chinese letters started below his right cheek and ran down the side of his neck until disappearing under a black t-shirt. Don't get me wrong, I have nothing against tattoos. For a couple of years, I thought about having a sunburst tattoo on my right shoulder to honor a friend who had one like it before he died when a car ran a light and broadsided him on his bike. But I always felt like the face, neck, and hands were sort of off-limits as a canvas for this art form. The counter guy hardly looked up as I walked past. Still uncertain of exactly what I was looking for, I sat on a stool at the snack bar and ordered a Pepsi from the large man in a loose-fitting plaid shirt who had his back turned to me. He spun around, and I recognized the big smile.

"Matt, is that you?" he said immediately.

"Hello Mac. I can't believe you remember me."

"Aw, Matt, I remember my friends. And your Daddy came to see me twice just a few weeks ago. He told me you were doing fine. He said you might come see me, but I had to keep it a secret. I did Matt, I kept a secret. I can keep a secret good."

I didn't know what to say. My head was spinning yet again, as too many thoughts at once seemed to shut my mind down. "He did? He came in here?" was all I managed to say.

"Yeah, Mr. Boykin came in two times. One time and then another time," he said. "He talked with Mr. Jimmy. He didn't bowl none though."

Jimmy Lynch owned the bowling alley, along with most everything else for two blocks around. He owned the strip shopping center across the street where the Books-A-Million and Kroger grocery store anchored each end. Not bad for a guy who started his career at fourteen polishing bowling shoes and had never worked anywhere else in his life. He and Dad had been friends for many years since Dad bowled a lot when I was young, and he often came to sit with us for a few minutes on Saturday mornings.

"They talked? Did you hear them?" I asked.

"No, I didn't hear nothing. They went into Mr. Jimmy's office.

Then they went and hung around the lockers for a long time," Mac said.

The hair was standing up on my arms again. The lockers! Of course. "Did you see what they were doing at the lockers?"

"Your daddy was putting some of his stuff in your old locker."

"I'll be right back, Mac." I was off the stool and walking quickly toward the metal lockers, fishing in my pocket for the key as I weaved through a row of new pool tables along the floor that was elevated above the bowling alley so people in the back could watch bowling tournaments. No one was playing pool. It occurred to me that these were the tables where I first learned to play pool.

I went straight to our old locker, which was still the same cream color. The room was in the same place, near the front corner of the building. Above a half wall, the same row of windows with tiny safety wire mesh sandwiched in the thick greenish glass like our high school had in the gym doors. I couldn't remember the number, but I knew where the locker door was. Top row on the left corner. As I stood in front of the locker, I noticed the odd padlock. No name or trademark anywhere, no writing of any sort on the lock. It was an odd pewter color, with a completely square body. I slid the key in and turned. The feel of the key in the lock and the way it sprang open with a soft click reminded me of the solid feel of a Mercedes car door. Not your typical padlock.

I removed the lock, which I noticed was very heavy for its size, and placed it on top of the locker, looking around to see if anyone was watching. No one was near, so I opened the small door.

Though I had no real expectations, what I found left me in shock. A stack of papers sat at the bottom of the locker on top of a metal container. On top were three passports, each with a different name and birthdate, each with my face in the ID photos. A different driver's license matching the various passports was paper-clipped to the front. The photos weren't absolutely new, but they were recent, and they were really me. Where they came from I had no idea, but my Dad must have had someone take shots of me with a telephoto lens and put the right background in place. My hair was a little different in each one, and the shirts were totally different.

Beneath the passports was an eight-millimeter film inside a metal film can, like the old home movies we made as a child before video cameras came along. Someone had written C4 on the container in black marker.

The film had no label, nothing to identify the contents. I sat at a nearby table and spread the passports and film can in front of me, trying to make sense of it.

I had an idea of what to do next, so I went out to the car and removed the bag of cash, stuffing one band of hundreds in my pocket. I placed the passports in the bag with the rest of the cash and shoved the bag into the locker, taking care to make sure the mysterious padlock was really locked. I took the film with me.

After telling Mac to keep one more secret and not tell anyone he had seen me, I left through a side door of the bowling alley and into the sun.

chapter 8

On the way back home, I started wondering if it was smart to go to the house. I hadn't been thinking straight. I knew someone had broken in to kill mom. And the cops had told me they might need to talk again after they filled out the paperwork on her death. But I needed to go back one more time, so as usual my needs out-voted my brain.

I parked three blocks away and walked down the sidewalk to look for cars out of place or anything that seemed odd. Nothing. I cut through two yards where I could stay out of sight. I hopped the fence and used my key to enter from the back. I didn't turn on any lights and in the kitchen drawer found a flashlight that worked.

The musty attic of my parents' house was covered with dust. Cobwebs glistened in the light streaming through the small window. Old straight-back chairs lined the back wall. Funny, I didn't remember the chairs at all. Boxes were crammed into the spaces where the ceiling slants down on each side, many of them open or filled to overflowing with old clothes, bowling trophies, and books. I stooped as I reached toward a box with Christmas decorations to slide the carton out of the way. I began with the box on the end, shining the light inside each one.

About half way down the row of boxes I located Dad's old Brownie movie projector. I removed the familiar yellow and red box with the Brownie. It had to be at least thirty or forty years old, but the box looked in good shape, so I figured the projector might still work. I carried it down from the attic.

In the study, I grabbed the white handle on top of the projector and lifted the machine onto the desk. The curtains were closed, as always, to protect Dad's books from sunlight. The paint on one side was still a shiny metallic brown and looked almost new. As a kid, I had helped dad set up home movies, and the operation seemed simple enough.

I removed the reel of film from the unlabeled canister, pushed it onto the top spindle, and threaded the film. I popped an empty reel from the box into place on the bottom spindle and held my breath as I turned the knob to Project.

I was lucky. The light came on and the reels began to spin, throwing an image onto the wall beside a large portrait of my great-great grandfather who'd had his arm shot off during the siege at Vicksburg but lived long enough to dictate a letter and send it home before he was buried in Vicksburg's Confederate cemetery. His one slave had returned home to Fairfield on horseback to deliver to the family my ancestor's pistol, Bible, and a letter from his commanding officer. We'd visited the grave once when I was a kid, but I could remember only the shock of seeing the acres and acres of white markers in the graveyard.

The images on the wall brought me back to the present. The black and white images were grainy and out of focus, mostly dark shapes despite it being obviously daytime. I turned the focusing dial and the picture came much clearer, so I kept adjusting the framing until the black strips along the edges disappeared.

Trying to make the scene explain something about my father

was useless. It was clear only that four men in black clothing and ski masks were breaking into a house in broad daylight through what seemed to be a back or side door. As one man picked the lock, the others stood close by with handguns drawn and held ready, pointed at the door. The door opened and the four were through it instantly.

The camera followed them down a hallway, and the picture grew darker as they slowly climbed stairs. The picture stopped momentarily before it opened on another scene in a bedroom. A leg came into view as someone dressed in loose fitting light-colored clothing kicked at the man leading the group. The camera backed up, and things were mostly a blur on the film as the four men fought one man for a few seconds before they were able to subdue him. His face wasn't visible, but his bare feet and legs kicked and struggled against the four who were sitting on him to hold him down.

One of the four reached into a pants pocket and retrieved a syringe, which he opened and jabbed under the arm of the man being held. Within seconds the man stopped struggling. The four men picked him up by the arms and dragged his dead weight into a bathroom, laying him face down on the floor as if he'd passed out there. The film went dark.

For half an hour I rewound the film and watched it over and over. I could have been a pouting child, sitting emotionless in a chair, repeating the same actions as I rewound the film and watched in stunned silence.

———

I tugged the string on the attic light, made my way down the stairs, and remembered my childhood friend Andy Simmons, Bugs we called him, who had shown up at dad's funeral. Not much can be said in the receiving line at a funeral service, but I remembered he said he'd read about my father in the newspaper. He mentioned he worked on computer graphics for movies and corporate training videos when I asked him what he did now. Bugs was brainy, always a geek, so learning he worked with computers had been no surprise. Even in high school, he was the one who ran the projector whenever we got to see movies or had to gather in the lunch room auditorium to watch film strips on some kind of disease. Bugs also told me something touching. He said that as a child I was the only friend he had who wasn't another nerdy guy. I decided to call him.

———

Bugs told me he still lived in the house he grew up in. His parents had given him the house after they retired and moved out to Shoal Creek to live on the golf course.

I grabbed my clothes, filled my travel bag, and left through a little-used side door so I could again go over the fence and take the back way to Bugs's house without anyone seeing me from any street. Within five minutes, I was knocking on his door, film in hand.

Bugs reached out to grip my shoulder. "Matt, come in. Man, I'm so sorry to hear about your mom," he said. "I'm sorry I didn't make her funeral, too, but I was in Atlanta for three days working on a film right after your dad's funeral. I didn't know about your mom until Dad told me when I got back." He hugged me. My eyes had to be shining as I choked back the tears.

I said, "It's all right. You know you were one of the few people I knew at Dad's funeral. I saw you with Kristine. It meant a lot for you to be there."

"I haven't forgotten how you stayed my friend all the way through high school even after you were in with the cool kids and I didn't fit in. That meant an awful lot to me," he said.

We walked into the living room and I was surprised at how small it seemed. As a kid I'd never noticed the size. On one wall hung the biggest television I'd ever seen, in front of a brown leather couch. Bugs pointed for me to sit on the couch. After getting us two beers from the kitchen, he shoved a two-foot tall stack of magazines onto the floor from a rattan chair across from the couch and plopped down.

"You said on the phone you needed help. What's wrong? I'll do anything I can," Bugs said.

I looked at his thick glasses and remembered where his name came from. In second grade, his drink-bottle-bottom glasses had given him bug eyes. When the first kid called him Bug Eyes, it stuck. Later he shortened the name to Bugs after he accepted that he'd never shed the label and may as well make the best of it.

"It's this old film. A sort of home movie thing. I need help figuring out what it shows," I told him.

"What do you mean? What is it?"

"Bugs, I'm afraid to say, but I have to tell you a weird story first. I think my parents were murdered."

"Damn, man. You serious? Murdered? Look, I've got all night," he said. "Come on."

"We may need all night. Apparently Dad got involved in

something at his job that was a big nasty deal, and it must be some kind of big dark secret."

"Then let's figure it out."

I told him the whole story, starting with the stranger who rescued me from the bar and ending with the odd black and white film that bewildered me. I didn't hold back my feelings and even told him I thought I could kill someone right then if I knew who did it.

"That's a hell of a story, Matt. Let's see the film," he said. He took the film and just looked at me for a few seconds, as if deciding whether or not I could really kill someone. When he nodded, I knew he had seen the truth in my words.

He opened the canister and held the film to the light saying, "I think I might be able to digitize it and add contrast to it a little, maybe enlarge some scenes, so we can tell what we're seeing. Let's give it a try."

We walked upstairs and entered what had once been his bedroom. The scene in front of me felt completely out of place in the old house and would have fit better in a 1960s Hollywood film studio. The walls were covered with sound-proofing materials that looked like gray egg cartons. An unpainted wood counter ran around three sides of the room. One wall had been removed to combine this bedroom with another small bedroom, making a long narrow work space for his equipment. The studio was completely covered with computers, tape decks, TV monitors, and other editing equipment, some old, some brand new. The room was pristine, just the opposite of the messy downstairs, but somehow that didn't surprise me.

From the way the room was kept, it was obvious the equipment all still worked. It looked like he'd never thrown away a technology apparatus in his life. Electronic machines of all descriptions were stacked on the counter, lined up underneath, and the shelves on one wall extended to the ceiling with various sizes and brands of gadgets I'd never seen, all of which seemed to be blinking red or green or blue. The wires and power cords were expertly bundled and had been run through openings in the counter so it all looked neat.

"Looks like you've got NASA mission control here," I said, turning in circles to survey the dozens of pieces of electronics.

"Yeah, I can do just about any kind of computer animation, high-end graphics, and some neat special effects," he said, as he sat in a swivel chair.

"How'd you get into this?"

"I got into computers early and owned one of the first Apples in Birmingham. In college a friend made a home movie as a project in class, and I did the graphics. I was hooked after that."

"Is this a job or a hobby?"

"I do animations. I've got film production company clients as far away as L.A., Chicago, and London that want my work on their movies."

"Let's take a look," he said. "I do still have some old projectors. A few years back it was a fad to use old home movies in TV commercials. I still get calls for that once in a while, so I keep a couple of projectors. They're eight-millimeter Brownies like your Dad had."

While Bugs rummaged around in his closet for a projector, I walked to a window and looked at the huge tree limb stretching over the garage roof. As kids we'd slip out the window after his parents were asleep, scoot across the garage roof holding the big limb, and shimmy down the oak tree.

Without turning toward me, he said, "By the way, Kristine lives somewhere here on Southside. I first ran into her a few weeks ago, eating pizza at Cadillac Café. Then I saw her at the funeral. I guess you still haven't talked to her since you've been back? I should have gotten her phone number, but I didn't think about it."

My relationship with Kristine had long been my greatest failure in life, the one thing I would change, the one thing I put out of my mind whenever I could. I answered, "No, I haven't really had a chance to try to look her up."

Those words were more than just a white lie. Kristine was on my mind from the moment I made the decision to come back to town. I'd checked the phone book but didn't find her name. She'd been someone I really cared about, but when I had my meltdown in college I left without even a goodbye. I didn't intend that, or to lose contact, but that's what happened. I called half a dozen times right after I left, but her mother always told me she was not home and promised she'd tell Kristine that I called. I wrote her two or three times right after that, then again a month or two later, but I never got a reply. After a few months it somehow seemed impossible. For seven years I'd carried that guilt and hurt around, thinking of her almost every day and wondering what had happened. But eventually I'd given up the idea that I would ever see her again. Now hearing her name for the second time since I returned home made me realize how much I really wanted to find her.

"How was she?"

"She got divorced."

"Divorced? From who?" I guess I'd never thought about how she would move on after I left. I still pictured her as the teenager I left behind, but clearly that was just where my own memories of her ended, with her suspended in time.

"She married Gerald Blass not long after you left," he said, as he slid a monitor over and plugged in the projector. "Everyone was in shock. Now she has a son in second grade."

I was stunned to learn that. Is that what Mom was referring to? I did the math in my head. She must have gotten over me in a hurry. I knew the day would come when I had to find her, to let her know I hated what I had done, if nothing else. We'd gone from childhood friends to best friends in junior high, and in high school realized we had grown into an item. None of our friends questioned it, and I can't even remember caring what our parents might think about us.

Before I could ask him more, Bugs finished threading the film into a machine, turned the switch, and threw the image onto the one blank spot on the wall he had painted white, next to a window that looked out onto the back yard.

"Holy Crap, Matt," Bugs said, leaning forward as the film played out and showed the man in front of the toilet. He ran it back and watched again in silence. "I've got some work to do. Give me a couple of hours to copy and digitize this onto the new DVD format and see if I can clean up some of these images."

"I guess I shouldn't ask what a DVD does?"

Bugs rolled his eyes. "Man, you have been off the grid. Just think of it as a music CD, with more storage and pics and vids."

"I can use a nap. I'll be downstairs."

chapter 9

When Bugs yelled down the stairs to wake me up, the horses scattered. It took several seconds to fight my way to the surface of the deep pool of sleep I'd fallen into. I sat up on his couch and blinked. Days of drinking and running on little sleep made me feel as if gravity itself had increased. The big German cuckoo clock on his wall showed the time was nearly ten. I'd been asleep for over two hours.

"Yeah," I said, "coming."

Bugs yelled, "Man, get your ass up here now. Right now. This is big. This is freaky."

Bugs sounded more excited than I'd ever heard him. And there was something else. Fear maybe?

The sound of his voice jolted my brain like a slap in the face. Adrenaline finally swept away the cobwebs. I pushed my feet into my beat-up Keds, hopping on one foot at a time and then running all the way to the stairs.

As I took the stairs two at a time, they creaked under my weight, each one signaling to Bugs I was almost there. I laughed to myself, remembering how impossible it had been ever to sneak out using the stairs at this house because they creaked so loudly.

I stood in the door of the studio that had once been Bugs's bedroom. Bugs sat back in a ratty stuffed chair with his hands behind his head. He stared ahead at a frame of the film blown up on a large monitor, not even looking over as I entered. The grainy picture showed a close-up of a hand grasping the wrist of the man who'd been subdued.

I froze and looked over at Bugs, hoping he'd say something. I couldn't speak. He didn't either. The missing finger told me something I expected but hadn't been able to believe until this moment. There was no denying it now.

"That's the same look I had," Bugs finally said as he saw my expression. He asked the question that was really a statement, "That's the same missing finger as your dad, isn't it? It's him?"

I recognized the hand immediately. Dad had some kind of accident when I was very young, and the last two sections of his index finger were missing. I managed only a soft, "Yeah, I think that's him." I slumped into an old wooden desk chair next to Bugs.

"Well, that's not the big shocker, Matt. This next one will blow your damn mind," he said, almost monotone, as if he himself was also in shock.

"There's more?"

"I don't know what your dad was into, but this is some scary shit. Look at this."

I leaned forward with my hands on my knees, breathing through my nose to help me calm down, hoping whatever Bugs wanted me to see would somehow make this whole thing make sense. I couldn't have been more wrong, and the next scene he showed me changed my life forever.

Bugs twisted a dial, which fast-forwarded the film. Somehow Bugs had lightened the dark scenes. Even at this advanced speed, I could tell much more detail, watching the fight in fast motion and seeing how easily the attackers had managed to overcome the man despite his karate kicks and punches. As the end of the film neared, Bugs slowed the speed, advancing the picture frame by frame to show two men dragging the man in pajamas by the arms.

Bugs stopped the film and zoomed into the frame. The man's head was down so low his chin touched his chest, his face mostly covered by long dark hair. His feet stretched behind him. When Bugs advanced the film one frame at a time, the man's head rolled to the side, and the hair fell aside just for a moment. Bugs froze the frame and zoomed in on the face. You couldn't see this detail at normal film speed.

Almost shouting, I gripped the arms of the chair and rose up in the seat. For the second time that week I felt the hair on my arms sticking up. I stared at a lifeless face that virtually everyone in the civilized world knew by name. His first name. "No, Bugs, this can't be real. No way."

"It's him, man. It's damn sure him," he said. "And he has left the building."

chapter 10

"Is he dead?" I asked Bugs, knowing the answer, but somehow hoping this was not really the way Elvis had died.

"Seems like it to me. I looked it up on the Internet, and it said he died in the bathroom."

A loud creak on the stairs made both of us freeze. I grabbed Bugs's arm to keep him quiet and looked toward the door.

Someone was creeping through the house.

Bugs looked at me, his eyes wide.

I pointed toward the computer as I reached for the film canister beside his keyboard. He pressed a button, and the disk tray opened. I snatched the DVD and placed it inside the film can, sliding the container with original film and disk inside my shirt as I stood quietly.

I whispered, "Can we still get out that window?"

Bugs nodded as he tip-toed toward the window over the garage. "My Vespa's in the carport. Key's right here." He patted his jeans pocket.

I was relieved when he raised the window easily and climbed through. I crawled head first right behind him into the darkness.

We'd almost reached the edge of the garage roof when I heard two loud pops from the window behind us. Bugs never made a sound or looked up, just went face forward over the side of the roof. I'll never forget his body landing with a splashing sound like the water balloons we once threw from this same roof as he hit the driveway fifteen feet below us. It was the sickest feeling of my life. I had to swallow the sobs trying to blow up in my throat like grenades.

I plunged forward into the tree, grabbing the trunk and spinning around to the back side as I half climbed, half fell down through the rough limbs. I heard shot after shot tearing through the limbs and leaves around me, and then the bullets stopped. I realized the shooter must be empty and reloading when no more shots followed. When I hit the ground, I dragged Bugs under the carport. I knelt down and felt his neck, but there was no pulse and even in the dark I knew he was dead. A large pool of blood was smeared across the concrete. I felt inside his sticky pants pocket and found his keys.

The Vespa cranked easily and lurched forward. I blinked away the tears so I could see. At the end of the driveway, I glanced back to see two men run from the front door toward me. I heard shots behind me and tried to will myself smaller, leaning forward and ducking my head as low as I could. Rounding the corner, I was able to look back and see the lights come on in what was likely a dark Lincoln Towncar.

The street curved around a long tall hedge enough to hide me. As soon as I knew they couldn't see me, I switched off the headlight, turned left into the first driveway, and cut through the back yards, hoping there were no new fences built since the times I'd run through these backyards as a kid. I stopped in deep shadow behind the second house and looked back to the street to see the Lincoln speed past.

When the car was well out of sight, I eased back into the street and drove the opposite direction as fast as I could without lights. After a mile or two, I switched on the low beams and began looking for a convenience store with a pay phone. I stopped two feet from a phone at the edge of the lot, dropped two coins, and dialed 9-1-1. When the operator answered, I said, "Someone's been shot on 22nd Avenue in English Village." I hung up, crying so hard I couldn't breathe, and went to my knees, throwing up until I was dry heaving.

chapter 11

Half an hour after using backstreets and alleys to hide from the men who shot Bugs, I pulled off into a dimly lit strip shopping center just south of Birmingham and parked in the shadow of a building facing the entrance. My shirt was wet with sweat. I'll admit it—I was scared, I was mad at myself, and I was pissed at someone I didn't know. I hated myself for leaving Bugs, for not fighting back. I hated myself for leaving home years before. And now for coming home. All at the same time.

In my life I have never felt more helpless, and I hammered my fists against the handle bars. I wanted to just find a ride west and run. But too many were dead. Family and now a friend. I put my head back and closed my eyes, willing my heart to slow down. And I decided this had to end and it had to end on my terms. First, I had to find someone who knew what was going on. That meant hiding while I figured this out. At that moment I knew I would not stop until someone was made to pay. I decided the first move was to get out of town, at least for tonight.

I took a highway and soon found myself thirty miles south of Birmingham in a quiet community known as Montevallo, home to the University of Montevallo. Although it's a state-run university, the campus looks and feels more like a small, private liberal arts college. Old brick buildings and tall thick columns. Manicured lawns. Clean sidewalks connecting the buildings. I parked the Vespa in front of the student activity building where I'd visited a few times with friends during college. A sign on the door showed it would stay open until two a.m. Two other motorcycles—a small-engine Honda and an older Triumph—were parked there among two dozen bicycles.

No one paid me any attention as I bought coffee and sat in the corner facing the front door, wondering what to do next. The film canister was a block of ice under my shirt.

Three pay telephones on the far wall caught my attention. You didn't see as many pay phones as we did when I was a kid. There was only one person I could talk to.

I asked for change from the young man behind the cash register whose dreadlocks seemed somehow out of place with his starched, white button-collared shirt. I dialed directory assistance for the number of David Collier in Jackson, Mississippi. I paused at the tenth digit, uncertain what to say. I took a deep breath, looked around one last time to be sure no one was close enough to listen, and pressed the number.

On the fifth ring the answering machine came on. I left the number of the pay phone and said it was an emergency, hoping David would call in the next half hour before the student union closed.

One minute later the pay phone rang.

"Hello, this is Matt."

"Matt, what's wrong?" David asked.

"David, Dad and Mom were murdered. And someone is after me or might be setting me up or something. It's all crazy."

I was relieved when he didn't tell me I was nuts or tell me to call the cops if I really believed what I was telling him. After he confirmed he had heard me right, he stopped me from going into detail and said to meet him in Tuscaloosa the next morning at ten at the Huddle House on McFarland. It was like he already knew what I said was true and was expecting my call.

Like most kids, I'd grown up with the fantasy of being a hero. Cops and robbers, Yankees and Rebels, Robin Hood against the king. We played them all, and I played every role on every side. And each time, I was a hero, making the quick-draw shot or throwing the knife to kill the last bad guy when my gun jammed. In my imagination, I sank the shot to win the tournament and hit the homerun in the bottom of the ninth. But here I was in real life, with real bad guys, with a real-life reason to be both angry and afraid, and all I could do was tell myself that when the time came to get back at the guys who killed my parents, I would let my anger win over my fear.

My drive on the back roads through Centreville to avoid Birmingham was uneventful. The most memorable attraction about the small town was the Twix 'n Tween Barbeque, a place people packed on their way back home to Montgomery or to South Alabama on Saturday nights after an Alabama football game in Tuscaloosa.

I arrived early at the Huddle House and was on my third cup of coffee when I saw a man park near the door. Even though I'd recently seen him in Dad's hospital room, I didn't immediately recognize David with his silver hair.

The restaurant had that appetizing Saturday morning coffee and bacon smell of leisure. We sat in a booth in the corner and ordered without looking at the menu. My two eggs sunny-side-up were cold by the time I slowed down enough from talking to take a bite. I motioned to the waitress leaning on the counter and pointed to our empty coffee cups. I'd started my story at the bar in Sequin and sprinted through to Bugs's death. I leaned forward and spoke barely above a whisper. I'd had to look away and wipe my eyes when I thought about my parents and Bugs. David said nothing for a moment. He looked over his shoulder to make sure no one paid us any attention.

"I always knew there was more to Marshall's problem than just the drinking. A couple of times he came close to telling me something important, something big it seemed, but I could see a real struggle going on inside him. The closest he got was asking if I would be there if you or your mom ever called for help."

"What did my father do?" I asked. "I mean, what did he really do for the NSEO?"

"He worked in a department he couldn't talk much about. I honestly don't know much. But for an office guy, he spent a lot of time at the firing range."

"I figured out that much, but why was it such a secret?" I asked.

"He couldn't tell me. He said he dealt with sensitive security issues and it was best not to talk about it. I assumed he meant national security. I accepted that he couldn't say much." David looked past me into the parking lot as he talked. "He always said he was mostly doing accounting, but it was obvious he did more than paperwork."

"How so?"

"Well, he came home from a 'conference' one time missing a part of a finger. Not exactly what happens with a paper cut in a boring seminar. He wouldn't talk about it."

I stared into my coffee, thinking of my childhood and trying to remember that event. "I never cared much about his job. He always just told people he was an accountant. He was embarrassing to me as a teen, so I never paid any attention to his work. I just remember when I was pretty young that he started staying home drunk all the time."

David nodded and sort of sighed, saying, "Yeah, the drinking too much happened suddenly. Then he lost his job."

He motioned for the check.

"Did you hang with him when he started getting drunk?" I asked.

"That's when he shut me out, along with the rest of his friends. I did talk him into coming over for barbeque on the Fourth of July that first year, and after he was drunk I almost got him talking. He said something that makes more sense now."

I picked up a paper-thin slice of crisp bacon, then pushed my plate back without touching the eggs or grits. I wanted to know anything at all about my father and his work.

"What do you mean?" I asked.

"He said he'd screwed up everything. And put his family and friends in 'harm's way.' I distinctly remember him using those exact words. That's when I think he really wanted to tell me what was going on. It's why they never tried to get you to come home."

"But he didn't tell you."

"No, he just got choked up and turned around to leave.".

"And that was it?"

"I caught him at the front door and grabbed his arm. When I demanded to know what he was talking about, he just said that if I ever saw you or his mother in trouble to know it was life or death and to take the situation seriously."

"So here we are," I said. I knew why he didn't question me much on the phone.

David looked really serious and leaned over the table as he looked me right in the eye. "Matt, he really scared me. He said to trust no one and especially don't go to the NSEO if something goes wrong. That was the last real conversation we had."

I stacked my plate and cup and slid them to the side. "You didn't try to find out what he meant?"

"After that he wouldn't talk to me much, or else he was too drunk. After you called me that time from California, I reached him by phone. He was some better that day and I thought he'd tell me something."

"But he didn't give you anything that might help us figure this out?"

"Marshall said he already knew you were fine, but he wouldn't say how he knew. But he didn't mention anything that would help with this."

"Do you think Mom was right about them killing him?"

"Matt, I don't know, but your mom was a very smart lady. I have no reason to doubt her," he said. "But until we find out, you have to stay hidden. And be damn careful."

"I guess I know how to run and hide."

David hesitated, then asked, "Do you know how to use a pistol?"

"I've shot enough, yes."

"Here." He slide a brown paper sack across the table.

Inside I saw a pistol.

That conversation confirmed that I had to do what I had to do. "I'm going to find out who did this. You'll learn I'm a patient person, but I will find out what happened. And they will pay."

"Matt, something tells me you're not a person who bluffs. But don't go off trying to get some kind of revenge on your own. We'll figure this out. You watch over your shoulder and don't trust anyone. I mean no one."

———

When I pulled up in front of Wal-Mart, I slid the pistol David had given me inside the back of my belt and pulled out my shirttail. The Charter Arms five-shot revolver had .38 Off Duty Spl stamped on the barrel. He said the pistol was legal but untraceable because he'd bought it at a gun show in Jackson years before and there wasn't any paperwork. Lots of off-duty cops carried this exact gun, he said.

At first I just sat there thinking about what I was doing and how David said I had to assume that a lot of people were looking for me. I needed to hide. But was this really necessary? Maybe it was. I felt a little foolish, but I decided to change my looks. Hair color and a razor would be the first steps to that. I grabbed a few bottles of color, uncertain what color or products I should try. Losing the beard would help. And I needed a car.

After going to three stores picking up the things I needed to alter my appearance—including adding a white baseball cap, dark glasses, and a couple of pre-paid cell phones to the list—I grabbed a newspaper from the rack and sat in the parking lot reading through the used car section of the classified ads. The purchase should be from an individual so the paperwork wouldn't have my real name.

Two hours later, after a quick shave in a McDonald's, I was driving a dark blue 1997 Chevy Cavalier through the countryside on the outskirts of Tuscaloosa, taking the long way to Birmingham. The car had close to ninety thousand miles, but it ran like new and wouldn't be memorable to anyone who saw it. I'd left the Vespa beside a dorm at the University of Alabama, the key under a tire. Even if no one took the bike, it could sit for a few days before anyone noticed.

Kudzu created a blanket over enormous pines and in places crawled through the ditches on both sides to touch the asphalt. I had the key in my pocket for David's lake house on Lake Logan Martin, about forty minutes the other side of Birmingham. He'd kept the weekend place when he moved to Mississippi. I promised him I would stay in touch and told him I didn't need any money. I had Dad's stash hidden away and a folded stack of hundreds in my pocket. I figured I could get to the money in a hurry if I needed more.

I pulled off at a clay pit to test the pistol and to find a suitable place in the car to stash the film. Up high along the back wall of the trunk, a section of carpet was loose, and the film canister slid in easily. To find the canister, someone would have to be looking for something small.

The first round I fired missed an old five-gallon paint can completely, but I grazed it with the second and bounced the can two more times in three shots. I stepped closer after reloading from the box of hollow points David had handed me. From about ten feet, I put four holes in the can. I reloaded, and this time held the gun in both hands the way my dad had taught me when I was a child. Even through his drunk years, we went out a couple of times to shoot. I fired all five shots as quickly as I could shoot. Three more holes. I repeated this three more times, gaining confidence with each trigger pull as I got comfortable with the blast and the recoil. The last time five holes appeared in a piece of cardboard propped on the can. Close enough.

chapter 12

When I reached the edge of Birmingham, I steered the car into an asphalt parking lot at a tiny grocery store with front windows completely covered by beer and cigarette posters. I spotted two newspaper racks near the corner by a freezer of ninety-nine cent ice.

The Tuscaloosa News had reported nothing about Bugs. But there it was on page three of the Metro Section of *The Birmingham Post-Herald,* an afternoon newspaper. A small blurb about a suicide on the Southside. The brief story indicated that Andrew Simmons, lifelong resident of Birmingham and small-business owner, had died of a self-inflicted gunshot wound to the head. A neighbor had spotted the body on the driveway, it said. I couldn't imagine how they avoided reports of the numerous blasts people must have heard.

I'd read a lot in my life and I loved crime novels and thrillers and spy novels. All through them were conspiracies and forces of evil, networks of the rich and powerful evil people at work. Those groups of men and women who conspired behind the scenes were the stuff of fiction and not something I thought really existed in any big way. But my view of the world was shaken now and upside down. They did exist, and they did scare me.

Despite David's warning not to trust anyone, I had to start

somewhere to learn what Dad had done to get himself killed. Jim Robinson would be the best person for starters. I'd seen in his eyes and heard in his voice real concern for Dad. He had taken me fishing as a child. I needed to talk to him, even with Dad's warning to David not to go to the NSEO.

Jim surprised me when he answered his home phone on the first ring. I expected him to be at work, somewhere I wouldn't call.

"Jim, it's Matt. I need to talk."

He practically cut me off, saying quickly, "Not like this. Come to my house. I'm in Hoover. Where are you?"

I didn't want to say no, I had no reason to suspect Jim of anything. But I had promised David to do as Dad said and trust no one. And I'll tell you, that was the easy part. When he didn't ask why I wanted to meet, my internal radar gave a warning.

I said, "Can you just meet me on Southside? I'll be at the Five Points South Fountain. Four o'clock."

There was a long pause, and I was about to say something when he said, "I'll be there" and hung up.

———

At two, I parked in an alley behind the Highlands United Methodist Church. The main building sits between two of the east-running five streets that converge to become Five Points South, the unofficial heart of the Birmingham neighborhood known as Southside. The fountain area in front of the church fills with crowds of skateboarders, businessmen lounging to avoid being in the office, white kids with dreadlocks hanging from under knit hats, and assorted other college students and professors, young couples, and a surprising mix of Hispanics and Asians who collectively make up what people in Birmingham refer to as Southsiders. Near the fountain seemed like a safe place to meet since traffic builds there each morning and remains brisk until midnight.

The bench beside the church door gave me a little elevation from which to watch anyone approaching on the circular sidewalks around the fountain. I'd arrived early just to get comfortable with the area, spending that time to walk around and through the church and up and down the alleys in the area to look for places to run or hide. I didn't know what to look for, but it seemed like the thing to do. An hour and a half later, I saw Jim crossing the street from where I assumed he parked in the public lot beneath Cosmo's Pizza. He was early, too.

He walked to the fountain and looked around. He didn't see me at first. The clean-shaven face and the hat and glasses worked for a few seconds. I noticed a wry half-smile as he turned and walked directly toward me, cutting his eyes to one side and then the other as he got closer.

I looked around, but noticed nothing out of place.

"Hello, Jim," I said.

"Matt, what's this about?"

"What do you know about why someone would want to kill my father?"

"Matt, I told you there is nothing to that."

"Why do you think that?"

"I looked into it a little after you asked me about it in the hospital. Your father had an accident. Nothing more," he said.

I'd prepared myself to push back if that was his answer. I had to know if he knew something he wasn't telling, or this road could end right here.

"Cut the bullshit, Jim. I know he and Mom were killed. And I know more than you think about that illegal job Dad was part of." Time to bluff. "Tell me about C4."

The slight raised eyebrows told me I was on the right track. Jim knew something. I wanted to shock him into telling me what he knew. "I have the film. I know everything, Jim. I just wanted to know if you'd be the one person I could trust. Now I know I can't." I stood to walk away.

He glanced around and held up his hands, palms down. "Wait. Sit down, Matt. This story will take a while to explain. If you have to know anything, you have to know everything," he said. He sighed, audibly, with clear resignation. He leaned forward and spoke quietly. "I may be the only person you can trust."

Jim motioned to the bench. He sat and put his face in his hands, rubbing his eyes. He said nothing for thirty seconds. Then he looked up and spoke, his tone genuine and friendly. "Matt, you have no idea what you can stir up with this, what you have already stirred up. It goes higher and is more complicated than you could ever imagine. C4 is more dangerous than its namesake. For your own good, give me that film."

That's when I noticed Jim again cut his eyes a little to the side, and I thought I saw his shoulders tense up. It was not something I'd normally even notice, but it made me look, too.

Although this area has several businesses nearby and plenty of business people around, the two men in suits walking toward us seemed out of place. And I'd seen their short haircuts before. I looked the other direction and two more men half a block down walking beside the church on the sidewalk looked like their twins.

I stood, looking around. Jim grabbed my arm tight in his strong right hand.

"Matt, give me the damn film. Please," he pleaded. "I'll get you out of this."

I slammed the heel of my hand hard into Jim's cheek, which clearly caught him by surprise. His grip loosened. I jerked my arm free and sprinted up the church steps and through the front door. Two women inside screamed as I bolted down the center aisle toward them. I never even looked back as I brushed past them and ran through a door that I knew opened into a hallway leading to the back door. Out the side window of the hallway, I saw a man walking quickly toward the back of the building and felt my stomach turn inside out as I saw the black pistol, a Glock maybe, he held to the side of his leg. I opened the door a tiny crack. Wood splinters exploded into my face as the man fired a shot that hit the doorframe inches from my chin. About that time a delivery truck turned into the alley and the man tucked his gun into his coat. I ran to the window, slid it open, and saw another way out. As the truck moved between the shooter and me, I jumped through the open window to the pavement six feet below. I sprinted around the corner and pulled the revolver from the back of my pants.

Hard leather shoes echoed down the alley as the man with the pistol ran toward me. The Cavalier was parked on the opposite side of the alley, so I knew I couldn't get there in time. With nowhere to hide or run, I froze, looking for any way out. Just as I heard the steps reach the end of the alley, I turned in desperation, faced the corner, and raised the gun. When the man rounded the corner at a full run, his chest crashed into the gun barrel as he ran into me. The gun exploded with a muffled sound but still too loud. Dead weight slammed me backward to the ground. I felt warm blood soak through my shirt. It wasn't mine. I pushed the man off me and half crawled on my hands and knees, keeping low as possible, back to the Cavalier. I saw two men run down the alley from the other end and scramble into a Town Car parked behind the church. The Cavalier started easily. My hands and the front of my shirt were red as I squealed the Cavalier's tires the wrong way down the one-way street.

Nearing the intersection one block down, I swerved around a black Suburban pulling out quickly from a parallel parking spot, and I glanced in the rearview mirror to see the Town Car round the corner from the alley. The Suburban slammed head-on into the Town Car, which didn't swerve or hit its brakes. Metal pieces and glass rained down in the street, and steam rose from the front of the wreckage. As I topped the hill, I saw a man running from the Suburban. For a moment I thought he might look familiar, but it happened too fast to know for sure.

———————

The mug of draft beer in front of me had lost its frosty coating. My hands were still red, not from blood but from scrubbing them in the Eastlake Mall men's room. I'd parked the Cavalier in the mall lot and changed out of the bloody T-shirt in the parking lot, managing to get my hands fairly clean before I walked inside.

After I felt presentable, I hoofed it half a mile to the used car lot where I paid for a 1990 Ford F-150 truck with twenty crisp one hundreds. Then I drove straight to the restaurant a few hundred yards down the road. The old truck looked at home out front with assorted other trucks and a newer Tahoe or two. The tires were decent, and it ran good.

For nearly an hour, I'd been staring at the beer without a sip. I finally pushed the glass back and waved the young waitress over to order iced tea.

Someone had to know something. I knew I needed to find Kristine. She might be the only person I could trust, but calling Kristine's mom would be an awkward conversation. I finished half a cheeseburger and two glasses of tea as I thought of what to say. I played back in my head how I had left so suddenly years before and tried to imagine what that must have felt like to Kristine and her mom, to my few friends, and to my mom and dad. What seemed like the right and logical thing to do at the time now seemed stupid and childish. Was I really thinking back then that Kristine would somehow run off with me when I found a place? Was I just running from growing up? Whatever I'd been thinking then was gone like a faint dream, one of those dreams you knew was important and seemed so clear in the night but the next morning was nothing but distant fractured pieces of scenes and unrelated events. I had no excuse. Nothing explained me. I had nothing to do but face the truth and play out the hand.

The Iron Horse Restaurant in Irondale where I was hiding was plenty dark. I had no fear at all of seeing anyone I knew. From where I sat I could watch everyone coming through the door and could turn my head if there was any chance someone familiar showed up. I had already checked out the kitchen when I went to the restroom and knew I could easily slip out a side door. It was still early for dinner, so there were only two tables with customers. Two UPS guys in brown shorts and shirts sat at the bar eating burgers and dipping fries in ketchup. Tucked among the row of brick buildings alongside the railroad, the restaurant was surely out of the way enough to be safe and was on the way to the Logan Martin lake house where I'd be staying for a few days.

Every detail of this scene around me seemed sharp and focused, with hard edges. It was as if a fog had lifted. I was no longer in the old slow-motion, detached world. Now the neon beer-sign colored hues on the walls and the sounds of people talking in muffled voices and the smoke from the pit created a new kind of dreamy world where the scene was at once vivid and clear, yet nothing seemed real, and I wanted only to be back on my motorcycle spinning down some dry Texas highway with the sound of wind in my ears and my head as blank as copy paper. I leaned my head over with my eyes closed and drifted into that state of mind where I was neither asleep nor awake when a truck horn outside caused me to sit up, suddenly wide awake again and back in the present. I had to call Kristine.

Directory assistance found an Eleanor Masters for me near Atlanta. I dialed the number on the cell phone. Eleanor answered on the first ring. Although I had dialed the number, I wasn't sure what to say.

"Hello? Hello? Is someone there?"

I cleared my throat and said, "Mrs. Masters, this is Matt Boykin."

A long pause.

"Well, Matthew, this is a surprise," she said. Her tone flat, uncommitted. Then a little warmer, "Matt, I heard about your parents. I'm very sorry. Your father and I had been good friends for a long time."

"Thanks," I said. "I was wondering if I you could help me reach

Kristine. I can't locate her, and I'd like to say hello to her before I leave town."

Again, she paused before answering. "I don't think that's a good idea, Matt. She's moved on with her life. You hurt her, you know, even though you were young. Opening that wound would not be good."

"I just want to say hello and let Kristine know I was sorry for disappearing. I owe her that."

"Well, that's something we can agree on," she said, cold again.

I knew that once the story of the shooting reached the news Mrs. Masters would never talk to me. This was my one chance.

"Just give me a way to reach her, please. If she doesn't want to talk, I promise you I'll disappear and leave her alone."

We went back and forth for a couple of minutes, me trying hard to sound reasonable and not like some lost teenager. I repeated my promise to go away. I'm not sure I meant it. Finally she told me Kristine was divorced. And she agreed to ask Kristine if she wanted to talk. If so, she would give her my number. All I could do was offer my parents' number and say leave a message there.

The conversation was over, and the awkward pauses were growing longer between sentences. I knew this would be my only opportunity to ask about Dad and his work, so I took a shot.

I told her, "Some of the men my father worked with came around when he was in the hospital, but Jim Robinson was the only one I knew. I'd like to talk to some of the others to say thanks, if you could tell me some names."

"Who else came around?" she asked, the tone a bit more than just curious.

I told her the names I knew. Then I asked, "Who else worked

with Dad? What about a man named Mark Pugh? Do you know if they were friends?"

The voice at the other end of the line changed to flat, cold again for what I knew was the last time. My time was up with her. "I don't know of anyone he was still close to after the drinking started. Everyone had their own life, and Marshall made it clear he didn't want to stay in touch."

"But you worked with Dad for years. You must know someone."

"It was nice to hear from you, Matt. I just don't want to talk about the past."

"Talk about what? I just asked for names of Dad's friends," I said, knowing it was the wrong thing to say, struggling to keep my voice down.

"Look, leave me out of it. And stay away from Kristine. Giving her your information would be wrong. I'm calling her to tell her not to talk with you," she said. "I'm truly sorry about your parents Matt, but you should go back wherever you were and go on with your life. Don't call again."

The line went dead.

chapter 13

There was no Kristine Masters or Kristine Blass listed in directory assistance in Birmingham. Time was short. I had to find her today. I decided to burn up one of the cell phones while on the move, then toss it.

I began going through my list of friends that I thought she might have contacted when she moved back. I could only come up with a short list. The first couple of people were nowhere to be found. Each time I did connect with someone the conversation was awkward and difficult to keep short, as everyone had questions about where I went, what happened, why I dropped out like that. But on the sixth try I found someone who had run into Kristine in a bookstore, and they had exchanged numbers. A girlfriend of Kristine's said she was living on Southside. I shouldn't have been surprised. That's where I'd have moved if I'd come back. It brought back memories of the two of us hanging out in the record shops and parks in the area.

The phone number for Kristine stared back at me from the corner of the newspaper I'd torn off where I wrote it. I couldn't think of the words to use. *Hey, it's me, Matt. Sorry I haven't gotten around to calling in the last seven or eight years. What do you want to do Friday?*

I'd always thought this day would come, but I never once came up with anything to say. I decided I'd just call. When I heard her voice, I'd respond to whatever she said.

The phone rang and part of me hoped she wouldn't answer, but she picked up immediately with a simple hello. I couldn't seem to form the right words.

"Is someone there?" she asked, the irritation obvious. The line went dead.

I waited a few seconds and called again. This time Kristine picked up after one ring. The annoyance came through in her hello.

"Kristine, it's Matt," I said.

She didn't hang up, but said nothing.

Not waiting for her to say more, I said, "Kristine, I need to talk to you."

"Yeah? Just like that? You need to talk." she said. The irritation had turned to venom and irony.

"It's important."

She cut me off. "Oh, it's *important*," she said mocking me. "Well, I thought it might be *important* eight years ago to know if you were dead. Or hurt in some ditch somewhere with your motorcycle. For weeks I thought you must be dead on the side of the road. Did you ever think about that?"

I managed a weak, "I'm sorry, Kristine."

She went on, "I thought it might be important eight years ago to know why a person I cared for disappeared without a word. But that didn't happen, did it?"

I could only whisper again, "I'm sorry."

"Where in the hell have you been? Couldn't you even write one time?" she yelled into the phone. "If your mom hadn't called me a year after you left, I'd have thought you really were dead."

"Kristine? I did write. And I called. Your mom said you wouldn't talk to me," I said, the confusion in my voice probably obvious.

"Yeah right," she said, but her tone had softened a fraction. It was a sliver of an opportunity.

I took the opening. "I'm truly sorry Kristine, and I want to tell you what happened. And I really did try lots of times to contact you. But right now I need to talk to you about my parents."

"I heard about them, Matt. I'm sorry. Your mom was very good to me," she said, even sounding sympathetic. Then, cold again, she continued, "My mother called a minute ago and said you might contact me. She said I shouldn't have anything to do with you after the way you ran out on me. And she said you might even be in trouble."

"I know it's not worth saying, but I wasn't running out on you," I said. "At least that was never what I meant to do. I tried and tried to talk to you at first."

Silence on the line.

I continued. "Can we meet somewhere so I can tell you what's happened? If you don't believe me then, I'll leave and never call you again."

It took another five minutes of talking to convince her to meet me at the Steak 'N Egg Kitchen for coffee.

———

Nothing had changed in the restaurant. The same metal chairs with red cushions and backs, the same smell of steak grease and hash browns soaked into the walls. When she walked in, I had to swallow very hard to find my voice. She was more beautiful than ever, and not in a girlish way. Her hair was still down to her shoulders, but her body was both toned and full at the same time. She stood erect and walked with a strong, confident gait, making her look even taller than her five-ten. I stood up, not really knowing what else to do.

Kristine slid into the booth without a hug or handshake. She was all business. Her expression was level, with neither a smile nor a frown. "So what does anything about your parents have to do with me?" she asked.

"I guess you read all about Dad's wreck and about Mom's suicide. I saw you at Dad's funeral," I said.

"Yeah, I saw the obits in the paper and talked with Bugs. But I didn't know your Mom was a suicide."

I took a deep breath.

"She wasn't. They were both murdered."

She leaned forward, the skin on her forehead wrinkled and her eyes wide. "What? Are you serious? The paper didn't say that."

I noticed a couple of very tiny permanent wrinkles around her eyes, reminding me how long I had been away.

We ordered coffee, and she sipped slowly as I went through the whole story. For ten minutes she sat silently as I talked, just nodding now and then. I started at the point I was handed a note from a stranger—that I now know as Mark Pugh—to call home, downplaying and leaving out most of the details of the bar fight. I went through the events that led up to my discovery of my mom's faked suicide, ending with Bugs being shot. I didn't mention what happened at Five Points South yet.

After I finished, she sat back shaking her head. "It doesn't make sense, Matt. I don't see how I can help, and I really can't have anything to do with this. I'm sorry, but I have a child to think of first. I hope it works out for you," she said as she stood up to leave.

I threw a five on the chipped Formica table and caught up with her outside.

"Kristine, there's more. When I tried to talk to Jim Robinson, a bunch of men tried to kill me. It has to be some guys from NSEO."

"Yeah, right. The NSEO is trying to kill you. Exactly what did you do to become such a big national security threat?" she asked, sarcasm and disbelief dripping thick as motor oil.

"They fired at me for no reason. And I shot one of them a few hours ago."

She stopped me before I could go on, holding both her hands in front of her as if signaling to stop a car, and said, "You killed someone?" The look on her face was more of sadness than horror.

"I shot him. He may be dead, I don't know. I didn't want to. I mean, of course I was trying to protect myself, but I didn't want to shoot someone. He was chasing me and shooting. I pointed the gun, and he ran into me, the gun went off … it was so fast."

Her eyes were somber and narrowed almost to slits, not wide and angry.

"Oh, my God. You carry a gun now? Matt, who have you turned into? I don't know you anymore."

Her voice was soft, disappointed.

I shook my head no as I spoke, "No, I don't really carry a gun. Someone gave it to me after men shot at me and killed Bugs. I'm sorry, this was the wrong thing to do. I just didn't know who else to call, Kristine."

I took a step to leave, but she placed her hand on my arm to stop me.

"So what makes you think I can help?"

"I have to have someone I can trust and a place to get off the street while I figure out what's going on."

"So now you want me to get in the middle of this?"

I leaned closer to keep my own voice down.

"No one will connect us. I just need a place to hide for a little while." As I listened to myself, I thought of what I was doing. Were my feelings clouding my judgment? "This is wrong," I said. "I'll find some other way. It was really wonderful to see you, Kristine. I'm so sorry for how things turned out. It was my fault. I should go now."

I meant it. I pulled my car key from my front pocket to show I was leaving.

This time Kristine put both hands up, palms toward me, moving them slightly back and forth to stop me. For several seconds she looked at me, then rolled her eyes upward as if in disbelief at what she was about to do. She let out a big sigh.

"Follow me to my apartment. But if I say leave, you leave right then. No questions, no arguments."

She turned toward her car without waiting for an answer.

Her first-floor apartment was somewhat sparse, but the pieces of furniture there looked expensive, tasteful. A leather couch and two overstuffed chairs faced each other in the small living room. One wall held a small bookcase that appeared to be mostly paperback novels.

I walked over to see a grouping of photographs on another wall.

Every photo was of a small boy. In one he was riding a bike. In another he was holding a soccer ball and a small trophy of some kind. I realized I'd been away longer than it seemed.

"Bugs said you have a son."

"That's Winter. He's mostly with my mom for the summer until I get settled in at my new job. She quit working a couple of years back. I just moved back here in May."

"I had no idea."

"Well, there's a lot you don't have any idea about. Winter is the reason I can't really have much to do with this. I have someone else to watch out for."

"What grade is Winter in?"

Something about the photos held me there, taking in each one. Although I was still facing a wall of photos I could see from the side that she was staring at me and shaking her head as if talking with herself.

"He'll be in third grade," she said.

I'd already realized how soon she moved on to someone else when I left, and the child reminded me. I changed the subject and told her to sit down for a few minutes and let me tell her what I knew about Mom and Dad. When I finished with the story about the men breaking into the house I believed was Graceland, she smiled the same crooked smile that first broke my heart when we were only fifteen. That was the summer I first noticed she looked more like a woman than a child to me. Her expression was a question that needed no words. She was searching my eyes for a clue about the truth in me.

I leaned forward and took her hand. "Kristine, I know you have every reason to hate me. And you owe me nothing. But

I promise you I'm not crazy, and I'm not making up any of the things I told you."

"Then make it sound believable," she said, pulling her hand free and leaning back with her arms crossed.

"You know me, Kristine."

"Do I?"

"I'm not crazy. I'm not on drugs."

"You sound like you are."

"As ridiculous as it sounds, my Dad was involved in killing a famous person who couldn't possibly be a threat to this country. But I don't believe Dad was just a killer, so there has to be some explanation, as weird as that sounds. And in the last week, people in the NSEO killed my parents. Those two things seem connected somehow. I have to find out who killed them and why."

"Wouldn't the police be the ones to do that?" she asked.

"Going to the police seems like the last place I can go."

chapter 14

At Kristine's suggestion, I planned to take the day to write down everything I could remember about what had happened. Who I'd seen at the hospital. Who called. Everything Mom or Dad had said. The funeral. Who was there. What I'd seen on the film. Getting drunk. Everything. I'd already filled a spiral notebook she gave me, scribbling whatever came to mind.

I had wanted to spend the day in the downtown library scanning books about Elvis, but Kristine suggested I just use her computer to make better time writing down every detail before I lost something to the fading of time. She spent a few minutes and helped me learn my way around the computer on her desk so I could find things, create a document, and search for information. It wasn't as if the computer was new to me, but I had no idea how easy it was to find almost anything. I really hadn't kept up with stuff like that.

I opened a document Kristine had made on her computer and spent a solid hour and a half writing. By the end, I realized she was right, that even typing slow was faster than hand writing fast.

I came to a natural stopping point that was virtually to the present and decided to get back on the trail.

The amount of material about Elvis was amazing, and trying to sort out some kind of connection to the government was equally crazy. More than one reference theorized that part of Bill Clinton's appeal was his likeness to Elvis with his little sneer, his voice, and his smile. And Clinton's nickname was Elvis. I knew Elvis had tons of fans, but I had no idea so much had been written about him.

Later in the afternoon, I decided to check my parents' house. I put on a hat and sunglasses and drove past, sitting as low in the truck seat as I could. One block down I saw two men sitting in a black Lexus, an odd place in the neighborhood for two men in a car to sit. I didn't stop or look their way as I passed.

Kristine spent the next couple of days taking breaks at her job as a paralegal to do Internet searches for me. She let me use her computer at home. Each night we'd compare notes on Elvis. As the week went on, our conversations grew longer and the tone in her voice lost some of the hurt I'd heard at first. She told me what she knew of various friends I'd lost contact with. We laughed a little, even talked of some of the fun times we'd had exploring every back street on Southside. I began to feel like we might one day be friends again. I couldn't help but think back to all the times before we could drive when we'd met at the overlook on 20th Street, usually telling our parents we were with some group of friends when it was mostly just us.

When I arrived at her apartment around five-thirty on Friday, I saw Kristine's Camry parked on the street in front of the two-story apartment building. I used the key she'd given me to let myself in.

She sat at a wooden kitchen table she used as a desk, dozens of pages spread in front of her that she'd printed from the Internet. She'd started using what she calls a 'search engine' named Google that she said was the hot new way to find things. It really was amazing how much stuff she could find really fast. I'd known about Yahoo, but Google was something new for me. Apparently they were taking on Yahoo and making real progress to become the alternative place we could do the online research. Kristine said lots of people had already switched to Google.

She hardly looked up, just said, "Here's a copy of a letter from Elvis asking for a meeting with President Nixon to present him with a gift."

I stood there reading from the single sheet as she shuffled through stacks of papers from other things she'd printed off web sites.

"This thing got the White House stirred up," she said. "I found a memo from Nixon's top guys that talked about Elvis."

"You're kidding."

"You really have to see this. Here's the memo from 1970 to Nixon's chief of staff H.R. Haldeman from Dwight Chapin, talking about the request for a meeting from Elvis. The memo says Elvis believes he could help counter the drug problem if he's made a Federal Agent at Large."

"Wait, who were Haldeman and Chapin? I know I've heard those names."

"Haldeman was the guy talking to Nixon on those tapes that the secretary erased."

"Oh yeah, right."

"And Chapin apparently scheduled appointments for Nixon. He went to jail later for something to do with all the Watergate stuff. But he's the one who first said they should let Elvis come to the White House."

I couldn't believe there was so much about Elvis and the Federal government that was easy to find, and mostly on government web sites.

"Let me see it," I said.

I practically tore the page out of her hand. I didn't know exactly who all the people were. I remembered some of the names from the Watergate crap, but I hadn't paid that much attention to who did what. "This Chapin guy recommends that they meet with Elvis and that someone named Bud Krogh meet with Presley and provide 'some kind of an honorary agent at large or credential of some sort that we can provide Presley,' it says."

She laughed. "Wouldn't you give anything to have been there to see Elvis with Nixon?"

"Well it happened," I said. "Did you notice the memo is initialed by Haldeman, approving the visit with President Nixon?"

Kristine nodded and then folded her arms across her chest and leaned back as she said, "I never heard about Elvis and Nixon before, did you?"

"No, but I'd sure like to know more. This is kind of spooky," I immediately wished I hadn't tried to make a silly joke.

I was happy when she allowed herself a smile. I pulled up a chair and looked at her. I couldn't tell anything about what she was thinking or how she really felt about me. It had been too long for me to be able to read her anymore.

The moment seemed right to tell her how I'd felt about her. "Can I show you something that may surprise you?"

She frowned and shrugged. For a moment I thought it was the wrong thing to do, as her expression seemed to harden and her smile went flat when she realized this was probably something personal. Until then, we'd done a good job of keeping this about my parents and not about us.

I dug in my wallet and fished through a stack of cards and folded scraps of paper. Near the middle I found her picture.

I held the snapshot out and told her, "I've carried this for eight years."

Kristine took the photograph. The corners were rounded and the image faded from crisp blues and flesh tones to orange and brown, but she recognized the shot as her senior picture.

She turned the photo over and saw the signature. Always, Kristine, it said. She dropped her head. She wasn't crying, but I could see a range of emotions in her eyes.

"If you kept this, why didn't you do more to contact me?" she said without looking up, barely above a whisper. She seemed more hurt than angry.

"I don't really have a reason beyond what I told you. I tried several times to reach you on the phone, and I wrote two or three times. I got caught up in things that took me away from everything and everyone I loved."

She looked up at me with her eyebrows pushed hard together. I knew she was trying to say something, but I wanted to finish.

"There's no excuse and I'm not trying to start back where we were. I know that ship sailed," I told her as I pulled my chair closer to her. "I just wanted you to know I thought about you a lot. You can't imagine how bad I feel about what I did."

"I never got a letter. Or a message." Her voice had a tone of finality to it.

She turned back to the computer and started typing again, saying nothing more as she continued searching for more information about Elvis. I could tell she was putting her thoughts aside, focusing on the screen. I didn't know what else to say or even if she believed me.

Not knowing what I should do or say, I said nothing more. I picked up a stack of pages she'd downloaded and began learning everything I could about Elvis Aron Presley.

That moment was another unexpected fork in the road in this journey I recently started, one I could never have imagined. Just weeks before, I was living paycheck to paycheck, welding from early morning to mid-afternoon, then a quick nap before downing a Red Bull and hitting the bars around San Antonio looking for a game of pool. Now I had thousands of dollars in my pocket, no bike, and a mission to find out who killed my parents. Little did I know that my world was about to be turned upside down again.

After half an hour of silence, I heard Kristine grow quiet at the computer and stop typing. She sighed loud enough for me to hear her breath whistle over her teeth. When I glanced up from the couch where I was reading, she was staring at the screen. Her cheeks glowed red in the late afternoon sunlight slanting through a large window that opened up over the street.

"I loved you, you know," Kristine said, her gaze never leaving the screen. "It took me a long time to get over you. It wasn't just the schoolgirl crush I had when I was twelve."

Then she turned in her chair toward me. "I just need to know why you left me." Her tone was neither warm nor angry.

"I don't have the right words to explain it. I was a stupid teenager, full of anger at my drunk father, mad at my mother, and frustrated that I couldn't help her."

"But what's that got to do with leaving me?" she asked, looking at me now.

"I didn't mean to leave you. That's not what I thought I was doing." I looked right into her eyes, took a deep breath, and told her what I'd never had the nerve to say. "I have loved you since the first time we made out in your basement when we were fifteen. I always had some kind of romantic notion that I would come get you."

"Yeah right. That's why I cried myself to sleep for six months."

Now it was me who couldn't look at her. Instead I looked at my shoes. "Kristine, for weeks after I left I had no address, no phone number to tell you to call. I never thought I'd just keep heading west and leave my whole life behind, but as days of wandering around became weeks and then months, my priorities just faded. Then my travel became weeks of drugs and drinking too much and riding my bike until all that I had been and known was gone. The old Matt disappeared."

"A simple letter would have helped."

I stopped for a moment and tried my best not to defend something indefensible. "There is no good excuse and nothing I did deserves forgiveness. But I told you the truth. I did write. I guess your mom wanted me out of the picture."

"If you say so."

"It's no excuse, but when you didn't take the phone calls or write back, I gave up," I said. "I was stupid. I thought that's what you wanted. I guess from my warped perspective the situation seemed hopeless, and by the time I realized what I had lost, I was too afraid to try again to come back."

Then she dropped another piece of a big puzzle in my lap when she told me something I'd begun to wonder about. She said, "I knew where you were some of the time. Your mom showed me pictures of you in California."

I couldn't even respond. I'm sure I looked surprised to Kristine. I just stared, waiting for more information.

"You really didn't know they were watching you, did you?"

I managed to mumble, "No."

"Your dad had someone who found you after you were arrested for fighting. At least that's what your mom said. They had lots of pictures of you."

"When was this?"

"A couple of times she called me about a year after you were gone, and I went over there. She showed me pictures of you on a big motorcycle. Later she had one of you sitting on a bench at the beach. You looked different in some. In some your hair was short and others it was long. They were watching for a long time, off and on it seemed."

"I don't understand. Why would Mom show you those pictures? What did Dad say?"

"He never knew she told me. And she made me promise not to tell anyone before she would even show them to me."

"Are you the only one who knew?"

"I think so. I was married by then, but I suppose a mother knows things that others can somehow ignore."

Kristine didn't just say things. That was not an idle comment.

"There's something you're not telling me," I said.

"Damn it, Matt," she said, reaching her arm out to put her hand lightly on my chest, her fingers spread, moving her face inches from mine. "Are you really that dense?"

My head was spinning, and it was clear I was nowhere near understanding any of this.

"Just tell me Kristine. I don't know what you're getting at. Why was Mom confiding in you these things that were obviously secret?"

"Mothers know things. Women know things. They notice what's

going on even when men don't think they're paying attention."

"What are you talking about?"

She shook her head, almost laughing, but not like something was really funny, more like she was incredulous.

"Matt, did you look at the pictures of Winter?"

"Sure, he's a nice looking kid," I said, feeling pressure in my brain again.

"No, I mean *really* look at him," she said, almost pleading, as she reached over to the wall and took down an eight by ten of her son standing on a baseball field holding a bat. She held it directly in front of my face with both hands gripping the frame. The child was dressed in a Cardinal uniform.

"Doesn't Winter look familiar at all?"

I suddenly felt like I was falling backwards down a well, and there was nothing to grab. As I looked at the photo, I saw what could have been an old photograph of me.

chapter 15

There's a worldwide network of fans who want to know anything and everything about the King of Rock and Roll, always hoping for some new bootleg recording to surface or to hear news that he's really alive even after nearly twenty-two years. When you search his name, millions of entries pop up. Somehow I'd missed knowing that Elvis had surpassed stardom and had reached cult status. Of course, until Kristine showed me how to do it, I didn't know what an internet search really was. Perhaps neither of those things was important to me in that life that now seemed years ago, though it had only been a few weeks. I knew Elvis had millions of fans, and I guess it was no surprise to learn of the hundreds of fan clubs, books, tapes, and Web sites. Learning his favorite drink was Pepsi or that he studied both tae kwon do and kempo and reached the eighth level as a black belt in karate was interesting, but finding something that would help tie him to the NSEO seemed like finding the proverbial needle. Dozens of web sites list Elvis sightings. Who would have guessed? But this fascination seemed much more than fans who long for one more song from their singer-turned-movie-star who became a Vegas legend.

One of The King's enthusiasts who was well-known among passionate fans lived near Birmingham, so I tracked him down through a fan site.

After a few emails back and forth, I could tell he really did know the life history. He wouldn't talk over the phone but finally sent an email saying he would talk to me in person. I drove to his house the next morning around ten after he said it was the only day he could see me.

I didn't really want to go. I could barely concentrate. All I could think about for that past day was being a father. What should I do? Would Winter accept me? Would Kristine let me visit? How would it work?

Spotting the house was easy. The mailbox was in the shape of an acoustic guitar that I soon learned Elvis played early in his career. The house was small but tidy. White clapboard siding, recently painted. Black shingle roof. A neatly mowed lawn. The standard molded concrete steps and small square porch. Even the carport was orderly, like hundreds of others you'd see in the suburban subdivisions around the outskirts of the city.

I parked in the front. As I walked up the concrete sidewalk, a tall man opened the door.

"He ain't dead you know," the big man said as he held open a screen door, extending a hand as thick as a t-bone. "I guess that's why you're here?" He had long sideburns, and his black hair was combed back. He looked about six-two, maybe just a fraction taller than me.

"You're Matt, ain't you? You can call me E.A. All my friends do," he said.

"Hello, E.A. Thanks for letting me come visit."

Inside, things were different. Any expectations of a quaint, typical suburban home with shag carpet and overstuffed recliners aimed at a television soon evaporated. Just inside the door on the left was a life-size cutout of the man himself in a diamond-studded gold lamé suit. The narrow hallway had framed original performance photos covering almost the entire wall on one side. The paint was deep red.

"That's him in 1957 in Hollywood," E.A. said when he saw me staring at the cutout.

Behind the cutout was a bookshelf running the length of the wall. I scanned the titles. Every book seemed to be on one man. "These are all about him?"

E.A. nodded yes and just let me stand there. He folded his arms and smiled big to let me take it in. Finally, he reached behind him and lifted a yearbook from his coffee table.

"This is my prize book," he said. "1953 Humes High School yearbook. Cost me six hundred bucks in a auction twenty years ago. Worth ten times that now."

The cover said *The Herald*. E.A. flipped the book open to a picture of a teenager with hair long for the times and in the expected ducktail. A lock of hair curled down over his forehead. His thick sideburns provided the style E.A. had copied perfectly. Beside the picture the editors had listed the young man's "Major" as Shop, History, and English.

"Coffee?" he asked.

I took a cup black and sat on a large brown vinyl sofa. E.A. sat across from me and offered to answer questions.

"Everybody that really wants to know about the stories eventually ends up on that couch," E.A. said, the pride obvious in his voice as he sat back in a deeply padded gold recliner and sipped coffee. "So what you up to? You writing a book?"

"No, I'm just interested in learning," I said, realizing I didn't sound convincing.

"Um hm," he said, grinning like it was a joke. "Nobody just 'learns' about the Tupelo Tornado. Either he's under your skin or he ain't. You ain't telling me everything. Are you a reporter?"

"E.A., I promise you, I'm not a reporter. I became a fan late in life."

"He ain't dead," he repeated, watching me, like he had before. I guess to see if I had reaction.

"Tell me why you think that?"

"I don't just think it," he said, reaching to put down a Dr. Pepper and using that hand to point his finger at me for emphasis. "He's somewhere in Michigan. Always loved that part of the country, and when he'd had enough, that's where he headed out. I got a whole book on it."

"Why would he fake his death?"

I realized I sounded cynical, so I tried to cover. "I mean, he had so many fans that loved him and a family and all."

"It was the government that had something to do with it. He was a agent for Nixon. That ain't just no rumor. You can see papers and all in the Smithsonian. Here, look at the letters and all in this book," he said, handing me a slim volume called *The Day Elvis Met Nixon.*

On the cover, I saw it was written by Egil "Bud" Krogh, a former White House aide to Nixon whose name Kristine had already mentioned. I thumbed through the pages and recognized some of the memos and documents we'd found on the Internet.

E.A. pointed with his thumb over his shoulder to an eight by ten black and white photograph in a black frame on a shelf. In the photo, Elvis poses with President Nixon.

"Nixon did it," he said. "Made Elvis a agent. Elvis always did want to help the government, and Nixon made him a undercover agent. Look starting on page forty-nine."

As I flipped the pages, I found a long 1972 *Washington Post* article about Elvis getting a narcotics badge and also pictures of Elvis with President Richard Nixon in the Oval Office. I could tell the photos were from the same visit as the photo on E.A.'s shelf. It all seemed like a stunt to me, but something about it left me uneasy.

———

For the next two hours, E.A. told convincing stories and showed me enough references in various books about Elvis and his ties to the government to convince me I had to do more research. I struggled to pay attention as my mind kept wandering back to the son I wanted to get to know.

One thing E.A. said startled me more than the rest.

"There's a group that protects Elvis," he said. "It ain't big, but there's still something he's hiding from and some folks are helping him. Hard to figure it out exactly, but he knows something about somebody somewhere up high. There's too many people have seen him and talked to him to deny it."

———

When I left E.A., I drove to the downtown branch of the Birmingham library where they provided computer access to look up information. I wondered if Winter ever came here. Did he have a library card? While my mind was on Winter, I needed to find out more about Elvis's ties to the NSEO. And if the rumor that someone was helping Elvis or hiding him had any truth, I needed to know. I knew Elvis was dead. I had the film. But something didn't add up.

I chose the second floor computer room and began running searches in archived records. With a pen and yellow legal pad beside me for notes, I settled into a thinly padded chair.

Forty-five minutes later, I realized the bright afternoon light had dimmed. I glanced up to see a man walking down the narrow aisle toward me, blocking the stream of sunlight from the window. His suit seemed out of place here among mostly college kids in jeans and retired men in comfortable shoes and short-sleeved plaid shirts. It didn't take much to make me feel things weren't right. Someone stepped up close behind me and an alarm in my head told me to stand up and run. As I stood, a hand from the other side gripped my shoulder and pushed me back into my chair.

"Sit down," the man behind me demanded, as I tried to jerk free, managing to get my feet under me but with him still pushing my shoulders down.

Before I could react, the first man punched me in the side. I felt the wind empty from my lungs in a gush. I went down, missing the chair and landing on my knees between the two men. Gasping for air, I twisted around and managed to glance up and see them. Both were about my size, with short cropped hair and cut-from-stone chins.

It was like they had a mold for these guys, clones of the men who'd chased me around the church a few days before. And I'd probably killed one of their friends. I couldn't fight my way out of this one.

I kneeled there wheezing and trying to think. As soon as I felt I could get my breath, I dove forward under the table and rolled over, knocking chairs into the wall. I scrambled to my feet with the large row of tables between us and ran toward the door as the men both slid over the table behind me. I reached the end of an aisle, grabbed the corner of a bookshelf and pulled it over, dropping dozens of heavy volumes onto the men behind me. From the avalanche of fallen books, a hand clutched the back of my shirt and held me as I tried to open the door. The heavy pile of shelving and books pinned him to the floor, but his grip was solid.

I twisted and leaned all my weight forward, ripping my shirt and giving me enough slack to turn. I grabbed the man's wrist, bent over, and bit into the soft flesh at the base of his thumb. When his grip loosened, I fell backward through the door, ran toward the stairs, and leaped down several at a time. I heard the men's hard shoes echoing on the marble behind me as I crossed the lobby.

A uniformed security officer near the front door stood up, alarm flashing in his eyes.

I ran directly toward him as if I had been looking for him all along and shouted, "Help. These men tried to rob me."

I slowed as if to stand with him. He looked past me toward the men, then back at me, his expression showing confusion. His hesitation gave me an opening. Although he stepped forward and held his hand up to motion for me to stop, he was too late to hold me back. I pushed past him and ran through the main lobby door someone else was opening. Outside, a teenager leaned on his bike and began pulling a bicycle lock from his backpack. I shoved him aside, grabbed the bike, and pedaled down the sidewalk.

I soon left the two men behind, turning here and there at every corner to keep out of their sight, even going against the traffic when I could. Once I was sure I'd put several blocks between us, I ditched the bike in an alley when I spotted a cab parked in front of an old hotel.

I hopped into the back seat and saw the cabby was an older guy with the tire marks of a rough road wrinkled across his face and a smile that suggested a sympathetic heart. That seemed good to me. I held up a hundred and said, "Take me to the Golden Rule in Irondale. There's a hundred in it if you never had this fare and never saw me. I'm dodging a phony assault charge from my ex and I need to get away until this cools down."

"Screw 'em. I got an ex, too, and she's a lying bitch. I don't know you and never saw you," he said. He grabbed the money and turned off his meter as he pulled into traffic. I slid down in the seat.

The old restaurant was the first place that popped into my head where I had no ties. No one would be looking for me there. I knew from going to the Iron Horse earlier that the east end of Birmingham hadn't changed much.

When we pulled up in front, I glanced up at the rearview mirror and saw the driver was watching me. He gave me a reverse nod and said "Luck. Keep it between the ditches." I nodded back.

I found a booth in the back and ordered iced tea. The place was no different than when I'd been here last. The hickory smoke smell permeated the place, and the waitresses were all over sixty. Maybe over eighty. Every five minutes I called Kristine from the cell phone, but she never answered. There was so much I needed to talk to her about. Not just Elvis, but more importantly: us. Whatever that meant. I was a father now, and this time I wouldn't run. I bent over and put my head into my hands to try to stop the pounding of horses' hooves.

After half an hour, I decided to go to the closest source I knew to find out about the tie between NSEO and Elvis. Jim Robinson.

The woman behind the cash register telephoned for a cab. Twenty minutes later I was sitting low in the backseat as the driver drove past my truck parked two blocks from the library. After twice around the block, I made the driver let me out right beside my door and was soon half way across town in the truck no one knew was mine.

Next to Jim Robinson's office building, I parked in the lot where I could see the front door. I changed my torn T-shirt into a fresh one and tugged the brim of a baseball cap low over my eyes. A row of tall, skinny pines with branches only near the top divided the two lots that served identical five-story office buildings housing various law firms, financial consultants, and at least one government field office, from what I could tell reading the monument sign in front.

It was nearly five, and I could only hope Jim would leave on time today. The window motor buzzed softly as I pressed the button, lowering the glass to eye level. A breeze blew the smell of wild onions in my window as yardmen cut grass bordering the parking lot.

Fifteen minutes later, Jim exited the front door and turned to walk almost directly toward me. When he reached his car, he was within fifty feet of me. I opened my door, closed it quietly, and walked toward him.

"Jim, wait," I said as he started to sit behind the wheel. I kept my hand on the revolver tucked into the front of my pants so he could see it.

"Matt?" He was obviously surprised and looked around. For what, I'm not sure. He closed his door and stood there with his arms folded, shaking his head. "What in the hell were you thinking?

There are arrest warrants out on you for murder."

"We need to talk. You know I didn't murder anyone. Those guys opened fire on me the second they could. I'm taking this whole story to the police."

"What story, Matt? You don't know a damn thing about what's really happened."

"Well then why don't you tell me? You're the one who tried to have me killed."

He shook his head as he answered, "Those men weren't with me, Matt. Just give me the film, and I'll help you. You can't deal with these people."

"Yeah, right. They just happened along when we were meeting and decided they needed to shoot me," I said.

Jim's face twisted into a silent scream as he jerked back against the car. A mist of blood splattered the front of my shirt. At the same time, I heard two shots from behind me. Jim slid down the car door to a sitting position. The car windows behind Jim shattered. I tasted the copper of Jim's blood on my lips, spit, and swallowed, forcing down the salty bile rising in my throat.

Car tires squealed, and a horn honked long and loud. I dropped to my knees on the asphalt. Jim sat with his legs splayed in front of him and leaned against the car as a dark red spot grew on the right side of his chest. He'd managed to pull his pistol from under his coat, but it merely lay on top of his limp palm beside him on the pavement. The car engine grew quieter as the shooter weaved through traffic and disappeared.

Jim smiled softly through the obvious pain. He began to make wheezing noises as he breathed, each breath coming faster and shallower. He could talk only in a whisper. I knelt close to listen as he talked. I pressed my handkerchief against the wound but couldn't stop the flow, and soon my hands were covered in blood for the second time.

"The film. I was in it. With your father. And Leopold," he said.

"Charles Ryan Leopold was there? I've seen it, Jim. I know what happened."

"No … you … don't," he said. I felt his chest fluttering up and down uncontrollably under my fingers.

"The film doesn't lie, Jim."

He began blinking rapidly, and his chest heaved harder as he tried to breath.

"It's all a lie. There's more to the story," he said, his voice growing softer. "So much more, and other people. I thought that if I just said nothing about the wall you would soon leave and this would all go away. You'd be safe."

So Jim was the friend who was supposed to tell me about the hidden wall space.

"Who was the other man in the film?"

No answer.

I yelled. "Jim, who else was there?"

No answer.

Jim's eyes started blinking rapidly. He took a deep breath and spoke barely in a whisper, "Find Mark Pugh. He's the one. The shooter is the key."

"The one of what? Jim, the only one of what? Who is the shooter, What do you mean?"

But it was too late. Jim stopped blinking and his eyes froze, staring from that place where time stops. His chest grew still, and I couldn't feel a pulse as I pressed my fingers into his neck. There was nothing else I could do for him. Sirens screamed in the distance.

I crawled between the cars until I reached the edge of the lot where I could wipe my hands on the grass. I stood up with my hands in my pockets as I noticed people murmuring in small groups of three or four, those who had sensed something wrong or heard shots or the ambulances. I mingled with several people emerging from the buildings and walking to their cars, unaware of the shots fired, until I could get to my truck as part of the group.

As I drove from the parking lot, I heard a woman scream from somewhere near Jim. I had to get to Kristine and tell her the apartment might not be safe. It was a call I didn't want to make. Two police cars sped past me from the opposite direction, their lights flashing blue.

Kristine didn't answer her cell phone or home phone. I could feel my own pulse speeding up.

chapter 16

Kristine keeps her routines the same. She always has. I never really watched, but I'd bet before she goes to run she puts her first sock on the same foot every time, then ties the same lace first. At her house, Wednesday was always spaghetti night, and I can't imagine it's not the same for Winter and her. Winter. Every thought seemed to circle back to him. Would he have the same kinds of routines and patterns in his life?

Anyway, I knew which streets she would take driving home. In my mind, I could see her stopping for meat, sauce, and salad fixings at Western and then driving this way.

I spotted a parking space open three blocks from Kristine's apartment. I made a u-turn and backed into the spot to face the direction she'd be driving. A stop sign three cars down would give me time to step outside and wave her down well before she reached her building.

A few minutes later I tried her cell phone. Then her home phone again just in case I had it wrong about her habits. I did. This time she answered, out of breath. She'd run to the phone, which she said was ringing as she unlocked the door. So much for knowing her routines. Rather than risk driving around for ten minutes looking for another parking space, I decided to walk to Kristine's as we talked.

"Your apartment may not be safe," I told her.

"What? Are you serious?" she yelled.

"I'm just trying to be cautious. Some men were after me at the library."

"Damn you," she said. The way she growled "damn" let me know she meant it.

"You can be mad at me all you want and I deserve it, but there is a lifetime to do that. You still need to get out of there. Go look out your window right now. And lock your door."

"I can't just leave my apartment," she said. "To go where Matt? And for how long?"

"Grab some things for a day or two. I'll be there in two minutes," I said. "Kristine, you can't imagine how sorry I am, but there's no other choice. I'm walking there from two blocks away." I closed the phone.

Thirty seconds later, I turned the corner of her block and waited for a car to pass. Across the street from Kristine's apartment, a man leaned against the side wall of a brownstone townhouse. A tall hedge gave him cover from Kristine's view. A black Town Car was parked in the alley nearby. From there he could see Kristine's front door and her bedroom window, but she wouldn't see him or the car.

I crossed the street going to the side of the apartment where the man couldn't see me. As soon as I was behind a house I called back.

I told her, "Someone's out front. Don't go that way. Is there any other way out?"

"There's a back door," she said.

"There may be someone there, too. What else?"

"I don't know any other way. Wait, the basement laundry room has an exit onto the alley."

"Go there. Go now. Don't worry about packing anything. Just go. The alley's on the north side right?"

"Yeah," she said.

"Okay, go to that door and try to see if anyone is watching. If you don't see anyone, run straight across into the yard across the alley. Go through that yard and the next one. Keep going north to the corner of Washington and 7th. I'll be on the street with my truck. Go now."

———

As I drove down Washington, Kristine ran from the bushes beside a house, waving her arms and carrying a bag. She jerked open the passenger door as soon as I stopped. No one had followed her. In ten minutes, we were halfway across town. Kristine had not said a word since she jumped into my truck. She just sat there with her arms crossed, staring ahead and hugging a quilted overnight bag stuffed with clothes as I recounted all the events of that day and the shooting at Jim's office.

"We have to call your mother."

Kristine cut her eyes at me. Her lips were pressed tightly, and she breathed deeply.

"If you've put my son in danger ..."

"I don't know that he's in danger," I said, hoping to keep her calm, but I was already madder at myself than she was. "I just think we should play it safe. Call her now. Tell her everything. And tell her to go somewhere safe with Winter."

Kristine spent the next ten minutes on the phone. She left out nothing, including Jim's death. They agreed her mother would take Winter away and stay with a friend no one would connect with them. They agreed to talk every day as we sorted things out.

After she finished talking to Eleanor, Kristine asked to talk with Winter. She told him she had to go away on work but would be home soon and would call him whenever she could. She just stared out the window for a few minutes.

Traffic was heavy on every street. At each light, I found myself spinning around to look into every car, especially big dark cars and black SUVs. Kristine could see my concern, but she just looked down at her hands.

———

I drove on past the city limits, veering off the main roads as we plowed deeper into north Jefferson County and finally into Blount County. The sun dimmed behind the forest of mostly pines replanted over smooth rolling hills from reclaimed strip mines along the highway.

Going to David Collier's lakehouse was not an option now. I spotted a one-story motel with a red neon flashing Vacancy sign in the front window. I registered under a fake name and paid cash. The clerk didn't bother to ask for ID and hardly looked up from the tiny television behind the counter. We took the end room of about a dozen identical rooms side-by-side in the pale green cinderblock structure. I parked around the side so that the car would not be visible from the main road.

Kristine, refusing to sit, paced around the room.

"What's going on here, Matt? What have you gotten us into?"

"I only know that I was right, and someone did murder my parents. And I've made us targets. I'm so very sorry that I didn't think this through. I wish I had something to say to make it better, but I don't," I said. I felt like an idiot. It might not be a stretch to say I hated myself for putting Kristine and Winter at risk. At one time or another, we've all said we hated ourselves. But this was more than just forgetting a birthday or driving off without your wallet. This was true, down in the mud, gritty anger at myself. I wanted to bash my own head in or throw myself off a roof. But what I had to force myself to do was to face my mistake and make damn sure I found a way out for Kristine.

Kristine didn't say anything.

I plopped down in the ratty, stuffed chair beside the window air conditioner and sank almost to the floor. I put my face in my hands, realizing how I had made things worse with every move.

Finally, Kristine spoke, sounding resolved, "Well, being sorry won't get us out of this will it? What are you going to do now?"

I looked up. She was not going to allow me to withdraw or do nothing. She was like that. Look ahead. Move on. Be an adult. She might not ever forget what had happened, but she knew what happened next was what mattered.

I thought for a few seconds about what to do. Winter. Winter. Winter. What about Winter? How could we protect him?

"First, Matt and Kristine have to disappear," I said, as I rose and headed to the door.

I went to the car and returned with a bag containing electric clippers and red and blond hair coloring. I had also bought a stack of temporary tattoos that I thought might help throw someone off if we used them in visible places people couldn't forget.

Kristine looked through the things I had bought and walked to the trash can where she began tossing various items that didn't seem right to her. "Matt, this is shit. If we're going to change our hair color, we have to do it so we don't look like freaks and stick out even more. Give me your keys."

"Where are you going?"

"Just give me the damn keys. And how much cash do you have? I shouldn't use my credit card, should I? I'll just go back to the Walgreen's I saw down the street and get something that won't make us look like we're in the circus."

"You can't use this stuff?"

"Some of it maybe, but you can put blond dye on your hair all day long, and the most you will do is turn it red. Now throw me your keys."

Half an hour later Kristine returned with a hair dryer, gloves, plastic containers, Vaseline—which I learned would keep my forehead and neck from burning at the hairline—and hair bleaching kits. Two hours later, I was a clean-shaven, crew cut blond. I had a dark blue cross tattooed on the left side of my neck. Kristine was a redhead with bobbed straight hair just below her ears and long bangs. She had temporary rose tattoos on the back of each hand. They looked real from a distance.

chapter 17

In the morning, we dressed in jeans and T-shirts and decided to have coffee and breakfast before we called Eleanor Masters. We ate eggs and bacon at the diner across the parking lot.

Back in the motel, Kristine pressed the speakerphone button on her cell phone so we could both listen as she talked with her mom about what had happened. When Kristine started to say where we were, her mother stopped her. Her mom's voice sounded far away, but the concern was easy to hear.

"Kris, you remember me telling you of the place where my parents used to take me in the summers?" she asked.

"Only a thousand times," Kristine answered, flat, annoyed maybe.

"Meet me there this afternoon. Make sure you are not followed. Get a room, and leave me a message at the front desk, but don't use your last name. Don't call me back on this line," Kris's mom said as she hung up without a goodbye.

As we drove, my mind kept drifting back to Winter. How could I ever make up to him and to Kristine the years I was away, not helping raise him or support them in any way? I had to find a way to start. Whether she liked it or not, I was the father. I would do my part. Now I had to figure out what that was. Fortunately, Kristine was lost in her own thoughts and said little. She stared out the window at the passing billboards, occasional cinder block shops with small gravel parking lots, and long stretches with no development. The Holiday Inn on Lake Guntersville was about an hour from where we were staying, just up Highway 79 on a stretch of highway bordered on both sides by wide pastures planted on the land reclaimed after strip mines cut their way through the county. Grazing cattle huddled in patches of shade created by huge oaks sprinkled here and there in the fields. We crossed a bridge over a shallow river where canoeists had pulled off the road to unload bright red canoes from the top of a green Toyota 4Runner. Kristine leaned against the door, continued looking out the window, and said little.

Forty years ago, the hotel on the lake where we were meeting had been an American dream, a great getaway weekend for middle class Birmingham. Sliding glass doors opened onto a patio where you could watch the ski boats. Picnic tables rested in the shade of huge oaks. Swimming in the lake and cookouts hosted by the hotel manager filled the Saturdays. Several makeovers later, the building reminded me of an older beauty queen who was still attractive long after the outside showed a bit of age. The structure was there, but even with fresh paint the years showed through.

We checked into the Holiday Inn after one o'clock, again using cash my father had left in the wall. Our room was on the back, facing the water. Bass boats and pontoon boats loaded with kids and families cruised by constantly as we drank beer from a six-pack I'd bought at the gas station across the street. We sat on the freshly mowed grassy slope leading down to the water, a view unchanged for decades. An hour and two beers later, we returned to the room.

I called David and told him what was happening. He thought

that Kristine's mom could help and that she might have good friends still inside the NSEO, friends she could trust.

Kristine started doodling on a pad she found inside the desk. She drew circles and filled them with the names of the people involved. At the top she wrote DOJ inside a circle, then NSEO and Charles Ryan Leopold in another circle below that, which she then connected to circles she labeled Marshall Boykin and Jim Robinson. She put Mark Pugh in a circle off to the side. She drew a line between the Boykin and Robinson circles. On the left was a circle with my name, and she connected it to both my father and Jim. Beside my name was a circle with Unknown Men at fountain and library. To Jim's circle, she attached one that read Unknown Shooter. Then she drew a circle with Elvis in it and connected that circle to my father and Jim. Right beside was a circle labeled Leopold. The circle on the other side of Elvis read Nixon.

For a few seconds she held the page by the corners for me to see before she lay the paper on the table, picked up her pen, and connected Nixon to the NSEO/Charles Ryan Leopold circle. Her eyes held a question.

"Is this about the FBI, Matt? Or the NSEO? Or the White House? Or Elvis? Or just someone wanting to keep a secret?" she asked.

DOJ

NSEO/Charles Ryan Leopold

Mark Pugh Marshall Boykin	Elvis	Jim Robinson
Matt Boykin		Unknown Shooter
Unknown Men		Nixon

I stared at the diagram. The connections were there somewhere, but the truth remained hidden.

Both of us jumped when someone knocked at the door. I grabbed the pistol David had given me and peeked through the eyehole in the door. Eleanor Masters was standing there with Harvey Sullivan behind her. Kristine put her hand over her mouth and stared at the gun in my hand.

I remembered Harvey well. He was the first black man I really knew. When I was growing up, Harvey was the only black man I'd seen inside a white person's house as a friend, not as someone who was there to do some kind of repair job or at best maybe selling insurance. You gotta remember this was Bombingham, as it was still being called in some circles. The 1960s were not that far in the past. He'd been friends with my dad when I was very young, and they seemed like genuinely good friends—something that had always influenced my views of race in a good way.

I opened the door and motioned them in, looking around outside before I closed and locked the door. I said nothing, but it was hard for a moment not to imagine how different things were today than just forty years ago. Eleanor Masters wouldn't have chanced traveling alone in Alabama with Sullivan back then, and I'm certain she couldn't have gone with him to a hotel like this without raising some eyebrows at the least.

"Where's Winter?" Kristine asked.

"I have him with a very close friend. You know Jay Jay. He's in good hands," Eleanor said, walking to her daughter and hugging her. "Sure as hell safer than you are."

She looked at me as she spoke with no smile and no doubt what she meant or who she blamed for the mess. And she was right, this was on me. I didn't start it, but I had handled things poorly. I didn't know what was right, but so far this wasn't it.

Harvey stood near the window and peeked through the curtains I had drawn tight.

"Could you have been followed?" I asked, alarmed that he felt he needed to check outside.

"Not very likely at all. It's fine, Matt," he said, holding his hands out with his palms down. "Just checking. Old habits, you know."

I didn't know, actually, but let it pass. "So why are *you* here?" I asked Harvey.

"Eleanor has briefed me," he said. "I was close to Eleanor and your father, Matt. We worked together for more than ten years. She thought I might help."

"Doing what with my father?" I asked.

He looked at me and smiled, sort of a crooked smile, maybe a smirk, but I couldn't tell. He said, "Eleanor said you really didn't know what your father did for NSEO. For one thing, your father saved my life."

"How?" I asked, having no reason to believe my father would have been in a position to save someone, unless it was from a papercut.

"We called in the FBI to stake out a bank robbery by a group we stumbled on during a routine background check. Your dad and I were assigned to be there with the FBI because we knew the players. It went south in a hurry. Three perps drove up with automatic weapons just as the inside guys came out the front door," he said.

I was still skeptical of this supposed news about the man I knew as Dad, despite all the new things I was learning that told me I had never known the whole truth.

"Both FBI guys with me were hit at the same time when they sprayed us with automatic rifle fire. I got pinned down and wounded in the leg. Couldn't get away. Bullets were dancing across the asphalt. Your father ran across an open parking lot to get to me and give me cover. He was hit in the hand and lost part of a finger over it. I owe him."

I'd never heard a word about how my father really lost his finger. He'd claimed it was a car wreck. I sat down on the bed. I didn't know what to say. And once again old feelings and new meanings to old events made me feel like I was driving through a fog.

Eleanor spoke up. "Matt, they say you killed Jim Robinson."

"That's crazy," I said. "I was just talking with him when a car pulled up and someone shot him. He died in my arms and I ran."

"Mom, you know Matt didn't shoot anyone. Not Jim anyway," Kristine said.

Eleanor wrinkled her eyebrows. "What do you mean *not Jim anyway*. Who *did* he shoot?"

"Everyone just sit down. I'll go over it from the start," I said.

For thirty minutes, I told Eleanor and Harvey almost everything that happened, not stopping until I was up to today. I didn't tell them about the money or what Dad said about righting a wrong. They asked me a few questions about the men I saw and what Jim had said, but they seemed to believe me when I told them what I knew. They both argued that I should give the film to Harvey and that doing so was the only way to get this resolved and keep certain people from chasing me until they had it.

Finally, Harvey walked over and stood right in front of me, leaned down, and placed his hands on the arms of my chair. Then kneeling, he brought his face so close to mine I could smell just a faint whiff of cheap aftershave.

"Matt," he said, speaking just above a friendly whisper, "there is nothing I can do to bring back your parents. I'm very sorry for that. But you have to give me that film for your own sake, and let me put it safely away."

"It's not here, but why should I give it to you anyway?"

"Just pass it to me. I can put out the word that you don't have it or know where it is," he said, "and as long as it stays hidden, you'll be safe. I don't see any other way."

"You could say that now if you really wanted to protect me."

"They would find out. They will find you, Matt. Just give it to me and get out of this."

I was tired of hearing that I should just walk away. I lost my temper. I pushed Harvey back, a little harder than I meant, and stood up.

"Why the hell does everyone think I should give them the film. That tells me I'd better just leave it in a safe place where no one will ever find it until I know what's going on," I said. Of course, the film was beneath the bed two feet away, tucked into a backpack with about nine grand in cash. Not exactly well-hidden.

I looked at Harvey and tried to be earnest and friendly but firm, "Why won't you tell me what's really happening?"

"We don't know anything else," Harvey said.

An obvious lie I was sick of hearing.

"I think you should either tell me or just get out of here. We're done if you can't tell me anything."

I opened the door.

"Kristine?" her mom said. "You have a son. This is not your fight. You should leave with me now."

Kristine closed her eyes. She took a deep breath before she opened her eyes and took her mother's hand.

"It didn't start out as my fight, but they dragged me into it," she said. "I may change my mind tomorrow, but for now I want to help Matt figure this out. Matt's Mom was my friend, too. We can't pretend that never happened."

Eleanor gave Kristine a hug before she turned and walked out the door without looking at me. Harvey followed.

As soon as they were gone, Kristine reached into her back pocket and removed a folded sheet of paper. "I felt Mom slide this in my pocket when she hugged me," she said.

"What's it say?" I asked.

Use this number only in an emergency and tell no one. NO ONE. 256 555-1177. Be careful. Do not contact anyone else from the NSEO or the FBI. Leave here as soon as we are gone and call me when you are safely far away. I love you.

Kristine sat on the bed and stared at the note.

"Why would she do that in secret? Obviously, she doesn't even trust Harvey. I don't get it," she said.

"As soon as it's dark, we're slipping out of here," I said. "And you better add Harvey Sullivan to your chart." I didn't say add your mother, but the thought crossed my mind.

I crammed the few things we had brought into Kristine's

overnight bag. We lay on the bed and flipped on the television to a news channel, but neither of us was listening. Kristine lay back looking up at the ceiling. The sunlight leaking through the curtain was just beginning to turn orange.

I picked up Kristine's diagram and studied it. Too many players. Too many connections. I found a pen in the bedside table and drew two circles beside my father's name. I wrote FBI in one and Harvey Sullivan in another and connected him to FBI and my father, then closed my eyes.

A noise outside the door made me sit straight up from a dead sleep. I'd been dreaming of horses. I was standing between two buff-colored horses close enough to put a hand on the side of each one when they suddenly galloped to the top of a hill and looked back, as if waiting for me before they ran out of sight, their drumming hoofs fading. Footsteps of children running down the concrete walkway faded, too. Kristine sat up next to me, blinking. The bedside clock said eight thirty. We'd fallen asleep for half an hour.

"We need to go," I said. Something was not right about being there. The horses in my dreams of twenty years had never run away before.

Five minutes later we were completely packed and ready. I opened the door and glanced around, but I saw only the two boys playing in the light of the walkway, one chasing another who had a small football tucked under his arm like a running back.

In the truck, I saw we needed gas, so I pulled across the street. I was inside paying for the gas and two bottles of water when I heard and felt the shock wave of an explosion come from the hotel. I left my change and ran to the car. Kristine had her door open and stood up to look at the hotel.

"Get in," I yelled. I drove to the first intersection and turned left onto the road that ran along the dam behind the hotel so that we could look back at the rear of the hotel.

"What can you see?" I asked Kristine as I weaved through the cars pulling off to the side of the road to watch the fire.

"Oh my God, Matt," she said, her hand going up to her mouth.

"What?"

"Our room. It's completely on fire. And the one next to it."

chapter 18

We drove without speaking for nearly an hour. Kristine was convinced that her mom had been followed and that her son—our son—might also be in danger. Having a son seemed as shocking as my parents' death, and I was trying to figure out where I fit into this new relationship—or if I fit at all. Did I even have role in keeping him safe? I had taken every moment between our other conversations about what to do next to ask Kristine to tell me more about Winter. What was he like? A smiling kid with lots of friends. Did he like sports? Yes, especially baseball. Was he good in school? A's and B's. She answered, but the answers had grown shorter and shorter with each question, until I knew to stop asking, at least for now. It seemed that Kristine was drifting somewhere in her own mind, as if my questions were punches, each one making her back away. I shut up about Winter and focused on staying inside the white line down the edge of the highway.

A few minutes later, I turned to Kristine. I hated to ask, but my question just popped out. "Does your mom really know how to hide Winter. I mean, she worked at the NSEO, but she was like an office manager or something."

Kristine chewed her lip. She nodded these tiny nods like she was talking to herself.

"Yeah, she does. Harvey or someone would tell her if she needed any help."

I let it drop, and the subject turned to *what next*. We argued what to do and who to turn to as we drove back toward Birmingham, turning down various county highways and always staying off the main roads until Kristine used the new number from her mom. She put the phone on speaker.

Eleanor sounded surprised and as angry as we were when Kristine told her of the explosion and fire. I heard her voice take on a tenor I'd heard before, from my own mouth, when I was past anger and tired of fooling around. Eleanor was very stern with Kristine that we should stay away until things calmed down and she would keep Winter safer than we could. Neither of us could argue it. She said go somewhere away from Birmingham and wait for her call. Don't say where we were, she told us, and don't stay anywhere longer than a day or two.

———

In another half hour we were on the outskirts of Birmingham, near the airport.

"Birmingham is absolutely the wrong place for us," I said. "But we won't go anywhere near where anyone would be looking for us. I need to pick up more money and a couple of other things we may need."

"You said you had almost ten thousand dollars."

"Cars and IDs are expensive. We've got to change vehicles. Do you know a place with valet parking?"

"ID's?" Kristine asked, irritated. But before I could answer, she said, "Oh, never mind. Go to Tutwiler."

I drove downtown and parked on the street beside the civic park across from the Tutwiler Hotel. It wasn't really the famous Tutwiler from the early 1900s, though everyone liked to pretend it was. The original Tutwiler was a block away until the Financial Center's huge towers rose on its dust after it was demolished. So in the 1980s, the Ridgley Apartment Building became the home for the new Tutwiler. Kristine said it was the one place she knew with valet parking, which seemed like the easiest place to steal a car.

For half an hour we watched a handful of guests drop off bags for the head bellman, an older guy, around sixty-five or so. Two college-aged girls in matching white shorts and yellow golf shirts parked the cars and returned each time to hang the keys on a peg board behind the bellman's stand.

"You have to get his attention away from the car keys on the peg board, and wait until both the girls are away," I told Kristine.

We picked out a dark blue BMW parked in the lot around the corner from the hotel's back door yet near the parking lot entrance. We stashed our clothes bag across the side street in the bushes behind the BMW. I walked around the block and entered the front door while Kristine walked through the parking lot and entered the lobby from that side.

As I walked through the lobby, I saw Kristine pick up a map from a display. She opened the map and stood near the back door scanning the pages, but I could see she was watching the car parkers.

She glanced back at me and nodded slightly, then walked through the door and stood near the bellman. I was a second behind her and walked past toward the sidewalk. One girl was just driving off to park, and the other waited for a guest to unpack suitcases. As soon as both cars left, Kristine asked the bellman to point out a couple of restaurants on the map. I noticed she had unbuttoned the top button of her blouse.

As soon as she had him pointing to something on the map, I stepped back and scanned the peg board. The BMW key was easy to spot. I lifted the heavy key ring and slipped it into my pocket.

When I was ten feet away, I heard Kristine thanking the bellman.

I clicked the remote door opener before reaching the car and opened the back door, throwing our bag inside. I heard footsteps and turned expecting Kristine, but it was one of the girls in the yellow shirts, and she had a puzzled look on her face. She seemed to realize I had not been with the car when it came in.

"I just needed something from my bags," I said, trying to be friendly as possible.

She smiled, but then she backed up a step and cut her eyes both ways. I knew any second she might yell for help. Kristine came around the corner and immediately saw what was happening. She stepped up behind the girl.

"Is everything okay?" she asked.

The girl relaxed a little. She looked at me with a smirk and said, "I think this guy is stealing from that car."

When the girl turned to walk away, Kristine grabbed her arm and pulled her back, simultaneously putting her mouth close to the girl's ear, "Please don't scream. He has a gun. Now just walk down that sidewalk and don't make a noise. You'll be fine."

She turned the girl toward the street and away from the bell station. After she was ten feet away, the girl started running. I knew we had about fifteen seconds before she could make it around the building to the front door.

We scrambled into the car and moved into traffic quickly as we could. In the rearview mirror, I saw the girl talking to a man and a woman on the corner and pointing toward us. That was good and would give us a few more seconds before they called 911. I continued for another block west, but while they could still see the car, I turned south and disappeared from their view. As soon as I knew they could not see me, I turned down an alley, looped back north, and within thirty seconds took the entrance ramp onto Interstate 20. I turned east and five minutes later was parked behind the bowling alley where the money was stashed.

A back door was open, so we walked through the area behind the end of the lanes where Jimmy Lynch had once taken Dad and me to see how the machinery worked that set up the bowling pins. I was able to get within twenty feet of the door to the room with the lockers without anyone seeing me. I eased the door open and scanned the room. Nothing seemed suspicious, and no one noticed me. I pulled my cap down low and walked toward the lockers. When I got there and looked around, no one was watching or coming my way.

In five minutes I was back in the car with about half the money and all my fake IDs in the travel bag. I left the rest of the cash stacked in the locker. No one I knew had seen me.

We took secondary streets I had never before been on and weaved our way north. We then zigzagged our way west and under Interstate 65 until we connected with Highway 78 that led to Jasper, away from where police might be looking in the downtown area. We would be away from the Birmingham police jurisdiction in minutes.

Taking out-of-the-way back roads, I managed to make

Tuscaloosa, normally a fifty-minute drive, in an hour and a half. I found an all-night diner on the edge of town and backed into a space behind the restaurant so we could get coffee and decide our next move. It was nearly midnight.

"We have to switch these license plates," I said, as we walked to the café door.

"Why not?" Kristine said. "Shooting. Stealing cars. Threatening a college student with a gun. What's one little car tag matter now?"

———

I borrowed a phone book from the waitress and located a junk yard not far away that was set up to allow customers to pull their own parts as they roamed unsupervised among the vehicles.

I drove past the front gate twice and saw a watchman inside the check-in booth at the front gate. He seemed to be looking down at a television. I parked on a side road and was able to scale the fence without much problem. I walked down the rows of wrecked cars and was happy not to hear any dogs barking. The place was well lit from street lights at all the corners. I got lucky and located a similar BMW that still had its license plate, close enough in model year to pass, and soon had clean license plates.

I took the nearest ramp onto the interstate to make sure we would soon be out of the county and the sheriff's jurisdiction in case someone had seen more than I thought. I wanted to drive all night toward San Antonio. I had a couple of friends there who lived beyond the edge of what most would consider the norm. If anyone could get Kristine a new identity in a hurry, they would know who, how, and how much.

After only a brief conversation sitting in a rest stop off I-20 near the state line, Kristine agreed to keep going to Texas. She said she was completely confident Winter was safe—at least safer than with us.

Heading west was one way I thought I could regain control. We needed to get away long enough to figure everything out. I could feel Texas pulling me, the familiar landscape calling me away from the death and lies in Birmingham.

In the rest area parking lot, surrounded by pines, three long-haul trucks sat lined up. Their big engines idled and filled the area with a soft rumbling hum and diesel fumes, which oddly, weren't unpleasant to me. A yellow-orange glow from the parking lot lights gave the area the look of an old tin-type photo.

chapter 19

After three hours on the highway, I stopped for gas and to stretch my legs. I bought a large Red Bull and drank it as soon as we were back on the Interstate. With the cruise control on seventy-six, I tuned in a sports talk radio station to help me stay awake. Kristine curled up against the door and went to sleep.

I began mentally to walk through everything that had happened since that first night in the pool hall, not far from our destination. One thing became clear to me as I tried to connect the dots: everyone involved had a reason to lie.

We stopped once more for a bathroom break about an hour after sun-up. Kristine had slept for most of the night.

Just after noon we pulled in front of, you guessed it, a pool hall. On the eastern edge of San Antonio. Although it had only been a few short weeks since I'd left, it seemed a lifetime ago.

Green paint blocked any light from penetrating the front windows, like old-time pool halls that were still scattered around here and there when I was growing up in the eighties. In the center of the window, a large yellow-striped nine-ball above the name City Limits Pool Room signaled to serious players that this was a place for old-school money games. We parked in front.

If you've never spent time in pool halls, it's hard to understand them. They are a subculture all to themselves. Titles and jobs and backgrounds don't count for much. Your word counts. Your game counts. Your cash counts. Blue jeans and blue silk ties both can fit, if Joey or Stick or whoever runs the show in that hall gives their nod. Pool halls are the golf courses of the underground economy. You need someone to collect a bet, somebody knows somebody who knows somebody who does that. If you need a clean pistol without a history, somebody knows somebody. If you need to disappear, the door to the other side goes through a pool hall somewhere.

I told her, "This place has been here for forty years."

"If it goes another forty, that will be too soon for me to like being here," Kristine said.

"If you know someone here, you can get connected for anything that's for sale, and the government doesn't get a cut."

"And you 'know someone' here I guess. Figures."

I didn't bite. It was a tough time, and she was still mad and scared and frustrated. I got it. I held my tongue.

"This guy can get you an ID without us having to deal directly with the woman who makes them," I said. "We need to talk to my friend. I don't know anywhere else to go."

"How do you know it's a woman?" she asked, as she stopped just inside the door to let her eyes adjust to the dim interior.

I didn't answer and looked down.

She nodded, and I saw the corners of her mouth were pointing down. "Obviously, you've done this before."

I knew there was no good answer, so again I didn't reply.

As our eyes adjusted to the light, shapes came into focus. The hardwood floors shined the same as I remembered, scuffed and gray with age beneath layers of wax. Although the corners of the room were dim, the tops of the pool tables were well lit by fake stained-glass lighting fixtures that filled the table rectangle with bluish florescent light. The green felt was fresh, but everything else on the pool tables reflected light from being worn smooth. The leather pockets at each corner had been burnished from men in T-shirts leaning on them as they stretched to make shots. The air carried an interesting mixture of cigarette smoke and cheap air freshener.

The person I wanted there, as usual, sat back in an old barber chair with a *Maxim* magazine open across his huge belly. He laughed with two guys playing snooker at a nearby table. While snooker was more fun than regular pool—with smaller balls, smaller pockets, and its own set of rules—the Average Joe rarely played. Money games were harder to find. And there were almost no snooker tables in bars.

The man I needed to see ran his hand over his flat-top, as if the hair bristles could be adjusted, and cocked his head as I walked up. He was not smiling. His features instead were flat, as if uninterested, but I somehow sensed there was nothing casual or relaxed behind the look of indifference.

"I need to talk," I said.

"Heard you left town. Maybe had something to do with a bunch of bikes got turned to beer cans, bro."

"Nah, still around," I said, shrugging.

He glanced around, then leaned forward slightly and raised two fingers to motion me closer. He said nothing more, just sat with his elbows on his knees, waiting for me to talk. He wore an expression that most people would probably think was disdain, but I knew it was just the kind of tough-guy disinterested look that was as common as a tattoo here among these second-generation Mexican

Americans who ran everything from pool halls to pizza parlors in the south part of San Antonio.

I explained that I needed identification good enough to get Kristine out of the country. Three sets.

He answered with the slightest nod and whispered an address.

"Ten o'clock. Be there on time or don't come back," he said, barely above a whisper. He picked up his magazine and began reading before I had even turned around.

———

Nine hours, three sets of photos, and fifteen-hundred bucks later, Kristine had three new passports, with fresh stamps from Mexico already in place and a few scuff marks showing typical travel wear and tear. She also had a Louisiana driver's license and two from Texas.

We took a room just south of town. We both lay across the bed with our clothes on and slept until sunlight through the thin curtains woke us. It was a typical dusty hot Texas morning, and we were ready to move after quick showers.

Half an hour later we stopped for an American-style breakfast of toast and eggs at Waffle House in Pearsall, Texas, south of San Antonio on I-35 toward Nuevo Laredo. We scanned *USA Today*, but nothing about a fire in an Alabama hotel made the national news.

The sky that morning was cloudless, thin, and more white than blue. Both of us wore the large sunglasses we'd picked up in a drug store the day before when we had Kristine's photos shot. We hardly spoke during the hour-and-a-half drive in the BMW to Laredo, both of us second-guessing ourselves I'm sure, wondering if this was right. I worried about how to gather information this far from Birmingham and doubted I would ever really know what was happening or why. Kristine seemed far away, probably thinking of her son, our son, as I was learning to think, though I didn't really have the nerve to say those words to Kristine just yet.

I pulled into the parking lot of a run-down shopping strip center where the original signs were mostly replaced with gaudy painted signs made from plywood. Tax Returns, one said. No brand, just Tax Returns. Mystique Nails. I found a parking space in front of Art's Crafts, thinking, *Really, Art?* At the far end, I noticed an electronics store with a huge Prepaid Cell Phones sign with We Buy Gold added at the bottom.

I told Kristine, "We need a couple of those throwaway type cell phones."

"What about guns and knives?" she said. "Maybe a grenade or two? Or those cool red-colored smoke bombs."

She hadn't lost her sense of humor or the way she could use a joke as an edged weapon that was just about as useful in silencing someone as a razor to a throat. This was not getting any easier, but at least she was sticking with me.

In fifteen minutes, we were back in the car with our little starter kit, as the guy had called it, with chargers and SIM cards with a hundred prepaid minutes installed.

Kristine fished out the note from her mother and dialed the number. I could only hear one side of the call, but it was clear her mom still wanted us—or at least her—to give up the film, come home, and get out of this mess.

Kristine said, "If it wasn't Sullivan, who was it?"

"Uh huh," she said a bunch of times. Then, "I don't know. You're the one who should know. Maybe *you* were followed, and it wasn't Mr. Sullivan."

She paused, listening. I could hear that her mother was practically yelling.

Kristine butted in, holding a hand up as if her mother could see her. "But you hid that note from him for some reason. And someone you know or who followed you damn sure tried to kill us."

Kristine switched the phone to her other ear. Then speaking slowly for emphasis, though trying not to yell it seemed, she said, "You have to take care of Winter. I won't bring him into this, but I can't come home just now. They know who I am. I have to stay away from Winter."

Kristine listened a little more and threw in more *uh huhs* before she finally spoke, her tone much more even now. "Mom, yes, I do trust you. But that film may be the thing that keeps us alive. We're keeping it hidden. And we made copies."

We hadn't, but I was impressed that she said so.

Finally, Kristine said, "It's better if you don't know. Probably out of the country for now. Just please find out what in the hell is going on. I'll call you when I know."

Kristine closed the phone and looked out the window without speaking. I just sat there, letting her process whatever it was she had heard.

———

We decided to check into a hotel on the American side of the border for a day or two while we decided if Mexico was really the best thing for us. Although Kristine was unhappy with me and the whole situation, things were fine for a day. We discussed lots of alternatives. We decided maybe we didn't need to go to Mexico. We could go back and find a place somewhere near Birmingham where we could be safe as we tried to figure things out and where we had friends we could call if we needed something. We were sitting in a back-corner booth of the hotel restaurant that was off to the side of the lobby, drinking coffee and eating giant blueberry muffins for breakfast, when it happened.

What I saw made my heart freeze. I leaned over to Kristine to say, "Don't turn your head. Just cut your eyes over and look near the front door. Those are the two men I saw at the hospital with Dad."

"My god Matt, how could they find us this fast?" She whispered, angry, though I couldn't tell if she was angry at me or them.

"Maybe the phone call to your mom? I don't know. I don't think they know for sure we're here or they would already have us," I said, remembering the hand on my shoulder at the library. I knew it would take a miracle to escape twice if they got that close again.

"What do we do?" she asked, as if I would know.

"Do you have all our passports and IDs?" I asked.

"Right here in my purse," she said.

"Then we just go. I have the money with me in my pack. The second they leave, we just walk out the back and get out of here without looking back," I said, pointing to her sunglasses on the table as I put mine on and pulled my baseball cap down lower.

A minute later the men walked out the front door. I threw a twenty on the table and took Kristine's hand. I led her through the kitchen door. A middle-aged Hispanic man in an apron with grease spots and flour smudged on it turned around from frying eggs and looked at us.

"La puerta?" I yelled, hoping my tiny bit of terrible Spanish wouldn't fail us as we moved toward the rear of the kitchen.

He pointed with a spatula toward a hallway, and I noticed faint faded letters EXIT above the doorway. "Second door," he said in English, but with a heavy Hispanic accent.

I pushed the metal lever, and we exited onto a busy side street. We looked for a taxi and saw one at the corner, near the front of the building. The driver was out of the car, talking with a man at a news stand. We walked toward the car. As we reached the corner of the building, I knew I had made a mistake. The two NSEO guys were standing outside the hotel under the awning, just a half a block down. One of them saw us about the time I saw them, and after only a moment it became obvious he recognized us when he said something and the other guy jerked his head around to look in our direction.

"Get in," I told Kristine, as the men began running toward us, knocking two young guys down as they pushed through the people walking along the sidewalk.

I ran around the front of the taxi and jumped into the driver's seat, hitting the door locks as I did. The keys were in the ignition. Just as the men neared the car and grabbed at the door handle, I had the taxi started and squealed the tires as we lurched forward toward the side street. In the rearview mirror, I saw the men standing in the middle of the street, not chasing us. One was on a cell phone. I fumbled to turn off the blaring Mexican music.

"Damn you, Matt," Kristine said, not even looking at me.

"Damn you."

"I know," I said, remembering that was the same thing she'd said when this started at her apartment. "Just watch for anyone following us."

I turned the corner and drove as fast as I could without risking being pulled over by a police officer. Two minutes later I drove into some kind of farmers' market parking lot just a block from the border crossing into Mexico. I stopped without bothering to find a parking space and left the car running as we walked toward the border, hoping someone would steal the taxi.

By mid-afternoon, we had rented a Ford Fiesta in Nuevo Laredo after we crossed the border on foot. We drove south and checked into the Hotel Fastos in Monterrey. The new IDs wouldn't be traceable, so I figured we had some time. I had driven my Harley to Monterrey twice before and knew it was a big enough city to hide us, with at least a couple of million people, I figured.

There was a new supermarket named Soriana in walking distance from Fastos. We bought a few things to eat so we could hang out in our room and make a new plan.

Kristine threw back the covers and lay across the bed. "Obviously, going home isn't as safe as we thought," she said, falling onto the bed and wrapping her arms around the pillow. "Will you just leave me alone for a while?"

I wasn't sure what this meant.

"Leave you alone?"

"Yes," she said, not looking at me, her face toward the open window where a thin pink curtain hung motionless.

I stood there still uncertain.

She turned over and sat up, holding the pillow to her chest.

"Just go. Come back in an hour. I need to be by myself."

I pushed the backpack with our money under the bed with the toe of my shoe and walked out into dry air and car horns and children laughing. For half an hour I wandered through the neighborhoods around the hotel until I found a little bar named Rosa Cantina. I ordered Negro Modelo and wondered how we could ever go home.

By the time I finished the third beer, I found myself looking over my shoulder. Stupid was the only word I could use for myself. It would not be fun to tell Kristine we could not stay here, where even among these crowded streets they would find an American couple in a day or two. Even rented under my passport name that I now knew my dad made just for an event such as this, they would find the rental car. The afternoon sky turned orange as I walked back to the hotel. I crossed the street again and again and walked into shops and out their back doors into alleyways as I'd seen guys do in movies. No one seemed to be following me.

chapter 20

I knocked softly before opening the door.

"It's me."

Kristine sat up in the bed holding the yellow bedspread in front of her as soon as I opened the door. She didn't appear to have been asleep.

"Kristine, I think we need to leave. Get deeper into Mexico."

"I'm taking a shower," was all she said as she stood up and stretched her arms straight above her head, bending her neck backwards and rolling it in circles. She picked up her jeans from the floor and tossed them onto a straight-back chair.

As I watched her walk into the bath in only her T-shirt, I realized it was the first time I had seen her legs in nearly eight years. But I would have recognized her firm calves and small ankles even if I hadn't seen her face. She looked exactly as I remembered her.

Using bottled water, I stood at a small metal sink just inches from the shower curtain and washed the mangoes we'd purchased earlier before I cut away the skin. I sliced the fruit into chunks, laid them on a paper plate, and sprinkled chili salt over them. I also sliced into wedges one of my favorites, Queso Criollo from the market, a cheese I had discovered similar to Muenster.

By the time Kristine stepped out of the shower, I had arranged the plates on a tray I'd placed in the middle of the bed. I opened two bottles of water and a small bag of shelled pecans to go with the fruit and cheese.

"So, we have to leave. Vamonos. Hightail it," she said, only a little of the chill dissipated from earlier as she dressed in a fresh T-shirt and the same jeans. "I guess we're a modern Bonnie and Clyde. Do I need to get a big hat?"

This was yet another one of those moments that has no good outcome, no correct response. I was having them too often. I could go along with the not-really-a-joke and make her mad for not being serious. I could argue I'm doing my best, always a weak answer. I could argue she was as much a part of the problem as I was, another bad idea I quickly realized. I opted for the same answer guys come up with ninety percent of the time—fall on the sword.

"Kristine, I'm sorry," I said. "Believe me. I never meant for any of this to happen."

As usual, that didn't help much either.

She said, "Well it did happen. I knew the first time I met up with you that this was going to go bad. I'm such an idiot."

"We can't tell your mother," I said.

"Maybe for a day or two. But she has to know where I am," she said. "If something happens to Winter, I have to be reachable. What if he gets sick or falls and breaks an arm?"

"No," I said, "right now you just can't risk it for his sake. She's raised a child. She can keep him safe. We can't. Not yet." I couldn't look at her. "We really have to disappear for a while. Being gone for a few weeks is not as bad as being gone forever."

Her eyes were slits and if she'd had death-ray power, I'd have been cut in half.

"Why? Isn't this place 'gone' enough?" she asked.

"Damn it, Kristine," I said too quickly, immediately sorry for my tone. I started over, slower. "You know how fast they found us before. That wasn't an accident. They had to be listening to your mother's phone and figured it out somehow. Or maybe they were checking all my old haunts."

Kristine sat down and began cramming cheese and mangoes into her mouth, staring away at nothing in particular. She was thinking, so I shut up. She turned up a bottle of water and drained about half of it, put the top on it, and reached to put it in her purse. For an average-sized person, she could really put a lot of food down her throat.

Kristine sighed, one of those big-breath sighs that sort of puts an exclamation point on a sentence that never needs to be spoken. Then she began folding her clothes strewn on the floor and chairs, placing them into her travel bag. I sat there waiting for her to say something. She looked over at me and said, "Well, come on, Clyde. Don't we have to go?"

———————

I stopped by the front desk to check out. "Can you give me directions to Chihuahua?" I asked, as I was pulling a hundred-dollar bill from my wallet to pay for the room.

The young desk clerk said, "One moment, senor." He waived over a gentleman about forty-five.

This man was obviously the manager or someone of authority. His hair was coal black and combed back from his face. He was dressed in black pants and a starched white shirt buttoned to the neck. He stood very erect and still with his hands behind his back and listened to my story of needing to get to Chihuahua the fastest way by car. He nodded the whole time. When he finally spoke, his English was perfect, the accent masked as much as possible. He directed me west through Saltillo and on to Torreon where I could pick up Highway 45 North that would take us into downtown Chihuahua. "Once you reach Mexico 45, stay on that highway all the way to Chihuahua. I hope you and your lovely wife have had a pleasant stay. Please visit us again soon."

Kristine and I walked through the front doors as a happy couple and loaded the trunk with our clothes and a new green backpack full of cash and IDs. Two blocks from the hotel, I turned the opposite direction from the way to Chihuahua.

"That's not the way he said turn," Kristine said.

"I know."

She sighed that big sigh again, which still needed no words but was punctuated by a head shake and a disgusted fake smile as she turned to stare out the window, her arms crossed over her chest. Glancing over casually, I could see tears on her cheek, but she made no effort to wipe them. I knew they weren't for us.

We drove south toward Mexico City, Ciudad de Mexico, following a full country map I'd purchased in the gift shop. For the first half hour neither of us spoke. Kristine broke the silence.

"What's your plan?" she asked, the words a bit warmer. "You obviously know the tricks for how to hide. I won't ask how you honed that skill."

"By now they know we're in Mexico, and we can't hide well even among the tourists. A redhead with a blond guy sporting a crew cut seems like an easy pair to spot."

I waited for that to sink in.

"I'm thinking Europe," I told her. I glanced over and saw her nod slightly, not so much in agreement as to acknowledge she'd heard me.

The car was quiet again for half an hour when she said, "You have to write all this down in a way that explains to others what we're doing. Or make a tape or something. If we don't know who to talk to, we have to tell several people what's going on. Someone somewhere has to get this out in the open if we're ever going to be safe again. We need lots of people watching. People who know what happened."

So that was the beginning of me telling the story on tape. She'd figured out how we might survive this mess. Later that night, I lay in bed thinking of the horses and wondering if they would visit when I slept.

part **II**

EUROPE

chapter **21**

When we reached Mexico City, I showed a different passport and booked a room in a hotel near the airport. We visited a nearby market and decided to change our hair color again.

"I'm the blonde this time," Kristine insisted. She had picked up some blonde clip-in extensions at the market, so I had suspected as much.

I went back to my usual dark brown, which better matched the ID I was using. I learned that going from light-colored hair to dark was much easier than the other way around, something that had never registered with me. I had not shaved in three days, so I decided to let it grow.

After spending an hour in the airport checking flights, we settled on a flight to Brussels, which had one problem—a short stopover in Chicago. We discussed the risk of going back through the US, but we wouldn't have to go through customs on the stopover, and I didn't think anyone could have found our new identities that fast. We decided it was fine.

We were back in the airport just after seven the next morning for a nine-fifteen flight. We'd booked our flights separately and had split the cash between our suitcases, carry-on bags, and pockets.

We slept off and on, talking little on the plane, and the stop-over in Chicago went without a hitch. We arrived in Brussels at eight in the morning and went through customs separately, but we made eye contact, and I signaled to Kristine to follow me. We'd purchased unmatched suitcases with rollers, so we walked through the airport. We found seating where we could face away from each other but sit back-to-back close enough to talk.

I felt a little ridiculous to be honest, like I was in some sort of spy movie. I knew that if they were as good as I thought, this kind of thing was useless once they knew generally where we were. I could only hope they were a step behind us. I wanted to give Kristine a little hope that I could get us out of this alive. If she were to give up or quit moving with me, the game would be over.

I told her, "Take a taxi to Hotel Bedford and check in. A sign said it's downtown. I'll be right behind you, and I'll check into the same place. Rest up, and let's meet out front at five this afternoon."

She just shook her head and walked through the front doors without saying anything or looking back. I waited five minutes and followed the same route.

When I walked outside the hotel at five, Kristine was already there, standing near the corner. She motioned with her head to follow. Three blocks later I saw her duck into a small café. Inside was dark, and my eyes took a moment to adjust. I found her in a booth near the back.

"I couldn't really sleep," she said as I slid in across from her. "I walked around and found this place."

A waitress walked to the edge of the table and smiled at us. "Deux cafés," Kristine said. Two coffees. I'd forgotten that

Kristine spoke French.

"Did you sleep?" she asked me, her tone back to normal it seemed, at least not as harsh as it had seemed in Mexico.

"Yeah, a couple of hours I think."

She leaned in on her elbows. "I walked around for hours this afternoon, thinking through all that has happened and how we got here."

"I'm sorry." I started to say, but she cut me off.

"No. We're past being sorry," she said. "I realize this whole thing isn't your fault. You just got caught up in something your father started. It doesn't excuse what you did to get Winter and me involved, but I see now you didn't cause all of this."

I didn't really know what to say. "I'm still sorry. I would never have called you that first time if I'd known what was going to happen. I wouldn't have done that to Winter, either." I realized that Kristine was giving me a huge break when I spoke of Winter. After all, I hadn't even met him. I had all sorts of mixed thoughts and feelings about how either of them would accept me in Winter's life, even if I had any role there or not in the future. But I knew that ignoring him as if he were not at the center of our mess was not the right thing.

"I know," she said, barely above a whisper, looking to the side. She'd never been one to cry much, and even now she wouldn't.

I swallowed hard to push the lump in my throat back down. "I think we have to move one more time, just to get away from the city where we arrived. I know we're not as good at hiding as they are at finding."

"I agree," she said. "I've thought about it. There's a train to Munich we can catch. Let's go there. And use a fresh ID."

Our coffee arrived. We both used the heavy cream and sugar on the table to mellow out the strong, almost bitter brew. We just sat there sipping the coffee as the café filled up with men and women getting off work. Soon every table was filled with people drinking beer in tall mugs. The sounds of conversation grew louder and the tinkling of glass could be heard mixed with laughter. We both switched to a local beer, and I convinced Kristine to eat a steak with me. I was guessing she didn't eat steak often since cooking steak for her and a child wouldn't seem to be the way to spend an evening very often. And from how hard her body looked, it was clear she ate healthy food. Of course, after the steak came and she ripped into it like a hungry dog, I wished I'd ordered us both one.

The next morning, we boarded the train separately, but after we left the station we found seats near each other for the trip that would take all day and into the night. I pulled a copy of an Elmore Leonard paperback from my backpack and began reading, glancing ahead once in a while at Kristine two rows up and across from me where I could see her. She folded her jacket into a pillow and turned sideways in the seat to take a nap as the train gained speed and rocked gently.

I knew nothing about Germany. We were in the station walking out when I learned that Munich was really Munchen in German. Never knew that. We hadn't even left the train station when I began to suspect this was not a place I wanted to stay.

"You sure this will work for us? I can't read anything," I said. In Belgium and Mexico, I could at least figure out what most signs meant, but nothing here seemed remotely decipherable other than signs like Marlboro and Budweiser.

She laughed. "Give it a chance." She was standing in front of what appeared to be an information booth, reading an English brochure on hotels, so I wandered into a newspaper and magazine stand to find something in English to read. I'd finished the Leonard book halfway through the train ride. I picked up a copy of *U.S. News & World Report*, something I hadn't read in years.

"Hotel Dolomit," Kristine said, glancing up from a map when I walked out of the news shop. "It's walking distance. They've got Internet, too, and modern rooms."

She saw the funny look on my face.

"We need a computer," she said. "It's the safest and fastest way we can get the information we'll need from here."

For the first time, I realized her mood had shifted. Now she was into this search for answers as much as I was. And it seemed that maybe her attention had shifted away from being angry with me. Just get on with it seemed to be her attitude now. I hoped it would last.

We checked into a double this time. I figured we had to be way ahead of anyone looking for us now. We could blend into this city easily if we didn't talk much in public. We dropped off our small suitcases in our room and stuffed half the cash from my backpack behind a vent I unscrewed with a coin. I kept the backpack with me. The bellman told us about a computer store. Kristine said that almost everyone under forty here spoke some English now. He directed us to a huge mall called Olympia something or other.

The taxi ride in a Mercedes left me queasy, with its quick acceleration and sudden stops. I think the car was one of the older models, maybe a 450, but in any case it was the best cab I'd ever been in, and although fifteen or twenty years old, it was in mint condition. Leather seats, clean carpet, and spotless windows. The streets alternated from straight, broadly divided boulevards to narrow winding streets too small for cars to pass. But the one thing every street had in common was that everything was clean. I never saw a piece of stray paper or even bit of a lawn that was not perfectly manicured.

When we pulled in front of the enormous mall, I was shocked at the glass dome and the immense parking deck. We paid the driver and walked through glass doors. It felt like I was back in the States for a second. Teens everywhere in tight jeans and Adidas or Nike sneakers. And even the young girls had tattoos.

Obviously, Germans liked shopping as much as Americans, and the mall could just as easily have been in the middle of Milwaukee or Atlanta, other than the signs and directories, of course, where every word seemed to have a few extra Es and Us, not to mention consonants that looked like they were just sort of jammed into the middle of words. I could make no sense of the language. Mrs. Peters' tenth and eleventh grade Latin wasn't helping the way it did in Mexico. I didn't see many stores I knew, though I remember being surprised to see a Woolworth's. I wasn't shocked to see McDonald's or the lines of German kids there. How many sausages can a kid eat without wanting a burger?

"Kristine, I can look up something on Google, but that's about it for me and computers," I said, as we found a computer store and stood there looking through the window. "I've never even owned one, just played around with some friends' or used one at the library."

"I'll handle it, and you can keep trying different terms in Google," Kristine said, rolling her eyes and walking into the store and leaving me there.

———

Back in the room, I helped Kristine unpack an HP laptop and power cords.

She sat at the desk and began inserting various DVDs into the computer and installing software. "This may take a while. Especially making connection with the Internet," she said.

I sat on the bed and watched, having no clue what she was doing. After a few minutes, I propped up on some pillows and began reading the magazine I'd bought. The second article that caught my eye was by a guy named Peter Clay Thomas, who was writing about corruption in the New York City government. About half way through it, I sat up in the bed. "Kris, listen to this. 'New York City Deputy Mayor Standridge may be unindicted, but his inability or unwillingness to explain seventy-two calls on a cell phone provided by the city to known crime figure Alfonso Neopolis leave me with no option but to believe something is rotten in the State of Denmark.'"

She looked at me. "Well, the guy has nerve to write that about someone who hasn't been charged. I hope his wife has good life insurance on him."

"That's my point," I said. "Here's what else the guy has written. Let me read his little bio. 'Investigative reporter and author Peter Clay Thomas is the recipient of the Associated Press's Sevellon Brown Memorial Award. He is best known for his expose' of illegal activities by Washington lobbyists and governmental officials, which he chronicled in *High Times and Low Life Inside the Beltway*.'"

"I've heard of that book. He names names, I hear. Maybe he's your guy," Kristine said. "Write this story, and send it to him."

"I think you're right. And I want to get his book."

The next day, I found a bookstore to order Thomas's book. Kristine managed to get online and create a new email account. We figured she could use it just once to contact her mom and check on Winter, but then we'd need to move to another city, so we held off on using it. Kristine began researching more about Elvis.

For the next two days, we slept late, walked for miles around town, and enjoyed bratwurst with hot mustard and beer from street vendors. We sat on benches under unfamiliar shade trees and read the Elvis books we'd ordered. Dead or alive, one thing was certain about the man: how much passion people felt for him.

We talked for hours about how to get help. How to expose the situation. Playing out scenarios about what really happened back in 1977 and why people like my parents were dying twenty years later. We decided she needed to assure her mother we were fine and to check on Winter. The Peter Clay Thomas book arrived on the third day, and I spent most of that afternoon and evening scanning each chapter. By the end of the book, I knew Peter Clay Thomas was the person I wanted to write this story. Now I had to figure out how to get it to him.

"Writing's too slow," I told Kristine after I put down the book. "But I think I can talk it through. Tomorrow I need to buy one of those little tape recorders."

*Uh huh w*as all I heard. She was face down on her pillow and half asleep. I stared at her hair down over her shoulders. She was wearing one of my T-shirts as she had begun doing the first night we stayed in the same room. I can't say the tension was gone yet, but things between us were much better. And she'd laughed a lot more often the past couple of days.

As I lay there beside her leaning on my elbow, watching her try to sleep, I reached out and stroked her hair. After a moment, she turned over and looked up at me, blinking. She looked puzzled but not angry. Neither of us moved for several seconds. She reached her hand behind my head.

"Come here," she said and pulled my mouth to hers.

She tasted of lemons. I became weightless. I could feel myself rising through space when I closed my eyes and focused only on the slender shape of her firm tongue as she ran it across my lips. She squeezed me so hard I had trouble taking a breath. I squeezed her back and ran my hands over her back under the T-shirt. She sat up and pulled the shirt over her head, fell back, and pulled me on top of her. Her kiss was so rough I thought my lips would be bruised, but I didn't care. Her hands were hot on my skin. For the first time in a long time, the moment was perfect, suspended, the world a faded reality that no longer mattered.

Afterward I woke first and lay there not moving, not wanting to do anything that would end this magical spell, listening to her breath make a tiny whistling noise as it rushed over her teeth, like wind through a screen door. I pushed my hair off my forehead and realized it was wet. The night was still and soundless. I fluffed my pillow and lay back, staring up, fingers clasped behind my head, trying to visualize life as a father. The future was hard to imagine. Was this just sex or something more? Would I coach soccer? Little League? Could I go to work wearing a tie? Would we be a family? I had a sudden fear that Kristine could never trust me to stay, and my past would keep us apart. I began to drift into the darkness again, weight coming back, the damp sheet pressing up into me as I closed my eyes. Soon horses were crowding around me, jostling me, scaring me, pawing the ground as black-edged clouds rolled above. Lightning flashed silently on the far distant horizon, and the horses' nostrils flared as they seemed to smell rain approaching.

chapter 22

The glowing sunlight worked its way around the edges of the dark curtain. I put my feet over the side of the bed and sat there, waking up. I saw my T-shirt on the floor and smiled. Kristine lay facing away from me, still curled up on her side with nothing but the thin sheet bunched around her waist, revealing a large tattoo on her back. I could not stop myself from studying it, even though I felt I was invading her privacy. What I saw left me surprised, perhaps shocked is a better word. I left her there asleep and tip toed into the shower.

I bathed and dressed in jeans and a new flannel shirt Kristine had brought back from her walk the previous day. She sat in a chair with her feet tucked under her, sipping coffee she had made in the tiny coffee-maker on the desk. "There's another cup if you want it," she said.

I poured the coffee, trying to figure out what to say about what happened between us the night before. Instead I avoided the subject, telling her, "I'm going to get that tape player. I saw a little electronics shop a few blocks down. I think they'll have it."

"I need to contact Mom," she said.

"We'll have to leave once you do," I said, worried I sounded a bit like I was scolding her, which I wasn't.

"I don't care. This is important," she said. "It's not like we have a house full of furniture or a dog or something. I can leave here in two minutes."

I stood up. "Just let me get everything ready to go. We'll figure out our next stop before we contact her," I said. I was at the door when she stopped me.

"Matt," she said, waiting for me to turn and face her as I stood in the doorway. "I wanted that last night. I'm not healed from the hole you created in my heart when you left, but I think I still love you."

I nodded. "Yeah. Me, too," was all I could think of. Not very romantic, I know. I stood there, awkward as a teenager, not knowing exactly what I was supposed to do next.

"There's one more thing. I suppose you noticed this morning."

I had, of course. "The tattoo?"

"The tattoo," she said. "I hope it doesn't weird you out or anything. I know it's a lot more ink than the average tramp stamps the college girls have."

"No, of course not," I said, but the truth was that I was more than surprised when I had first seen her bare back that morning for the first time in many years, one of the most incredibly intricate tattoos ever, running all the way down the center of her back with elaborate designs and colors, carefully placed so that none of the design would be seen wearing normal clothing. A huge flowering tree dominated the center of the design, surrounded by a tiger and a lioness staring at each other. The most stunning thing was the herd of horses, smaller in scale, running across a field in the background. They were my horses, our horses, the ones we had dreamed about as kids that one day we'd own together, on some faraway ranch with mountains in the background. Exactly like the tattoo. Exactly like my dreams. I had questions, lots of them.

But what I said was, "Being around biker guys for years, I've seen thousands of tattoos on men and women, and even kids. Nothing surprises me for long. But I have to admit that did a little."

That was a lie. I was in shock.

"Yeah," she laughed. "Not what you expected of me, was it?"

"The truth? No."

"It started with the lotus. Lotus was a nymph, if you remember Mrs. Peter's mythology class, and she turned into a lotus tree when some guy tried to rape her. She was the daughter of Poseidon. A lotus was both an escape and medicine. I wanted a reminder that I had to be both for Winter."

"I guess it makes sense." My guilt came roaring back, and I was sure she would see my face and ears growing red, but she said nothing of it if she did. "And the horses?"

"Yeah, they're what you think. Our horses. The thing I kept as part of you. So now you know."

"I'm not sure what to say," I said, feeling lame for saying it and wishing I had something eloquent and touching and memorable to say.

"Only two or three people have even seen it. A few months after the lotus I added the lioness, since the female takes the lead in the hunting for the family group, and then the tigress."

"I guess she means something, too?"

"Female tigers stay close to their mothers but stake out their own territory. Still, they get along with the males, too. I just wanted that reminder. And the horses were added last. So now you know my big secret. My life story inked on my back."

"Makes sense," I said, remembering suddenly my mother's words that there was much about Kristine I needed to know.

"It's meaningful."

Finally, she laughed and waved me out. "Go on. I'll have things packed when you get back. I'll go online and look at the train schedules, too."

I stumbled out into the light, feeling like I'd had sex with someone I'd just met. This Kristine was not the teenage girl I had left behind. At least now I knew why she had laughed so hard when I apologized for asking her to put the rose tattoos on her hands.

———

"Why not Venice?" Kristine asked when I returned, tape recorder and cassettes in hand. I didn't have anywhere else in mind and knew nothing much about Europe anyway. We spent the rest of the day learning what we could about Venice and waiting for the afternoon train.

"We're seven hours ahead of Birmingham," Kristine told me. "I'll try to hit Mom's email about seven-thirty in the morning, two-thirty here. That gives us time to make the late afternoon train and get there early this evening. It's not that far, maybe two or three hundred miles."

Kristine emailed her mother through a new email account she had set up locally at an Internet café. Our hope was that whoever at the NSEO was involved in this didn't really have eyes out for us world-wide. Either way, we wouldn't be here long after sending the email.

We didn't have to wait long to know if it worked. Within a couple of minutes Kristine heard back from her mother who like clockwork was checking her email with her morning coffee. Winter was fine, though asking for his mommy. She said "our mutual friend" had been on her every day to find Kristine. We assumed that meant Sullivan.

Kristine looked at me hard when I said to say we were in Northern Mexico, but she did it.

When I tried to put my arm around her, she shrugged it off and grabbed her suitcase. "Let's just go," she said as she turned and walked out without waiting to see if I was ready. I didn't think words would help much to make a mother separated from her young son feel better, so I just followed her out of the hotel. In the taxi, we decided to travel in separate cars in the train and meet up in front of the station when we arrived in Venice. Venezia, she told me.

chapter 23

Even in the dark, I sensed the countryside had a look all its own. As we rolled through small towns, stucco buildings and red tile roofs shown here and there under streetlights, and the stone streets passing by the train windows gave me a feeling of security. Things here endured. They weathered whatever the world offered, and somehow my own troubles seemed smaller, if only for a fleeting moment.

Almost as if reading my mind, Kristine spoke. "Venice is literally the end of the line. This railway delivers us into Venice, which is actually 117 tiny islands. "

"It looks like it's about six inches above sea level to me."

As we lumbered onto the island, I was fascinated by a bridge alongside the rail trestle, heavily travelled with tiny cars, refrigerated delivery trucks, and small flatbed trucks with cargoes under canvas tarps. It was the lifeline of the city, pumping the oxygen of commerce as steady as a heart. Trains backed out the same way they came in, on one of the several parallel tracks on the rail bridge.

We soon found ourselves standing on a sidewalk, a bit uncertain of our next step. "A water taxi, I guess," I said, shrugging my shoulders.

"Yes hon," Kristine said. "That's how it works here."

The word "hon" made my breath catch in my throat, but I turned away quickly. The sarcasm of the past days seemed to have dissipated like fog, and I could think of nothing more welcome than her tone of voice with intended humor. I didn't allow her to see my reaction to her use of the endearment, but it took me back eight years. The memory was good.

I waved toward a man, about twenty-five, black pants and white shirt with a bow tie, standing near a powerboat, under a TAXI stand. He ran toward us across the street, ducking between passing cars.

"English?" he asked.

I wasn't pleased that we were that obvious. I made a mental note to figure out why we couldn't blend in better.

"Yes, we need to get to…" I said, trying to remember.

"… Hotel La Calcina," Kristine finished.

"Ah, Pensione La Calcina," the water-taxi driver said in perfect English. "Very good choice. A nice place and easy to get into. About half an hour from here, on the other side of Venice. Many famous people stay at this place. Small hotel, cozy. I hear the rooms are nice."

The water taxi swayed in the water, choppy from ceaseless waves that seemed to have no pattern, churned by a stream of long work boats, gondolas, and sleek water taxis. The boat gleamed with teak covered in thick shiny varnish and fresh glossy paint.

We settled into the back of the boat, which rumbled low tones as we entered a larger canal. The city was like nothing I could have prepared for. Towering buildings of gray stone rose from the water, with intricate chiseled designs and large windows. Busy sidewalks ringed every building, and pedestrian bridges arched over the canals around every corner. A constant stream of boats glided past in every direction as their drivers anticipated one another's moves. It was a world of water, stone, and blue sky. Through it all, Kristine held my hand, and for a few minutes nothing about death and murder and deception crossed my mind.

The hotel wasn't exactly what I expected for a place that apparently dated to the 17th century. It was better. I felt like I had stepped back in time to a place that wanted us. Kristine had read about this famous guy named John Ruskin who had often stayed at the hotel and about whom the hotel owners seemed very proud. A large plaque with an inscription praised Ruskin, who lived in the hotel in 1877, it said. The plaque was presented by The Council of Venice in January 1900.

I laughed silently when Kristine asked the desk clerk if the very room Ruskin had used might be available. I was more surprised when he said yes. Mr. Ruskin had stayed in more than one room, but one of his favorites was in fact available. We took it. Yeah, the word sucker did come to mind, but who cares.

Kristine loved the room with its old furniture, plush linens, and modern Internet connection. I was not used to being asked if we wanted a room with a bath, but I was glad they had one available.

After checking in and dropping off the bags, we walked aimlessly for an hour, finally stopping at a sidewalk café where pizza and wine seemed to be on every table. I've moved around enough to know that the best food is wherever you find a few locals mixed in with the tourists. This looked like the place.

We had the same thing we saw everyone else ordering, and both food and wine convinced our taste buds this was a good place to hang out. The pizza was obviously hand-tossed and not quite round, with a tangy red sauce, a few spicy pepperoni slices, and a rich cheese perfect for this dish. Kristine made sure we ordered the house red wine, a good call. For six bucks, we had a bottle of wine better than any I'd tasted in a long time. After dinner, we noticed gelato vendors on every other corner, so we each had a chocolate ice cream cone. I knew I'd sleep well that night. I wasn't used to this much food.

The next morning, I had coffee downstairs in a room off the side of the lobby where I read the plaque that told about Ruskin living in the place in the late 1800s. They had copies of all his books behind glass cases. I asked the desk clerk if I could read any of Ruskin's books. He reached behind to hand me two books that were reprinted copies of *The Stones of Venice.* He said the entire body of work had originally been three volumes, but this reprint shortened it to two. I spent a couple of hours browsing it. Heavy stuff. Mostly, Ruskin seemed sad that as government had changed its interests, they had let the city rundown, deteriorate. At least that's what I got from it.

On the third day at La Calcina, when I came out of the shower, Kristine stood at the window and watched the boats, mostly work boats loaded with lumber or bricks. "We can't just hide here, Matt. You have to record this and send something to that guy."

She was right. I didn't really know how to start, I'd stalled by looking up things about Elvis on the computer, reading the Ruskin books, or just wandering around Venice. "How do I start?"

"I'm going to leave you so you can begin," she said. "I've already put in a tape and numbered ten tapes for you. Just say what tape number it is and start talking. Go all the way back to when the guy told you to call home. It's not a novel, Matt. Don't worry about making it perfect."

She slung my backpack over her shoulder, kissed me on the cheek, and walked to the door. "Two hours. Don't leave here until you spend two hours on it, okay? We must get this over with. I miss Winter." She closed the door quietly behind her.

Two hours later, I was tired of talking. But I also discovered something. None of this would make sense unless I could figure out what was behind the attack on Elvis. And I had to get Peter Clay Thomas working on this story from his side. If he would even listen to me.

———

The next day, Kristine was helping me create a Yahoo email account at an Internet café across the city. "What are you going to say?" she asked, the anxiety very high in her voice.

"Just the bare facts, and something that no one would know who wasn't there in Birmingham when this happened," I said. "I have to convince him I'm not just some crazy."

"Won't this get us found, like in Mexico?"

"I think it's safe. They won't know any connection between Thomas and me, so they have no reason to be watching him," I said, trying to sound more confident than I really was.

chapter 24

"I'm going to look for a new Internet café somewhere near the Academy of Fine Arts of Venice," Kristine said as she closed the door behind her.

Kristine was pressing me to finish figuring out how we could go back home. But piecing together my own history was not at all like I thought it would be. It was more like writing a history of my parents. To tell that story, I had to go back to a dark time with them that shaped who I am and who they were.

When I was almost eight, everything changed in our happy family. And the dream of horses squeezing in around me first started.

I'd just walked home from second grade, my books held together by my belt and slung over my shoulder, imitating the big kids. My mother sat on the top front porch step crying, so I asked, "Mama, what's wrong?"

She tried to smile and pretended those weren't tears on her cheeks. "Nothing's wrong, Honey. Come sit by Mama." She put her arm around me, and we sat there for a long time not speaking.

"Why are you crying?"

She didn't answer.

I cried just because she did. I was afraid to ask any more. Things were never the same after that day. I remember the moment vividly because I'd never seen my mother cry before.

Inside I found Dad asleep on the couch. I ran over to him, all excited, and yelled, "Dad, I hit a home run at recess today!"

Nothing.

"Dad, you should have seen it!"

Nothing.

I put my hand on his arm and shook him a little. Still nothing. I thought he was asleep, but I couldn't wake him. I noticed an empty whiskey bottle on the floor beside the couch. He rolled over with his back to me and mumbled something I couldn't hear.

Mom rushed into the room. "Come on, Matt. Your father's not feeling well. He'll be fine later," she told me.

I still remember her grabbing my shoulders and turning me around, sort of guiding me away. One day at school a few weeks after that, I overheard one of the boys in my class say, "My Dad said his dad's a drunk." When I walked up, they grew quiet and looked down, scuffing the toes of their Converse sneakers on the sidewalk.

Dad progressed from quiet to withdrawn to drunk in just a few months. Eventually, he must've lost his job because he was always in the house, just sitting in his easy chair for hours staring at Alex Trebek running *Jeopardy!,* an open half-gallon of Jim Beam on the floor next to his chair. The only good thing I remember about our house for the next dozen years was that although Dad would yell and act mad at us half the time, he never hit me … or Mom either. From then on, I didn't watch much television like the other kids. I didn't want to be in that room with Dad, and we just had the one TV set. To this day I still don't like television.

Kristine only knows a little of this stuff that happened at home. I never liked to talk about it. When she gets back today, it's time she hears the whole story.

chapter 25

The sunlight in Venice added a warm yellow tone to the buildings and boats as I sat near the window making a recording late in the afternoon. Kristine napped. I switched off the recorder and watched her. The silence woke her, and she rolled over and looked up at me.

"Time for gelato?" I asked. In the week we'd been there, a routine had already developed that included long walks in the afternoon and ice cream. The weather was warm, and there had been no rain.

"I'm ready," Kristine said as she sat up and pulled on her jeans.

We left the front of the hotel and turned right at the first street, as usual. From there we'd learned to let the crowd sweep us along, with no particular place in mind. Each building along the sidewalk had its own shade of gray, a hundred different grays, colors that had no name in English. The buildings not gray were earth tones or yellow.

Everywhere pigeons fought for position. Some were daring, landing at our feet while others held vigil over some bread crumb they'd found. A few were patient and cunning, awaiting the tiniest scrap of food we might drop from a sandwich or a crumbling cone from our ice cream.

"I love the glassware here," Kristine said, stopping in front of a large window filled with wine and champagne flutes, crystal and hand-blown Christmas balls of red and blue hanging from fishing line. We'd window shopped here three or four times before.

"But you've bought nothing," I noted. "When did you get so into decorative stuff?"

"Uh, eight years ago maybe?"

"Ouch, I guess I walked into that one," I said, joking, but I hoped she didn't look closely at my face. I couldn't get past what I now knew was more or less desertion of my lover and the mother of my child, no matter how much I tried to claim it was just a youthful bad decision. I had been a child, too, I told myself, but I still couldn't shake the feeling that what I had done by leaving so suddenly was a holy transgression beyond forgiveness.

"Matt, this isn't a vacation. We have lives waiting on us. I have a …" She caught herself, then continued. "Winter needs me. Maybe even us. But whatever he needs, it's not to live with my mother."

I hadn't mentioned the email I received earlier in the afternoon. I guess somehow I thought that if I ignored it this time with her could go on longer. When she said that maybe Winter needed us, I realized for the first time that I really did want Winter, or at least to experience whatever notion I had of fatherhood.

———

"I heard back from Peter Clay Thomas," I blurted, surprised to hear the words coming from my mouth. This was not how I meant to tell her. I wanted a plan first, but here it was, and the words were not something I could now ignore.

"He's beginning to believe me."

She crooked her head and looked at me. She was more startled than disappointed.

"When?" She asked.

"Just today. He checked out what I said. I told him a high-powered rifle had killed Jim Robinson and that it was one shot to the right side of his chest. That wasn't in the news," I said.

"Why would that matter?"

"He said he had friends in the police that could check it out if I knew something that was not in the news, so I guess they told him I must be for real."

The lines on her forehead wrinkled as her eyebrows rose. "I don't remember you saying all that when we emailed him."

I hadn't told her of the skeptical reply I got almost immediately the first time, or the two long emails I sent back with all sorts of details to check on. I immediately felt the dread of someone whose secrets are being revealed. I didn't much know how to open up to anyone and had been on my own so long I just forgot how to share information.

"I had to write again. I didn't want to worry you," I said, knowing from the look on her face it was the wrong thing to do.

She closed her eyes and slowly shook her head side to side. "Matt, I'm in this, too. We can't have any secrets in this."

"I just didn't think it would help if you worried about somebody tracking his email. I won't do it again. I'm really sorry, I just didn't think."

So, there it was, once again the easy "I'm sorry" as if that made everything right. I was learning fast how the I'm sorry card had to be played at exactly the right time or else the words simply evaporate like steam.

Kristine threw her gelato into a trash can on the corner and turned quickly toward the hotel. "I'm ready to go," she said over her shoulder.

"Kristine," I said to her back as I hurried to catch her. "I didn't think it would be a big deal. I just did what you wanted and tried to make this happen."

"I know that," she said, pulling her arm away as I reached to take her hand. "I just want us to do this together. You dragged me half way around the world and had me leave Winter, all based on trusting you after not seeing you for eight years. I think I've earned a little trust from you."

I didn't know exactly what to say. "I do trust you. Look, he believes me now, or at least he's interested in hearing more. Isn't that what we wanted? What you asked me to make happen?"

"Yeah, I guess it is," she said, but her tone felt like a cold breeze on my neck. "But I didn't mean make it happen all by yourself. We don't need any more secret agendas."

"Kristine, there's more."

"Isn't there always?"

"He said he'll give me a number to call when he's sure it's safe. He'll do it now for sure."

———

Sitting at a table in front of the hotel drinking red table wine that night, I realized that the stakes were going up for Kristine and me with each day and each action we took. The risk of email to Peter Clay Thomas seemed low, though maybe I underestimated the NSEO. And now I'd soon make a phone call and increase the odds of being found. There was only one thing I could think of. I needed a gun, having tossed the one from David into a dumpster behind the hotel in Laredo.

My argument with myself had me almost talking aloud, to myself. Should I tell her? Should I just keep it to myself? Could I afford not to have one if something happened? I decided I would tell her, but only after I had bought it.

Buying a gun in a place where you know no one, in a way you want no one to know, presents interesting challenges. There wasn't a pool hall in sight, so I didn't know where to start. I walked to the far end of Venice and began talking with some shop owners and found that Italians can own guns if they have a permit, but few do so. Mostly they have shotguns for hunting if any gun at all. Fortunately, I found that two US one hundred dollar bills can buy good information. When I laid them on a shop owners' counter and said all I wanted was information, he hesitated for about two seconds before asking me exactly what I had in mind.

An hour later, I was sitting where he directed in the back booth of a nearby bar. I was to do nothing. Just wait. Don't talk to anyone.

Most of the light came from the front glass windows. Only a couple of lamps with small globes dangled above the tables. I felt like I was sitting in the back of a cave, but the place was clean. A boy about thirteen years old in a white apron and with long hair tied in a ponytail swept around the tables. He had tiny headphones over his ears and listened to his Walkman so loudly I could hear it whenever he came near me. A middle-aged guy with huge arms and two chins worked behind the bar, wiping down the counter and straightening glasses on shelves that lined the long mirror on the wall at the back of the bar.

I was sipping a Peroni from a green bottle when a short round man with black hair combed straight back pushed through the front door, hesitated only for a moment as his eyes adjusted, and then walked quickly to my table.

"Is perfect," the man with a huge gut said as he spilled heavily into the booth and immediately slid across the table a new-looking Beretta pistol wrapped in a white linen handkerchief. No hello. No question about who I was. He wheezed from the effort of simply walking into the bar. He pulled from his back pocket an off-white lacey handkerchief and wiped droplets of sweat from his forehead.

"Weapon of choice for police. Forty caliber, M92G," he said, sucking in air. "G for Gendarmerie. Military grade."

I didn't ask how he obtained a police weapon, but I chuckled when he placed a box of American-made Smith & Wesson bullets on the table. He put his hand over mine when I reached for the bullets and held it there, but with enough pressure to hurt.

"If you are working for the police or the government, you will not make it to the sidewalk. Are you?"

I pulled my hand free.

"I'm just a man who needs protection."

He smiled, what appeared to be truly a friendly look, and spread his hands. "Very well. One thousand US."

I slid ten Ben Franklins across the table. He folded the stack with one hand, slid the bundle into his pocket as he rose, and nodded slightly. He walked away without looking back.

chapter 26

Italy changes you. I realized it while sitting outside at a small wooden table and drinking my third cup of coffee while reading a three-day-old *International Herald Tribune*. I was searching for news from the States and wondering if that man walking past was ready to slide a pistol from his coat and explode the back of my head. I felt at my belt just to reassure myself I had the pistol. Only a few weeks had passed since the bar fight, but it felt like years, a lifetime, perhaps a different incarnation altogether. I was hiding and trying to sort through all the death and pain and desperation, but I couldn't shake the constant urge to look over my shoulder.

I think most of us in my generation of the late seventies and eighties grew up unaware of the rest of the world. Viet Nam was over before I started school, so it didn't affect my friends or me much at all. We were focused on what Little League team we'd play on, believing that unless you were in the good old U S of A, you lived a life of gray days of drudgery and came home to eat half a boiled potato to survive while soldiers in shiny black boots and crisp brown uniforms glared at you from every street corner.

Then I ended up in Venice, where magnificent buildings rise as if floating above the streets. The imposing architecture and stone blocks made me feel small but not insignificant. The people were vibrant with laughter and conversations. Life was good, and they were living it well.

I practically wore the soles off my shoes walking the stone sidewalks of Venice as I worked out a plan to somehow tell the story about what the US government did to my family, or, in fairness, I guess I should say, what a group of misguided evil people did to us. To my parents. To my friend. To Kristine and me.

It's funny in a way, but I don't think any of the government guys chasing us started out as evil. And yes, I do believe there is good and evil in the world.

As for righting wrong, I'm not naïve enough to believe the good guys always win. Or the bad guys always get caught. We'll see how the Presidential election comes out next year, probably between Gore and the little Bush. Maybe one of them can clean up Washington. I'm certainly not saying I can have much to do with changing the way guys who answer to no one run our lives.

I learned that the world wasn't always as it appeared from something my father said at dinner one night when I was a kid. Dad leaned on his elbows, just watching me. "There's something you need to know," he said, pointing a finger at me and staring through his bloodshot eyes.

His look made me uncomfortable. Had I done something wrong? The moment flashed and became one of those snapshots of memory that I run across in an old drawer in my head sometimes.

He went on. "Friends are a good thing, Matt. They can help you, but don't ever believe they can make things right for you. That's on you. Good guys can lose. And a man who's not his own man makes himself a loser. Don't be that man."

About then Mom brought out a large bowl of steaming mashed potatoes. "What are my boys talking about tonight?"

We just looked at each other, not sure how to respond to that. I don't remember what I said, if anything, but I never forgot those words when he said good guys can lose.

I suppose that's what brought me to this point, this telling of a story that's bigger than life as I knew it before. Telling what happened is the best thing I can think to do right now.

———

I hope no one takes it the wrong way when I talk about my new hero John Ruskin. Just because I'm staying in Ruskin's hotel room in Italy doesn't make me some great crusader like he was. I know that.

Anyway, I don't have any illusions that what I want to do compares to what Ruskin did, but I love the way he took on the big guys. Over the past days, I read part of his books and the books written about him. Ruskin exposed the government in Venice a couple of hundred years ago for sitting by and letting the city's monuments and great buildings almost completely ruin and fall into the sea.

Now I'm laying low in Italy in Pensione La Calcina in Venice. Sitting right where Ruskin sat. Watching gondolas just like the ones he watched.

The hotel where I'm staying sits right on the water just a few blocks south of this cafe. Out front a big canal is always busy with boats of every size—from row boats and gondolas to yachts and loaded barges and water taxis. I love watching a barge heavy with lumber and building supplies glide past the front dock every morning about breakfast time, barely making a ripple, like a giant alligator low in the water. By mid-morning, the streets fill with college students, each one with a backpack slung over a shoulder. Tourists with ice cream cones from the gelato vendors mill around on every other corner, peeking in shop windows and gawking at the girls in short shorts.

I mentioned Ruskin. I ran across John Ruskin by accident. As I said, he stayed at the hotel Kristine picked, sat in the very room where I often read on a tiny sofa off to the side of the lobby. Opposite from where I sit, an oil portrait of Ruskin hangs beside a large desk piled with books. The guys in the hotel make a big deal about him, so I sat in their reading room one day and skimmed one of his books. He was highly pissed and decided to tell the world about a government he believed refused to do the right thing. The books were his way of shouting. There was no Larry King Live on CNN to listen to you complain and to nod knowingly as you told the world how offended you were.

In some ways, my story—or my father's story, I suppose— parallels Ruskin. Okay maybe that's a stretch. I'm not a reporter. I'm just a guy telling a true story. Just a guy who wants nothing more than to hold hands with his girlfriend on long afternoon walks and find some kind of job that's useful.

Maybe taking the time to tell this story is too easy, too simple, but it's what I believe needs to be said. I think I know now what my dad wanted before he was murdered by people he thought were his friends—he just wanted people to understand: even good guys in government can lose their way.

chapter 27

Kristine and I sat on a stone bench in a plaza near an internet café. The stone was cool to the backs of my legs. Pigeons gathered at our feet, milling about, hoping for some morsel of a sandwich we might drop. A woman with a stroller pushed past us. Canvas bags hanging on both sides of the buggy overflowed with leafy vegetables and long loaves of bread that poked out the top.

Kristine wrote a list on the little pad she always carried in her purse. The list included about a dozen Elvis books we kept running across and one called *Bureau—The Secret History of the FBI*. We couldn't find anything about NSEO. She went back inside and ordered the books online for immediate delivery, using a special account we'd set up and pre-paid.

———

In a week, the books began arriving. For several days around noon we began to receive calls from the front desk announcing that "i pacchetti sono arrivati nella posta." A parcel had arrived in the mail.

The first book to reach us was *The Elvis Files* by a woman named Gail Brewer Giorgio. And a day later we received her earlier book, *Is Elvis Alive?* Two more books, one titled *Elvis' DNA Proves He's*

Alive! by Bill Beeny and the FBI book, arrived together.

I was only a third of the way into *Is Elvis Alive?* that evening when I placed the book face down on the bed and opened to a chapter called "Clues." Giorgio was looking for evidence that Elvis might have faked his death.

"This Giorgio is a pit bull," I said to Kristine, who was reading the FBI book. "I don't know if she's a conspiracy chaser or genuinely interested in finding the truth about Elvis' death, but this stuff is crazy. Once she sinks her teeth into something, she just hangs on."

"Like what," Kristine said, her hair pulled back into a bun and looking over the top of the glasses she wore only when her eyes were tired. The schoolteacher look was working for me. "I'm sure it's truly fascinating."

I ignored the vinegar in her voice. She never hid the fact that she thought all the Elvis mania was nuts.

"She's catalogued much of the same stuff we've already run across a few times, like the letter to Nixon from Elvis and the White House memos about Elvis' visit, but she's also interviewed and written about all sorts of people who claimed to have seen Elvis alive after his funeral."

"You don't believe that stuff, do you?" Kristine said.

"No, but there are a lot of people she says who claim the figure in the casket was just a wax dummy."

Kristine laughed out loud. I realized it all sounded crazy.

"Hey, you're the one who insisted we had to look at all this stuff," I said. I grabbed my pillow and hit her across the stomach. Kristine was quick and on her knees in a wink, whacking me on the side of the head with her pillow. A puff of white feathers floated around her head when she sat back, suspended as if part of the air itself.

———

I put aside the Elvis book when Kristine turned out the light on her side of the bed. I picked up the FBI book and spent half the night reading, skipping the parts that didn't seem to matter. I found nothing about C4 or my dad or NSEO or any of the men around him, but I learned plenty that showed me small groups inside a federal agency would cook up their own projects and have their own agenda. Maybe NSEO was the same. If Hoover really would blackmail Congress, kidnap Soviet agents, and bug foreign embassies, why wouldn't NSEO do whatever they needed to do to protect themselves from being exposed? I still had no idea why my father and his team had committed such a horrible act.

———

After going through all the books, we had the same questions as everyone else about Elvis' death, assuming the seemingly silly claims in these Elvis books had any truth at all. Why did the medical examiner's report say Elvis was a hundred seventy pounds, when there was plenty of film footage from right before his death showing he had to be well over two hundred pounds? And why didn't anyone ever claim his life insurance? Beeny said flat out that Elvis was part of a three-year undercover operation and the mob was out to get him before he could testify. There was no shortage of theories about how Elvis might have died, or why, or who might have wanted him dead. The only thing that was clear was that Elvis' death created more conspiracy ideas than President Kennedy's assassination.

We also noticed that despite Elvis visiting the White House twice in the same day in December 1970, there was no news coverage of it. Apparently, the first time it appeared in news coverage was two years later on January 17, 1972, in *The Washington Post* in a story by Jack Anderson. I remember telling Kristine, "Listen to this sentence from the story of what one guy did when he heard about Elvis's interest in police badges: 'Deputy Narcotics Director John Finiator a few months ago sought to enlist Presley in the anti-drug fight.' Hell, maybe they did cut a deal with Elvis to do something undercover."

I was half-way kidding, I mean, it all seemed so ridiculous.

At some point I woke up with the book open across my chest and turned off the light.

———

After sleeping in the next morning, we walked to a café for eggs and coffee. "Let's go check our email and let me look up a couple of things that FBI book mentioned," I said.

"You go on," Kristine said. "You kept me awake with the light on. I think I'll go back to the room and browse those books."

I held my tongue. There was no win in any comment, straightforward or smart-ass. Maybe I was learning something about how to have a relationship after all.

At the internet café, I Googled (that's what Kristine called it) a few words and phrases, but after reading a dozen articles I found only the usual dead ends. When I was about to leave, I checked one last time and found that a cryptic email had just arrived from Peter Clay Thomas, except it was a new email address. He said simply:

Have acquired FBI files on E. Not sure if they worked closely with NSEO or not. Incredible number of lines redacted during and after pages dated 1977. Have listened to first tape you sent. Send more. I'm in. Keep your head down. Do not call. Use email address below one time. I will send a new one later. PT

Beneath his signature was an address in New Jersey. I had ten minutes left on an hour I'd purchased, so I used the email address to tell Peter that I'd send a couple more tapes and gave him an overview of what had happened with Kristine's mom and with Sullivan. I suggested that it would be interesting if he could find anything about the operating group C4.

The sun was high overhead and made me squint for several seconds as I pushed through the door to the street. Sweat beaded on my chest and soaked through in wet bands across my shirt as I hurried to the room, barely keeping myself from breaking into a run. I swerved around people on the sidewalk, darting between an older couple strolling and two teens carrying skateboards. I thought that both seemed too young for the multiple tattoos on their arms and legs. All I could think about was telling Kristine about the email. We both believed Peter might be the best we could hope for, if he would believe my story. Now we had hope.

Kristine sat on the curb in front of the hotel talking with a woman and a young girl maybe twelve years old. Kristine stood up when she saw me, waving to the mother and the girl who I could now recognize as her daughter, their chiseled features and straight hair identical. They walked away holding hands.

I couldn't wait to tell her about Peter. "He says he's in."

"He's in!" she said, smiling big. "That's good. Who's in for what?"

"Don't be coy," I said. "Peter Clay Thomas. He's done his homework, I guess, and said to send more tapes."

———

For dinner we decided to celebrate with pizza and wine at da Mamo, the best trattoria pizzeria we'd found so far. The smell of fresh baked pizza crust and the almost sweet aroma of broiled shrimp, fish, and lobsters filled the room as we were seated along the side wall beneath a row of huge lamps that lined the wall from the front window to the back of the restaurant.

"So where are we?" Kristine asked as soon as the waiter left with our order of a seafood pizza. "I mean, is this going to keep dragging out or can we go home now?"

"I know you miss Winter. I want to see him, too."

"Can't this Thomas guy put the pieces together for us," she said, more as a statement than a question. She held her napkin in front of her on the table, twisting it into a rope.

"The correlation between my folks' murder and the film just isn't there yet," I said. "It feels like we're close, but someone has to connect the dots and make it very, very public. They've covered too many trails."

The waiter showed up with the house red wine we'd ordered. Kristine slid her glass toward mine, and he poured us both a glass.

"Then tell me what we do know," she said.

I'd been down this road with her at least three or four times, but I started back at the beginning. I suppose we were good that way. She could react with urgency while taking deliberate, careful steps. She was impatient and cautious—somehow melding those opposite traits into a personality. I was worried about knowing all the details but wanted to make something happen. So far we'd managed not to be impatient at the same time and make a mistake.

"Okay, we know—at least I know—that my mom and dad were murdered. We know someone used your mom to try to kill us. We know Bugs is dead and Jim Robinson. I shot a man and was almost shot, too."

She nodded and said, "And someone thinks we know enough to follow us across the country." She smiled her little crooked smile. "Jesus, Matt. All these people dead, including three agents. Your friend and your parents. How can they ignore all that? Someone will have to do something."

I swirled my wine until a little splashed onto the table. I took a deep breath. "I know, it seems like that much death and shooting should show up as some kind of big conspiracy issue in the papers. But look at it this way. Dad was a car wreck. Mom is listed as a suicide. Bugs, too. And I'm charged with murdering Jim. Who's going to believe the NSEO had anything to do with any of that?"

Kristine's lips were pressed tightly, and she looked past me, not at anything specific I guessed.

I went on. "But if Peter can get someone to string all those things together and get to someone high enough to look at the film, then maybe it gets their attention. The trouble is: who to go to?"

"There's got to be someone at the NSEO we can trust. This is over our pay grade, Matt."

"Maybe so, but how do we find them? Jim told me that Leopold was involved. Who's going to go against the director?"

Kristine leaned in closer and spoke in a whisper. "You can't tell me there is no one out there who will tell the truth."

"Maybe that's true, Kristine. But let me ask you this in case we can't find that person and I have to go another direction. What kind of man would you think I am if I don't see this through and do whatever I have to do to expose who killed my parents? Is that the man you would respect as a father?"

chapter **28**

I read the last page of *Elvis Undercover* and slammed the cover shut. I placed the book neatly on top of the stack, sitting back to look at them. All five books were now marked and underlined and had yellow sticky notes on half the pages. I'd read the books in three days, all while running back and forth from the Internet café to do research, and I was burned out on Elvis and the NSEO. I slid the stack to the back of the bedside table.

Kristine sat on a stool in front of the mirror and brushed her hair. She had finished reading the books the night before.

I walked up behind her and could see she was smiling. Actually, a smirk would be more accurate. The fresh smell of her skin after a bath gave me the urge to wrap my arms around her.

"What?" I asked, though I had a good idea.

"Are you done with this silliness yet? Is Elvis around the corner at Baskin Robbins? Did he really hop a jet to South America? Or is the NSEO hiding him somewhere and feeding him fried peanut butter and banana sandwiches?"

"Funny."

She turned toward me and pointed with her brush, touching it lightly to my chest. "I don't mean to make fun of you. I know you're trying to make some kind of sense of a mess. But it's all just so much conspiracy and intrigue. If there's really something to any of this, why doesn't anyone in the mainstream media ever pick it up and run with it? It would be the story of the century."

"You've got a point. But after knowing what happened to Bugs, I know things really can be covered up."

She turned around and began brushing her hair.

"Alright, I'll concede that one," she said, looking at me in the mirror. "But these books seem to point in several directions at once. They don't come together to explain what might have happened that fits with that film."

"I don't disagree, but I don't know what else to do."

"Maybe the answer is back home."

We had always ended up in an argument when we talked of going home, so I ignored her and changed the subject.

"Kristine, I've got to take a couple of hours off and let some of this settle out for me. I'm going to the library to look up stuff on Ruskin. You wanna go?" I asked.

"You're taking a day off?" she asked, surprised, holding the brush loosely as she looked around at me.

"Is there something you wanted to do?"

"No. That's fine," she said, turning back around and brushing her hair. No longer catching my eye in the mirror. Her meaning clear, that it was anything but fine.

I had little experience in how to respond.

"No, really. What did you want?" I insisted.

"Go. Just go. It's nothing."

I still didn't know how to deal with Kristine, so I didn't. I gave up easily like most men who know 'It's nothing' sure as hell is something, but you'll have to wait to find out what. "I'll be an hour or two. Then we'll do whatever you want. I have to clear my head."

On the way to the library, I checked email and had this note from Peter: *The official reply is that C4 was the unofficial name of a former recruiting and screening department for internal NSEO hires or White House staff, but has been discontinued for many years. Sounds unlikely to me. Will keep checking. They will be watching now. Do not use that other email. Use this one for a few days, and I'll contact you with a new one. PCT*

The library made me feel small and perhaps a bit insignificant. The ceilings were thirty feet high. Leather-bound books stacked half-way up the walls made it feel like the knowledge of the world was all in this one room. Marble columns rose three stories in the circular atrium, where railing circled the opening on each floor to allow patrons to stare down from the upper levels. A domed ceiling above it all was painted with various saints and cherubs frolicking in a luxurious garden with bubbling streams and lush shade trees.

I pulled down Ruskin's *The Seven Lamps of Architecture* and had the book open on a long oak table, reading. I had read that it was written before *The Stones of Venice*. I hardly noticed the old man who sat two chairs down until he spoke.

"Avete scelto un interessantissimo autore, un mio amico," he said in a friendly tone.

"I'm sorry, I don't speak Italian."

"Ruskin. An interesting man, a fine writer," he said in English without hesitation, sort of reverse nodding as he pointed to the book with his chin. "That book had a lot to do with building on the momentum for Gothic Revival architecture that had begun a comeback a century or so before Ruskin."

"Yes, I think I've figured out he was outspoken against the government's priorities."

He laughed. Then a smile spread across his face, and he gestured with his palms up, shrugging.

"Yes, yes, yes. You get it. Let's just say, he and his friends were skeptical of the trends that industrialization was bringing to the world. They wanted the older styles to remain strong and protected. Sort of a protest, I suppose you might say."

I noticed his haircut was perfect and he wore an expensive light-blue silk shirt open at the collar. The age was difficult. At least sixty, but maybe eighty. The hair, combed back and slicked down in a way that suggested confidence, was two-thirds silver but with some black still there. His demeanor was sophisticated but friendly, and his English was precise despite the Italian accent.

"You know Ruskin?" I asked, though the answer was obvious. "I don't get all of what he was about. Does everyone here know about him?"

He smiled again, almost laughed, but then seemed to hesitate, as if reflecting on a thought. "Unfortunately, no. Not that many people remember Mr. Ruskin as perhaps we all should."

"But you do," I stated, opening the door for him to tell me why.

Chuckling because he knew I would not understand, he said, "Sì come insegnante presso l'università." He smiled at me. "I had the good fortune to teach some of his work at the University."

He extended his hand across the chairs between us. "Professor Niccolò Strozzi."

I hesitated half a second, hoping he didn't notice. "Bart Johnson."

"Ah, American I see," he said, noting my accent. "A Southerner, or perhaps a south Texan?" he asked. He sounded almost hopeful in his last question.

"Good ear," I said. "Alabama. But I've spent some time living in Texas, too."

He clasped his hands together and leaned forward smiling broadly, almost like a child who's been given a prize.

"Ah, Texas, fascinating place."

"How so?" I asked.

"Everything is enorme. Esagerato. Più Grande della vita. How do you say, ah, upsized?"

I laughed. "Yeah, you could say that."

He laughed with me, a kind laugh, with his inner self showing in the smile lines around his eyes. He sat very still and with a perfectly straight back in the wooden chair. "Grander, bigger, better. Dreamers of the first rate. Overachievers. Believers that willpower overcomes a lack of money or education or fortune. I am correct, no?"

"You're dead on," I said, realizing how the world had figured out Texas. "Have you been there?"

He nodded, and then as if changing his mind sort of shook his head side to side and shrugged. "Once. To a conference of academics. Houston. But only for three days, and I hardly saw more than an airport and skyscrapers out a taxi window. No cowboys unless you count the oil men I saw in the hotel lobby with their black cowboy boots and hats."

"Then you should go, and drive from state line to state line. It's really worth a month to explore."

"Perhaps," he said, holding his palms upturned. "But I'm old, and there is so little time left for travel. Perhaps you can tell me about Texas."

"If you will tell me about Ruskin."

"As you say, 'Deal,'" he said. We shook hands again, and our friendship started at that moment. We sat at the table for another hour, as he told me about Venice during Ruskin's life. The city he described didn't sound that different from what I was seeing here now. Stone on stone with buildings perched as if floating on the water, defying gravity. Students and families on holiday. Goods from the East shipping in by boat.

Finally, he said, "I must go. Prior dinner plans. But will you meet me tomorrow morning? I would love to exchange more Ruskin insights for stories about Texas."

"Sure," I said.

"Coffee at nine?"

I nodded. "That would be great."

He removed an expensive-looking black fountain pen and small leather note pad from his coat pocket and wrote "Caffe del Doge, Sestiere San Polo, 609" on a slip he tore off and handed me as he rose from his chair. "You will find this coffee shop two blocks north of here. Until then," he said, with a slight tip of his hat.

———

I arrived at nine the next morning. He was already there, with a very small coffee cup before him, empty. Spread across the table were three stacks of paper, each stapled and worn, covered with type and hand-written notes in the margins. Passages were underlined, and some were highlighted in yellow.

"Good morning, Professor."

"Ah, a pleasant day to you. What may I order you, Mr. Johnson?"

As we drank coffee, he explained that the stacks of paper were lectures he had delivered on Ruskin at American universities, so they were all in English. "Together," he said as he spread documents in front of me, "these papers will explain Ruskin's general outlook on the world and the major events in his life which led him to his strong feelings about Venice and the tragedy he felt was eminent for the city."

For three hours we talked. I told him what I knew about Texas, like it had twenty million people and was as much Southern as it was Western, but without really being part of the South. And how it seemed to me that most everyone there who didn't work in a retail store, a restaurant, a bank, or a law firm was in agriculture or natural gas. But what he really wanted to know was the people. What they were like. What they thought about politics, religion, baseball. How they felt about so many Mexicans and Mexican-Americans in the state. He knew a lot that I didn't. Like the Civil War went on for two months longer in Texas because they hadn't heard the news of the war being over in April. So Texas got Juneteenth as a sort of unofficial holiday because June 19 was the day the last slaves were freed.

For the next couple of days, I spent morning hours in the library and afternoon hours drinking red wine with Professor Strozzi as we talked about Texas and Ruskin and American politics, sitting in sidewalk cafes or the library when he wanted to point out passages in a book. I tried to give enough of my real background that I didn't feel like I was lying to my new friend, but I had to skip over large parts of my life, so I wasn't just making up a bunch of lies I couldn't remember. We traded phone numbers.

Later that week, we sat outside at a café on a small plaza, a pleasant day. Pigeons cooed around us. Women pushed babies in strollers. Long shadows of the buildings stretched across the cobblestones. We drank wine, as usual.

He turned to me and surprised me. "Bart, you have no idea how much pleasure you have given me these last few days. I have spent so much of my life with other professors, scholars, and teachers. How wonderful and refreshing to get to know someone who has been immersed in living life instead of trying to observe it under a microscope and label everything instead of just accepting it."

"I've enjoyed it too, Professor."

"No, let me finish. By sharing so much time, you have given me a valuable gift. At my age, you realize that the greatest asset is not money, it is time. And you have shared yours so unselfishly."

I was almost embarrassed, but he went on before I could think of anything to say.

"You have reminded me that to really understand a culture, a people, you can't get it from books or university or lectures. You have to talk to a real person who has—as you taught me to say—'been there, done that.' Someone who is honest and with nothing to gain. Someone who knows things about real people, who observes day-to-day living, not to study it but to fit in and be a genuine person."

It embarrassed me to hear this man talk about honesty, knowing I was lying every day by concealing who I was. I almost blurted out everything right there.

chapter **29**

Over dinner, I told Kristine about my conversations with Strozzi. She wanted to meet him, so I arranged it.

The next afternoon, Kristine joined us in the library, eager to meet the person who had made me so enthusiastic to learn about someone long dead. We sat for a couple of hours in the heavy wooden chairs around a long table that had almost turned black from the repeated coats of aged varnish. Strozzi paid her lots of attention and listened carefully when she talked. We both liked him.

Kristine and I had arranged to meet Strozzi for lunch the next day. Again, he was already there when we arrived. As we sat, our glasses were instantly filled with wine by a young man in dark pants and a white shirt, materializing at our table as if from thin air. I could tell Strozzi's mood was more somber than usual. I started to say something, but he held his hand up to make me pause.

He spread his fingers wide on each hand, then placed his fingertips gently together and held them under his chin, as if deciding something. "Now, you two. Why don't you humor an old man and tell me why you're here?"

Professor Strozzi then outstretched his hands toward us, palms up. "We have a saying in Italy: 'Tagliare la testa al toro.' I won't bore you with the history of this saying that means to cut off the bull's head. But the point we make in this saying is to get on with what you are doing. You are holding back something from me."

I had no clue about the saying, but I did have a good idea that his gesture and comment meant he genuinely wanted to know our story.

Strozzi went on, "In America you might say, 'Get to the point.' Or perhaps, 'Cut to the chase.'"

Kristine looked over at me, then back to Strozzi and spoke first, smiling and sounding as unconcerned as she could. "We're just taking a long holiday. Why would you ask?"

"Hmmm," he said. "It seems more."

"Why would you think that?" I asked. My whole life had taught me that I wasn't that good at lying. I always seemed to get caught and knew perfectly well that I was best saying nothing if I didn't want to tell the truth. But here I was, being called on it and knowing that Strozzi had likely already figured me out. I suddenly imagined myself on a horse, no saddle, just hanging onto the mane and galloping away into the wild. I wanted to escape. Or at least I certainly didn't want to face the truth. He knew. And I knew he knew.

He ignored my question. "If you're in trouble, perhaps I can help you."

Kristine spoke, her words clipped and abrupt. "Why would you say that? We're not in trouble." She leaned back in her chair, hands gripping the chair arms, again glancing at me for an answer. The concern was there beneath the surface, like the swirl of a current in an otherwise flat calm river.

"I'm so sorry, my lovely friend. Poor choice of words," he said, taking her hand gently. His eyes were kind, the wrinkles at the corners angling up to show his smile was genuine. "I truly meant nothing. But I have observed my young friend 'Bart' now for a few days and tried to piece together your story. And honestly, it's such a poor attempt to create a history. I can tell there's something going on, something unsaid, and hoped I could help."

I looked away down the street, away from his eyes. Children kicked a soccer ball, their laughter echoing down the stone buildings that lined the narrow alleyway.

I turned and faced him, sitting up and leaning my elbows on the table, our faces close together. The moment of confession was right there, that moment we all experience from time to time in life when we face the shame of lying and embrace the redemptive act of telling a friend what that friend had already figured out. And a real friend understands. I was hoping this was one of those moments. I spoke barely above a whisper. "If something were wrong, why would you think you could help?"

I saw the slightest hint of a smile and what was an almost imperceptible nod, like he was confirming something to himself not to me.

"My family has been very fortunate over the centuries to become successful, to make many friends, to build connections. We know many important people," he said, leaning forward, mirroring my posture. "I have resources, contacts. We are a nation of survivors. I myself was sixteen when I had to learn to survive the twin horrors of Adolph Hitler and that beast Mussolini. My family members were leaders in the resistance. If you learn anything about my country, you will find that it is built on strong families and their connections established over the past five hundred years."

I can't really say why I decided right then to tell Professor Strozzi my story. We didn't know him. Telling anything at all about our real identities added enormous risk. But this man beamed such a genuine, trustworthy personality that I believed him. And his admission of being part of the Italian underground in World War II showed there was more to this old man than appearances could reveal. I had already checked and found he was indeed a very distinguished professor from a well-known and powerful family in Florence.

"Matthew," I said. "My name is Matthew. And this is Kristine."

Professor Strozzi tilted his head back and softly snorted once, then a long slow laugh started deep inside him and shook him from the shoes up. He slapped both hands on his thighs in apparent delight. Soon his cheeks were shiny from tears.

After several seconds, he removed a white silk handkerchief from a coat pocket and dabbed his eyes. He leaned forward, his eyes wide as he looked directly into mine. "And so, my friend. Matthew. Let's hear your real story. Something tells me it's worth my time," Strozzi said. Turning his face toward Kristine, he said, "As I told Matthew, time is something to value far above money."

A waiter appeared and sat a large plate in the middle of the table. Cheese, olives, irregularly shaped crackers that looked as if they were baked fresh in the restaurant.

"Please try this stagionato, my favorite," Professor Strozzi said, pointing to the cheese. "It's a delicate flavorful form of Caprino. An aged goat cheese."

Strozzi ordered a second bottle of wine, though the first was not yet empty. I began telling the story from the point the Suit — Mark Pugh— pulled me out of the bar fight. I continued our story until I reached the present and told him about the tapes I was working on daily. We talked for two hours, right through dishes of pasta and roasted fish, with Strozzi hardly interrupting other than to ask me to clarify something here and there. Kristine filled in details about my parents from the years I was away.

When we tilted our glasses for the last of the wine, a flurry of waiters cleared the table. The professor insisted we pay nothing for the lavish meal and wine. When the bill appeared, he merely glanced at it and handed it back to the waiter with a nod.

"Let's stroll for a bit, my new friends," Strozzi said, rising and reaching for Kristine's chair.

We walked outside and strolled on the sidewalk, the sky just beginning to turn from clear and bright with a blue background to the promise of a citrus afternoon, lemon over orange stripes building in layers horizontally above the rooftops to the west. No one spoke as we walked half a block, each of us trying to figure out where this new friendship would lead.

Professor Strozzi glanced aside momentarily as if to make sure no one stood within earshot. "With your agreement, Kristine and Matt, I ask that you allow me the privilege of listening to your tapes." He stood with his hands clasped in front of his chest, his eyebrows raised in anticipation. "There are few you can trust with such information, but I can help."

Kristine and I looked at each other. This was unexpected, but I think perhaps we both wanted the Professor to step forward and give us a hand. He was the only person we had come to know since we began hiding.

"What about it?" I asked, looking at Kristine. The truth was: we knew nowhere to turn. We needed Professor Strozzi to see this situation through our eyes and tell us if he saw the same thing.

Kristine turned slightly, her back toward the Professor. I could tell she wasn't completely comfortable.

She looked back over her shoulder at him. "Please excuse us for a moment."

"Of course." He walked to the corner and sat on bench, looking away from us to provide us with a private moment to talk.

Kristine stood close and spoke softly. "I like Professor Strozzi. But what do we really know about him?"

"I looked up his family and him. There is plenty about him on the Internet. He is who he says he is. His family is famous for their role in the war, in business, and in education. It's almost like they're the remnants of the Renaissance."

"But why would he want to help us, to risk getting involved?"

She had a point.

I thought about it and figured it was best to tell him how she felt. We walked over and sat next to him.

"Professor, Kristine and I value your kindness and your friendship, and everything in my gut says we can trust you. Please don't be offended, but Kristine is trying to be very cautious, and I can't argue against that."

He smiled. "I understand. So how can I put your mind at ease?"

Kristine said, "One question. Why would you want to help us and risk being involved in something dangerous with people you don't really know?"

"This is a complicated story," he said. "and it may bore you as a history lesson."

Kristine smiled her crooked smile. "Bore us."

He laughed. "Be careful what you ask my friends. I told you about Resistenza Italiana, the partisan resistance."

"Yes," she nodded. "You were seventeen."

"Today our countries are friendly, and Americans love Italy. Our food, our wine, our art, and our architecture. Even our people. Many people somehow fail to remember that throughout the twenties and thirties, fascism was the rule of law in Italy under Mussolini."

She nodded. "I've heard about him, but I don't know the history."

"Our country did not side with the Allies but was part of the Axis in World War II. Did you know that?"

I shrugged. "To be honest, I never thought much about it."

"Precisely," he said. "Few younger Americans seem aware of it. They simply assume we were on the same side and America rescued Italy as it did other countries. But Italy was in league with Adolph Hitler. Mussolini had already clamped down on anyone who opposed his government, and by joining Hitler he thought perhaps he would get a piece of France."

"And where did your family stand on all this?" Kristine asked.

"Ah. Perceptive. We were what I suppose you could call part of the Catholic opposition. Mussolini outlawed many groups— communists, Christian Democrats, Catholics, socialists. And this unlikely group came together as the resistance."

Kristine smiled. "So how does that make a retired Professor fifty years later want to help a young couple who could be ax murderers?"

Professor Strozzi and I both laughed. He leaned toward her. "Let me ask you something. Did you know that for a while there were two Italys?"

We both shook our heads no.

He raised his finger, as if emphasizing a point in a lecture.

"Mussolini allowed Hitler to take over parts of our country as his Axis empire spread. But the Allies gained ground, and Italy's government under King Victor Emmanuel surrendered to the Allies in 1943 after working to depose Mussolini. His plan was to join with the Allies. But most of Northern Italy was still under German control, so to prop up Mussolini, Hitler created the Italian Social Republic in the northern half of the country, which lasted as a puppet state for about a year and a half."

"I never knew that," Kristine said.

"My point is this. I have seen and felt what happens when citizens stand aside and allow a government to run over its own people. Matthew here has convinced me that he wants that story to be told in your country. It may not be as big as a world war, but Matthew's war and now yours unfortunately, my dear Kristine, is a story that should be told."

Kristine stood up. "You're still fighting an old battle."

"I suppose that's one way to look at it," he said.

"One more question," Kristine said.

"Anything."

"Did your support help your side win?" she asked.

Strozzi laughed loudly. Then he hesitated for a minute, his smile fading some as he looked away and seemed to be thinking. "Yes, I can honestly say we did. I was a kid, playing a very small role, secretly running messages among underground groups. But my father was in a group of partisans that captured Mussolini."

"Really?"

"Yes. In 1945, the Allies had pushed the Germans north near Lake Como. My father was leading a group assigned to check German soldiers retreating toward Switzerland. Mussolini was trying to escape disguised as a common foot soldier, but he was discovered."

Kristine seemed fascinated. "What happened? Did that end the war for Italy?"

"More or less. He and his mistress Clara Petacci were hanged within hours along with other Fascists. I am not especially proud to say that their bodies were sent south to Milan and displayed upside down at an Esso station. Gruesome but understandable for the time."

"Was your father celebrated as a war hero?" I asked.

"He was killed a few weeks later as part of a final assault into Germany."

Kristine took his hand this time, in both of hers. "I'm sorry."

"Such a long time ago. Let's go now and retrieve your tapes, if you believe I can be trusted."

I looked at Kristine and she nodded yes.

"We can bring them in the morning," I told Professor Strozzi.

"No, Matthew. I can use the walk. If you will indulge me, let's get them now."

As we walked, Kristine took Professor Strozzi's arm. They talked for a few minutes, and he asked her about Winter. She told him about his love of roller skating, fried chicken, and playing on his Gameboy. I found myself longing to love the son I didn't know. I safely locked away every detail she said about him in a new room in my heart. There was much space to fill.

After the professor had tucked the tapes inside his pockets and was gone, Kristine unzipped her big purse and scrambled through it for the cell phone with her mother's number. She held the phone up perhaps to ask me if she should call, but without waiting she immediately pushed the speed dial number her mother had typed into the phone.

"It's me. We're fine. How is Winter?"

She listened, eyes closed and frowning for part of it, and nodded, for almost a minute, as if her mother could see her.

"Let me speak to Winter."

She waited a few seconds. Even though it was a phone conversation, her features softened, and she was smiling as she talked. "Hey Sweetie. Yes, I miss you very much, too. But Mommy is trying to get this job finished so she can come home and be with you."

She frowned as she listened. "I'm so sorry, Baby, but it's better if you have your own teachers right now. We'll get you back in school with your friends as soon as we can."

Her eyes were glistening now, but she kept her voice even. "Winter, you listen to your grandmother and be good for her. I promise I'll be home soon, but you have to be the big boy of the house."

She did not look at me when she said that. I was glad, knowing I probably turned red listening.

"Put your grandmother back on the phone." Kristine stood silently, her face blank.

"Thanks for taking care of him. He seems okay." She nodded as if agreeing with whatever her mother was saying and a few times said yes or sure.

"Yes, we plan to tell the story to a reporter."

More listening.

"No, Mother, I don't think we are playing spy. We're trying to stay alive," she said, slamming the phone shut. She had tears in the corners of her eyes but refused to give in, simply brushing the tears away with her sleeve.

The phone rang immediately. She looked at me, turned away, and answered.

"What?"

Kristine listened.

"Yes. Okay," Kristine whispered.

Again, listening for a minute.

"Fine. Okay. Yes, of course. Fine. Yes, we'll consider not releasing the tapes," she said, glancing at me. "But we still believe that's our best way home. Don't worry about us hiding. We're dug in as long as we know Winter is safe."

Kristine paced around the room while her mother talked for a long time.

She stopped at the window and pulled the curtain aside to look down at the street. She pushed her hair back from her face, put her hand on her hip, and spoke very deliberately, emphasizing each word, "Mother, we're not giving anyone there that film. The film is all that will keep us alive. And Matt is not going to ignore the fact that someone murdered his parents. Your friends, I might add."

I made note that she didn't mention the DVD copy. I wanted to ask her to put the phone on speaker, but this seemed like a conversation only a mother and daughter could have. Kristine again pulled the curtain aside a few inches and peered out, giving me a moment of alarm. I walked over to see what she saw where she was looking down the street, half expecting to see her mother standing there, but Kristine just walked away from the window and kept pacing. I saw nothing but a man walking past with a newspaper under his arm and a woman waving her arms and pointing toward the canal as she argued with two men.

"Why are you protecting Leopold, Mother? This is our lives we're talking about. You have to tell me everything. This is not making sense. What are you leaving out? I have to know."

Kristine put her finger in her other ear to shut out the noise of the woman who had begun shouting on the sidewalk outside. "Mom, let me just say it this way. Unless you tell me right now what you have been leaving out, I'm not sure I will ever trust you again. I mean it."

Suddenly Kristine sat down on the edge of the bed, slumping, her head cocked forward as if hearing something bad but expected.

"Yes, I can take it. Yes, I promise anything you tell me will not keep me from loving you."

I had to listen carefully to hear Kristine. She was talking barely above a whisper.

"But why now? Why haven't you told me this before?"

Seconds later, and louder now, "Oh, so he was married. Well, that just excuses everything, doesn't it?"

Another two or three minutes of listening and nodding, only saying uh huh once in a while, her voice once again barely above a whisper.

"Please be careful. Don't let anything happen. Let me know how I can reach you."

She hung up, turning toward me as she lay back on the bed, saying nothing.

"What?" I finally said, unable to stand it as we both lay there facing each other, taking shallow breaths.

"Leopold and my mother had an affair," she said. "That's her connection to him. Even though it has been over for a long time, she's trying to use that connection to find information from him to help us."

I couldn't comprehend what that meant and could think of nothing to say, so I slid over to put my arms around her.

She held her hands up against my chest and sat up. She didn't want to be hugged. Her mouth was a thin ribbon of anger. "Without the film, she said there are people who will not stop until they kill us. They'll use Winter if they have to. And there's nothing my mother can do to stop it."

"Well we knew they wanted to kill us. They've been trying."

"It's bigger than that. This isn't just a couple of guys gone rogue. It's much bigger, and worse. We're totally on our own to figure this out. And we don't even know who *they* really are."

"What does that mean?"

"Mom has gone into hiding now to protect Winter. She was afraid to tell me where they are in case the phone is tapped. She's contacting people from her old office, but she's not sure what will happen next."

chapter **30**

Kristine and I spent the day piecing together all our notes, jotting down everything that had happened and what we knew of every person with any connection at all. We stuck them to an empty wall where I had removed the one print of an unsigned Italian landscape impressionist painting of rolling hills with vineyards and mountains in the background. A couple of times, I tried to bring up Leopold and give her a chance to talk about it, but she cut me off each time. We drank caffé lungo from the little shop half a block down, then I made another two cups in the little coffee maker in our room.

We were talking aloud but not to each other as we folded paper and tried to tear clean edges from sheets she had printed in the Internet café about people, the NSEO, the DOJ, and Elvis. Our energy became frenzied as we bumped each other moving paper around and ripping tape to stick notes to the bottom edge of other notes.

By mid-afternoon, the wall was covered with square yellow notes and lined paper torn from a spiral notebook and shredded printer paper. We scrawled down names and dates and events and drew little arrows in black marker whenever there was a connection. It was as if we were crazed with paranoia, seeing spooks and conspiracies behind everything that happened, pointing and grunting and shaking our heads, seeing something here and there just beyond comprehension, connections or plots or schemes, but nothing that explained who was behind a conspiracy that touched so many people. Or why. Or how it started.

We planned to meet the professor at five at a small café on the street behind Palazzo Dario off the Grand Canal. Our plan was to tell him as much as we knew and ask his opinion. We finally lost our momentum. Both of us ended up sitting on the floor on top of scraps of paper, our backs against the bed, our legs spread in front of us, our eyes looking up at the montage we had created from notes and lines and photos.

"Don't you think the U.S. is big enough to hide two people no one knows?" she asked, though it was really a statement. Kristine wanted to fly home. She had more or less dismissed the implications of the clues that covered the wall, turning back to thoughts of Winter and her life that was okay and safe before I blew it up.

"Maybe, if you could get there without being caught. But that's a big if," I said.

After talking about it for a while, we agreed she would check flights to the U.S. and Mexico near the border, but after staring at the wall and seeing who might connect, I wanted to get out and research a few details that puzzled me. It seemed as though we had enough information put together to spur some kind of investigation, but how could we be sure?

"I'm going back to the new internet café we found. How about I meet you at the café with the professor after we both finish?" I asked as I stood up.

"Don't be late" was all she said.

I was out the door. I debated walking or taking a water taxi to the internet café we'd found a few days earlier on the far side of town. The café was a little out of the way, but we agreed we needed to use one we had not used before for our internet email. I decided to walk. At the store counter fifteen minutes later, I studied the price list and tried out the little bit of Italian Kristine was teaching me. "Tre Euros? Un'ora sola?" The attendant, dressed in torn jeans, a black T-shirt, and black lace-up boots he propped on the counter, cut his eyes up and nodded without really looking up from his comic book. I guessed he was in his best grunge rock imitation. I gave him three Euros for an hour and asked for a hookup near the front window. He mumbled something I was sure I didn't care to hear as I walked away.

When I logged on, I saw I had an email and figured Peter had a question. I clicked to open the email, but it wasn't Peter. It was from someone I had chatted with after meeting him in a chat room for Elvis fans.

I stopped breathing when I didn't recognize where the email came from. And what I read made me shiver. "This is the person you talked with last week, but this new email address will not exist after you get this, so don't try to contact me. I believe they're onto you. Don't worry, I am a friend. Those of us who have figured it out have to stick together. After our last chat, I knew you were near the truth that Elvis isn't dead and the government had something to do with his disappearance. *The Elvis Files* from Giorgio you mentioned may have a lot of it right I believe, even if the book is wacky in parts, but I think there's a lot more and she doesn't understand anything about why it happened. Anyway, this is what you need to know: right after we chatted, someone claiming to be in government reached out in the chat room about a "fugitive" who was obsessed with Elvis and said that anyone with information about someone like that should report it to the NSEO. If that is you, get underground now. And don't go back to the computer you are using. Good luck. Don't write back, this email account will be deleted now."

I had grown careless after too many days in Venice. I ran out of the cafe to get to the hotel so we could pack and leave. The professor would know where we could hide. I started half walking, half running, trying not to attract attention by sprinting full out. Within blocks, I had sweated through my shirt until it was dripping. I picked up the pace a little since it wouldn't matter anyway now. I wished I hadn't gone so far.

Taking the stairs three at a time, I was out of breath when I reached the landing in front of our door. "It's me," I said, as I knocked, intending to use my key but not scare Kristine. The door opened an inch as I knocked, and every muscle in my body seized as I stood motionless, listening. She never left the door unlocked, and I remembered locking it when I left. I felt a rush of heat in my chest as if I had leaned over and opened an oven. I pushed the door slowly all the way open and knew the room was empty before I took a step inside. A chair was turned over and a water bottle lay in a puddle in the middle of the white tile floor. The notes on the wall were gone.

Every drawer was upside down on the floor, and the small chest sat away from the wall. The mattress had been overturned and leaned against the window. The clothes in the closet were scattered on the floor. I knew instantly that someone had gone through every item in the room, looking for the film and tapes. I only hoped they did not know about Professor Strozzi, who had both. The DVD was hidden in plain sight inside a large magazine, and my father's money was in the hotel safe.

As I turned to leave, I saw a note sitting on a small table beside the door, along with a cell phone. The note was addressed to me. "Matthew, take this cell phone. We will call you." No name. I slipped the phone and note into my pocket and the magazine with the DVD copy inside the back of my shirt. I took three stairs at a time down to the lowest level and turned into the kitchen area and out the back into an alley.

chapter 31

The bricks at my back were warm as I pressed against them in an alley a mile or so from the hotel. I tried to call Professor Strozzi. I had doubled back and gone through two stores from the front straight through to the alley before the shop keepers could stop me, just to be sure I wasn't followed. I had twice stopped and watched backward from a hiding place to be sure. No one was following, or I had lost them if they had been.

After pressing the wrong numbers three straight tries, I finally forced myself to take a breath and slow down. My hair lay plastered to my neck and forehead.

"Ciao, sono il Professor Strozzi."

I blurted out one long thought. "Professor, they took Kristine. They found us, and the room is torn up, and they're obviously looking for the film, and maybe they know about the tapes too."

"Matthew, slow down. What happened?"

I was winded from the run and took a deep breath to try to slow myself down again. I started walking to the end of the alley to peek around the corner, talking as I walked. "Someone in an Elvis chat room warned me that the NSEO was asking around for information about us. This was someone I met online who is an Elvis fan, and I had been talking to them about their idea that Elvis is alive. I ran back to the hotel and she was gone."

"Are you sure someone took her?"

"I'm sure they have her. Everything was torn up, and they left a cell phone with a note for me, saying they would call. They may be coming for you if they saw us together. I'm worried they hurt her."

"Matthew, they are professionals, and I do not believe they will harm her if they want to bargain. I am safe here and your film is safe. Don't worry about me. Let's get Miss Kristine back. And don't go back to the room. Where are you?"

"In an alley. I'm not sure. I took a lot of alleyways."

"You need to get off the street. What are you near? Look down the street and tell me what you see? And are you sure you have not been followed?"

I looked around the corner and recognized the street. I saw nothing unusual, no one suspicious. "Okay, I know where I am. Near a trattoria, Al Corallo, if you know it."

"Okay, I know the place very well. Go inside and take a seat in the back. I will call the manager, whom I have known for many years. No one will be seated near you. You're only a block from Canale Marani. Do not go back on the street. If they call, don't agree to meet them. I will get a boat and be there in fifteen minutes." The phone went silent.

———

The three men who arrived at the restaurant with Professor Strozzi all wore jackets, despite the heat. They looked around for a moment, and I could tell they were professionals sizing up the room. They came straight to me. Strozzi entered behind them and nodded to them that it was me. They motioned me to follow them to the front door, and after sending one man ahead to check the street, they surrounded Strozzi and me as we all walked quickly toward the steps that led down to the water. We loaded onto a gleaming wooden powerboat, and within seconds were on the Grande Canal, slicing the smooth water into a giant V that rolled into the parked boats on either side, lifting them up and down like a series of heads nodding at our passing, the engine noise rumbling low and powerful and menacing as it echoed off the stone canal walls.

Weaving through water taxis and gondolas, we soon docked near the professor's office. A man walked on either side of us, with one in front. All three scanned everything around us. It was obvious they were professional security, but I couldn't imagine how the Professor had found them in minutes. Two of them stood outside on the sidewalk while one stayed just outside the Professor's office door.

"First, we make copies of the tapes," Professor Strozzi said as he placed the tapes into a deck on a shelf behind his desk. "I already had a grad student copy the film for me." He removed the original film canister from a desk drawer and handed it to me, noticing my look of panic. I hadn't told anyone of the DVD copy.

"Don't worry, she didn't watch the film. She is a niece of a cousin and part of the family business. She is discreet."

Professor Strozzi pressed a couple of buttons, and I could hear the tapes humming. The high-speed recorder clicked off in a few seconds. He placed a second tape in the machine.

"How can we find Kristine?" I asked him.

"They will call soon. Where is the cell phone?"

"Who are those guys outside?" I said, as I held up the phone.

"The tall one near the door is my grandson, Nick. Named for me," he said. "He runs the family gondolier service."

"They look like security guys."

He smiled that smile we all know means *you're close to the truth, but I don't want to talk about it.* He motioned for me to sit down. He pulled a chair around in front of me and sat down, too, leaning forward with his hands on his knees. "Matthew, these men perform many services for our family. We often need security that the local police cannot manage. If we are to get your Kristine back, these are the men who can do so. But that must be your call. Your other call would be the police."

"Should we go to the local authorities?"

He smiled again, and I felt like a child. "Matthew, that is of course your option and perhaps the best one. But from what you have told me, do you really think that's a good idea? That bell cannot be unrung. Your government can reach out to the government here. All of these men with us are former military. All are well trained. Our security in my family and in our business is never left to the authorities."

"If it were you, Professor Strozzi, and your girlfriend were taken, what would you do?"

"Matt, please do not think me some kind of lawless person. I am not that. But I would rely on men who are only concerned with getting her back safely and nothing else."

"Okay, you're right. I just don't know what to do."

"Then we'll just have to make a plan." He walked to the door and whispered something to Nick, who came inside with us.

"You may need this," Nick said, handing me a Berretta 380 from his coat pocket. "Do you know how to use a gun?"

I nodded, immediately wondering if this was really the right thing to do. "Yes, I've been shooting many times with my father as a child, and recently I did a little target practice. And I have this, which I prefer."

I handed him back the three-eighty and pulled the other Beretta forty caliber from the back of my belt and held it out.

He and Professor Strozzi's eyebrows rose exactly the same way when they turned toward each other, almost mirror images, but Strozzi also laughed. "Matt, you continue to surprise me," he said. "I won't ask how you got this in Italy, but at least we know you are resourceful."

Nick took the gun, removed the clip, and pulled the receiver to eject the bullet. "Police grade," he mumbled, as if talking to himself as he turned the gun over in his hand to read the information stamped into the barrel. He inspected the bullets and reloaded the gun, apparently satisfied everything was in good order. He left the room for less than a minute and came back in to hand me something. "Here's another clip." It was full. Same bullets. Same caliber.

I noticed his accent was almost flat and English was comfortable to him. He could have been from anywhere in Europe, even the U.K.

Professor Strozzi motioned for us to sit at a small round table. "My grandson Nick was educated in New York. Columbia. You notice his English is good, no? Then he served seven years in Aosta down in Sicily, part of a cavalry unit of the Italian Army. He specialized in planning ground assaults. Now he manages security for the family businesses. He can help us find Kristine and get her back."

An hour later, we had a plan. Nick left. The Professor flipped open his phone and began making telephone calls.

A small woman knocked at the door and brought in a coffee service she arranged on a side table.

"Ti ringrazio tanto, Giulia." Professor Strozzi said to her as he walked to the table. She nodded and left without speaking. He poured us each a cup of the steaming dark coffee.

———

We sat at the table for another fifteen minutes before the cell phone rang. I picked it up and looked at Professor Strozzi. He nodded, and I opened the phone and said, "This is Matt." The conversation was short, though not really a conversation. More like instructions. The voice named a time and place to exchange Kristine for the film and tapes. He didn't make threats or yell, but the tone of his voice almost made me nauseous. The person on the line was not someone I knew, but he was all business. Cold as a flagpole in winter.

chapter 32

It's funny the things I remember. The smell of fresh-baked bread blew in on the breeze from the west, but I never saw a bakery or a restaurant. Three stories above me a woman shook a rug out a small window. A dust cloud hovered around her in the still air. The sidewalks were almost empty, unusual for anywhere I had been in Venice, with just one older couple holding hands and walking away from me several doors down.

I eased up to the shadow at the corner of a marble block building, sliding along the stone to brace myself to spy at the corner. The surface of the stone was like fine sandpaper, which I'd learned happened when rainwater dissolved CO_2 from pollution and reacted with the elements in marble. Ruskin would be horrified to know how pollution was finishing the job of gradually destroying the beauty of the buildings he so fought to protect from neglect. I recognized the material as Istrian Stone, which Professor Strozzi had taught me to be aware of because it was the most widely used marble in Venice and was quarried nearby in the town of Trieste. Funny what goes through your head when you most need to concentrate.

The building had once been some kind of office building I thought, though it now appeared empty. Seeing nothing alarming, I stepped around the corner into direct sunlight that made it impossible to see well for a few seconds. I held my hand above my eyes, searching the rooftops and windows, and looking into the side streets. Dust from the woman's rug glittered in the sunlight.

They had Kristine, and I could think of no other option but to meet with the kidnappers, whoever they were, who demanded I bring the tapes and the film. Strozzi and Nick had agreed. I began walking toward the bridge where I'd been told to wait. I hoped Professor Strozzi was right about how good his nephew was at planning missions.

I stopped at the edge of the arched pedestrian bridge. There were seven steps. Each step was rounded at the leading edge from hundreds of years of people walking on them. Another useless detail that sticks in my memory.

Two men stepped out from a side street half a block down, each holding one of Kristine's arms as she stumbled along between them. Both men wore dark suits and white shirts, unbuttoned at the neck, no ties. They had the same short haircut, almost a flattop but shorter. They were wide at the shoulders and with thighs thick as telephone poles. At this distance, they could be twins. I didn't think I could pull Kristine from their grasp, and if any of Nick's guys were close by, I couldn't see them.

Something was wrong with Kristine. Her hair was down over her face and her head tilted to the side. Her steps were uncertain, forcing the men almost to drag her. I forced myself not to yell, squeezing my fists as I realized she had been drugged. A third man stepped around them, hands in his pockets.

Harvey Sullivan, looking tired and haggard as his years, took a few steps in front of the men with Kristine and stopped, folding his arms across his chest.

"Hello Matt," he said. "I'm truly sorry it came to this. We tried to get you to turn over the film and just walk away with no problems. This didn't have to happen."

"You sack of shit," I yelled, surprising myself a little at how much anger I was feeling and how it erupted without thinking.

"Kristine is fine, Matt. We just gave her something for her own safety so she wouldn't do anything stupid," Sullivan answered, holding his hands out, palms up. "Just walk to the top of the bridge. We can get this over and you two can go."

I took a few steps up the incline, and the two men led Kristine toward the middle of the bridge.

Sullivan walked ahead of them. "Just put the tapes and the film on the street and step back. We'll let her go."

"Let me talk to her and make sure she's alright. You've proved you're a lying son of a bitch."

"Everything I told you was true, Matt. I may not have told everything, but what I did say was certainly true."

"Considering you tried to burn us alive in a hotel room, that's not very comforting or believable."

"That wasn't me," Sullivan said, shaking his head. "Ask her mother if you don't believe me." He looked down for a moment, as if talking with himself.

"Kristine, are you okay?"

She slowly nodded yes, but didn't speak. Muted laughter from children echoed faintly inside one of the nearby buildings.

I turned back to Sullivan. "If not you, then who was it? Who else knew we were in that hotel?"

"You have to ask your mother-in-law about that. Not a word of this came from me. I meant it when I said I owed Marshall. Your dad saved my life. I haven't forgotten it, but this is bigger than you and me."

I stepped up right in front of Sullivan, looking over his shoulder at Kristine. Her eyes were narrow and focused. I could see she knew what was going on and was more aware than they realized. The anger was there, drugged or not.

"You have a great way of showing your gratitude," I told Harvey.

"It's complicated."

I would have laughed if things hadn't been so scary right then.

"Then educate me if you want that film," I told him.

He smiled, with that look parents give a child when they know the kid's not likely going to listen to good advice. "We could just take it, you know."

"You don't think I'm stupid enough to just bring it here do you," I bluffed. The original film was in a new canister in the professor's office safe with the tapes, but the copy was in the original canister, which I carried in a thin plastic bag with a few tapes, tucked into the back of my belt.

He sighed. "We were told that Elvis had become an informant for Nixon. People thought it was a joke, but that fool John Finiator who was deputy narcotics director actually cut a side deal and had Elvis sending him reports. It was Finiator's way to be a big shot in Vegas, get tickets, rooms, stuff like that. He didn't realize Elvis would actually find things to report. Elvis used his friendships in Vegas to get close to certain people, and somehow he stumbled across the guys we used for off-the-books jobs."

"So why kill Elvis? Why not just deny it? What proof could he have?"

"He was going public, and we were told he might have been wired during one meeting. He could have destroyed the entire agency. These guys were hooked up. They were the real mob, not just a bunch of hoods. The country wouldn't understand us working with them, and the country couldn't afford to have a security operation that was ineffective. What we did may have seemed wrong, but it was for the right reasons. And it worked."

"I don't believe my father and that team would have done that. You're still a liar."

"Marshall agreed after a while that it had to be done. We all did it once we were convinced this was for the country. But you're right. Not everyone could go through with it."

"What do you mean?"

"One team member began to think the whole thing just wasn't right, that there was more to the story. First your father. Then Jim Robinson wanted to back out."

My head was spinning to hear someone say it, though I already knew. Jim. My father. Who else was on that team? "Were you the fourth person on that film?" I asked him, putting my finger on his chest and leaning into him.

He brushed my hand away. "You're asking the wrong question, Matt. Yes, I was the fourth, but the question is who was the fifth? Who shot the film? And who signed the order?"

"Why is it important who shot it?"

He laughed. "Do you really think Eleanor was a secretary?"

Behind Harvey, I saw Kristine lift her head. Her eyes were suddenly wide open, and she strained against the men holding her arms.

"Eleanor was part of this?" I asked, unsure of the implications.

"Jeez, Matt, why do you think she wants that film as much

as I do?"

"To protect all your asses. That much is clear."

"Believe me, that's not the whole story." Harvey turned his head at the sound of a low, rumbling hum of a gasoline engine barely above an idle. A water taxi entered the canal two blocks down from the bridge, gliding through the glass-smooth water as if on rollers, leaving a widening V behind it to roll up against brick walls on both sides of the canal. He stared at the taxi for a few seconds and then looked back at me.

It was time to move. "If you want the film and the tapes and my silence, I want the whole story. No lies, no smoke. Right now. That's not too much to ask."

He looked at me hard, just standing there for a few seconds. He sighed. "Jim Robinson couldn't do it," Sullivan finally said. "Couldn't take out the target. He crossed the line and let it be personal. He realized the whole thing was cooked up by Leopold, who headed up the unit. Leopold was the one who would have lost funding and, worse, maybe gone down for cutting deals with organized crime to do our dirty work in exchange for not chasing certain cases. Careers, lives, and maybe the protection of the country were on the line."

It still made no sense to me. "But you did go through with it."

"Not really. Jim changed the drug without telling any of us. He was our chemist. Elvis didn't die."

My head thundered with the sound of horses running. "What do you mean he didn't die? I saw the damn film."

Sullivan went on. "Elvis was unconscious. Jim took his pulse and told us he was dead, but Jim had set it up for Mark Pugh to come back after we left and split up."

"Mark Pugh? He was involved?"

"Mark put Elvis into hiding and faked the death, but for years only Mark and Jim knew, and maybe some others they recruited to help later. At least that's what I heard."

"That all seems impossible to coordinate."

"Not really. They'd had almost a month to set it up, and the plan worked. No one knew, at least for a while. But nothing that big can stay a secret without working at it. And luck. Now I've told you everything, so let's get on with it."

The pieces were there, but I couldn't quite make them fit. My father's wreck. My mother's murder. Mom's insistence that "they" had killed dad made more sense, but who they were was not completely clear. Dad's note and plans he made after getting sober. The film of Elvis dying. All the sightings of Elvis over the years. Now the revelation that Elvis hadn't been killed.

Harvey walked to the side of the bridge and looked down as the taxi cruised slowly under the bridge. I thought of all the books I'd read about Elvis and how the body weight at the autopsy didn't fit, how people said it was a wax replica in the casket. How a photo taken weeks after the death seemed to show Elvis behind a glass door.

I wanted to hold Kristine, to give Harvey the tapes and film and get out of there. But I knew this had to end right here. If we were ever to be safe again, I had to know the whole story.

"One more thing. Why was my father killed?"

"Matt, I loved your father. I promise you I had nothing to do with that."

"That's not what I asked. Why?"

Sullivan looked at me like I had two heads. I waited.

"He figured it out, Matt. Can't you see that? He became a threat to someone. To everyone. Every person who was part of that unit or the brass who approved that godforsaken plan. From Eleanor on up. Leopold. Others above him. We never knew who had made Elvis a target to start with. We were just soldiers."

I needed the whole story and had to know. "But I don't see how he became a threat so much later. Who did he threaten?"

Sullivan looked back at the men holding Kristine, then stepped back up where his face was inches from mine. He was talking very low. "You saw how that whole thing destroyed Marshall. It ate him alive. Every day for years he thought about what happened. A few months ago, he figured it out. Began gathering the evidence. The film had been hidden in Jim's house. It disappeared one day without anyone leaving any evidence they'd even been there. Jim called me about it, and that's when I learned the story. Soon others knew that the film was back in play. Jim's little insurance policy got cashed in by Marshall, but no one imagined it was him at first. Not until he started showing up again, sober, did anyone suspect it was Marshall."

"My father really was going to tell the story?"

"Everything. For all I know he found Elvis drinking beer in some bar in Michigan."

"What about Mark Pugh? How did he fit in?"

Harvey was getting impatient with me. I could see it. He said, "No one has seen Mark for years. Some of us tried to contact him, but he disappeared from his home weeks ago, about the time your father had the wreck. We don't even know where he is. Now let's get this over."

I knew it was time. Now or never. "I want to talk to Kristine. I'll give you everything."

Harvey motioned the two men to bring Kristine over.

"I'll take her now," I said as I reached to hold her up.

Harvey nodded, and the two men stepped back a couple of steps.

"Now where are those tapes and film, Matt?"

I knew Harvey would have told me all of that story for only one reason. He knew I wouldn't be able to tell it. They would never let us leave here.

I put my hands on Kristine's shoulders and looked into her eyes. "Are you really okay?"

She said "Yes," but it was barely audible.

I hugged her, with my mouth near her ear and away from the side where Harvey was standing. "I need you to trust me," I whispered in her ear. "Do you understand? I need to know if you understand. They are not going to let us get away, but we have a plan."

"Enough talking. Let's get this done," Harvey said. "You see she's fine, now it's your turn."

I looked into her eyes to see if she could follow. She nodded, just enough to let me know she heard but not so Harvey could tell.

"I think she's going to throw up," I said, turning and walking her quickly to the edge of the bridge before Harvey could react. I reached behind me and pulled out the bag with the copies of the tapes and film, tossing it in front of Sullivan. "This is everything."

"Give me the copy, too. And don't BS me that you didn't make one."

I was glad I had thought to bring the DVD. I slid it out of my back pocket and laid it on the bag.

That was our signal.

Shots began popping down a side street. Harvey and the two

men dropped to the ground, guns suddenly appearing in their hands. The shots were in the air, but they wouldn't know it. At least not at first. I grabbed Kristine and pulled her over the side of the stone wall at the edge of the bridge, holding her hand as we both hit the water.

The water taxi that had just passed under the bridge spun around and sped back toward us. I pulled the Beretta from my pocket and pointed it up toward the bridge as three men leaned over the side. All three men on the bridge began firing, and I saw one of the two men in the boat beside me slump over. I fired until the gun was empty. When the water taxi reached us, one of the men above us on the bridge fell backwards and disappeared from sight. I dropped the pistol as I struggled to make sure Kristine could tread water. I was confused when I saw the second man slump over the wall above me and slide down out of sight.

The driver of the boat grabbed Kristine and pulled her onboard by both her arms. Harvey Sullivan stood above me on the bridge looking down. He raised his gun and slowly took aim at me, staring down the gun barrel. I realized it was too late for me to duck under water or swim away. Then his eyes grew wide, and his mouth opened in a large O as I heard a muted pop. He flinched just as he shot and missed me. The gun slipped from his hand. His chest grew red, and he fell forward to splash beside me, blood staining the water around him as he sank.

A second later, Eleanor Masters looked over the side of the bridge. Her face revealed nothing. No smile, no frown. She surveyed the scene and could tell her daughter was safe, and then she tossed a pistol that looked like an automatic with a silencer into the water near me and turned to walk away. I climbed into the water taxi and the boat lurched forward. As I looked back, I saw Eleanor raise her hands in the air. In seconds we were blocks away, making several turns down narrow canals, often where the passageway seemed to offer only inches of clearance on each side of the boat.

———

Within half an hour we were leaving Venice behind. Kristine's hair was pulled back into a ponytail, but it was still damp. Strozzi had told us of his men stopping Eleanor, but she had been allowed to go to her hotel after he confirmed who she was. The men were outside the hotel to be sure she was safe.

We both had on new sneakers, jeans and button-up shirts that didn't fit exactly right. But at least everything was dry. Diesel fumes burned my nostrils. From the deck of the barge where we sat, I watched the buildings of Venice grow smaller as they sank into the sea behind us, maybe five miles or so in the distance. The professor sat on a wooden crate in front of us, leaning forward with his elbows on his knees and with his hands clasped. Kristine and I sat on a stack of new two-by-fours held by a tight metal band. The pine smelled fresh.

The professor explained his plan. "Matthew, we have a car waiting when we arrive at the docks in Chioggia in about 15 or 20 minutes. The driver will take you to Firenze—Florence, you would say—where you will be perfectly safe at our family estate until we can decide what you need to do next."

"You're not coming?" I asked.

"I have some things to take care of first. I'll be there only a few hours behind you. It's an easy drive, about 250 kilometers, straight down through Bologna. You'll be there in three hours, but my sister will get you settled in when you arrive."

Kristine put her hand on my arm. "I need to call my mother," she said.

Professor Strozzi handed her a small cell phone from his coat pocket. "This phone will be safe to use. I'll go check with the Captain to be sure the car is ready for you. I can tell you that your mother is safe."

———

Kristine entered the number she had memorized, it being her only link to Winter. Her mother answered immediately.

"Mom, are you alright?"

Kristine nodded as she listened, swaying slightly.

I moved beside her and put my arm around her waist to steady her.

"He's here? You brought him here?"

She looked at me and shook her head that he wasn't here. I assumed she meant Winter.

Her mouth was open. "Germany? With whom? How could you leave him?"

Kristine listened again for a full minute, saying little other than "um hm" every now and then. Finally, she said, "Okay, you're right. I'll call you back in about three hours. We have a safe place to go."

Kristine held the phone tightly against her ear, nodding as if her mom could see her. Slowly, she said, "Mom, you'll just have to trust me this time. The same way I have trusted you." She flipped the phone closed.

The wind shifted, creating small waves that crashed into the front of the boat and caused a fine spray of salt mist that I could feel coating the side of my face. Exhaust fumes filled the air as we neared the mouth of a large harbor. Sail boats and power boats lined the docks on our left. Ahead were small commercial boats and barges loaded with various sizes of large, rusty containers, their bright orange long ago faded to almost peach.

Kristine turned to me. "My Uncle Shep has Winter in Munich. Mother thought she could protect him better outside the country."

I knew her uncle. A true tough guy when needed. He'd been a cop and then a railroad detective for Illinois Central. He was a big guy, intimidating if you didn't know how gentle of a person he could be. A good choice to protect Winter.

I asked, "Why was she here? And how did she find us?"

"Sullivan had asked her to help convince us to give up the film. She played along long enough to find out where they thought we were."

Kristine turned and looked toward the front of the boat, but her eyes did not seem to be focused on anything specific. She said, "You know, all that stuff from Harvey turned out to be true. Your dad really wasn't anything like an accountant."

I was puzzled. "Yeah, that's obvious now."

"And Mom wasn't a secretary, either. She said she was the fifth member of the team, the shooter, she called herself. She shot the film."

"She shot more than film."

"What do you mean?" Kristine asked. I realized she hadn't seen all that happened on the bridge. Just that her mother had been there.

I took her hand. "She shot Harvey. She saved my life."

Kristine shook her head, trying to make sense of it all. "My mother shot Harvey? They were close friends."

"I saw it. He was a second away from shooting me. What I don't understand is why she was with the group after us. Surely she knew they planned to kill us. They had already failed once."

"She said she thought she could protect us from the inside. But she figured out that Sullivan was only after the film," she said, standing up and facing me.

"I don't understand why she didn't try to warn us."

"She had just learned where we were. They traced our Internet searches. You were right. She knew they would kill us both once they got the film and tapes. She came here to try to get us out. And now she can't go home either until we expose the rest of them. She says she can help us."

Professor Strozzi walked up. I turned to him. "Professor, one of your men was shot. I'm so sorry."

"He will be fine," he said, removing a handkerchief from his pants pocket and blotting sweat delicately on his forehead. "But we have other issues now, do we not?"

"We've got to get our son Winter out of Germany," I told him. "He's with an uncle. A retired cop."

"Yes, of course. I can arrange it. Tell your mother to speak with my men at the hotel. Just tell them where your son is and who is keeping him."

"And Kristine's mom. You can arrange for her to meet us?"

He smiled his big smile, as always. "Matt, we will arrange for her to meet you. For now, she is safe. My nephew's men followed her and stopped her right after they saw her shoot one of the men shooting at you. They are outside the hotel where she is right now, making sure she is safe from harm."

Professor Strozzi took Kristine's hand. "I can help get you all back together in a very safe place."

"How can any place be safe from these people," Kristine asked, less confident than I had seen her before.

The Professor patted the back of her hand. "Do not worry. We will bring them to Palazzo Della Bella Luce, not far from Florence. It has been our family home since the mid-16th century, built to try to outdo the Medici's Piazza Pitti. You would call it 'keeping up with the Joneses.' No one can reach you there."

"But this is the government, Professor," Kristine said, needing his assurance.

Professor Strozzi said, "When the family built this home centuries ago, Kristine, everyone had to take care of their own protection. The police weren't there to guard you then. Now don't worry, you will be my guests until we figure this out."

chapter 33

After Venice, the pieces began to fall into place. Though the story may never be fully understood or told, we continue to fill in the blanks. We've learned there are lots of agendas, and different people want my film for different reasons, though they all seem personal and not about protecting NSEO or the United States.

We've been staying at Palazzo Della Bella Luce for nearly two weeks as I try to finish telling Dad's story on tape. The Professor's nephew recovered the tapes, film, and DVD from the bridge for me, so I have what I need. We're trying to decide our next steps, but for now the focus is to finish telling what I know and to get that and the film to Peter Thomas. Along the way, I'll have to figure out Kristine and Winter and me.

Professor Strozzi proved himself a gracious and kind person to bring us here and make sure we are safe. I have learned something about friendship from this man, though I barely know him, if the truth be known. He says it was just the right thing to do, but I'm not certain I'll ever be able to really understand why he has helped us so much and why he continues to take such risks for us.

Kristine's mom and Winter have their own rooms across the hall from each other and seem to be busy with a game or making a pie or something all the time. It's clear that Eleanor adores Winter. I can see now why she also risked so much to help. I spend time daily trying to trace the activities of Dad's unit so I can finalize these tapes. Peter and I email once in a while, and he is anxious to hear the tapes. Sometimes I ask Eleanor about Dad's work to help me speed up finishing the tapes, but she doesn't like to talk about it. I guess I can see why. But I think she has finally forgiven me for running off and leaving, or at least she understands now.

Winter and I are getting to know each other, and after only one week we had already found ways to do boy stuff like walking the huge property, skipping stones on the pond, or discovering animal tracks along the creek. Kristine and I sat down with him last week and told him the truth. That I was his father. He was amazing. His questions about why I had been away were perfect. The tougher questions were why I was back and what it meant for him and his mom. We did our best to explain that I had to do things that took me away, but now we had a chance to be a family. I told him he could ask me anything, and he keeps asking really tough questions, but I guess I deserve it.

The weather is changing as fall settles in. One cool morning a couple of days ago, Kristine and I were sitting in a lush garden, surrounded by a stand of lemon trees on one side and bamboo on the other. A fountain bubbled nearby, covered in water lilies and with sculptures of fish dancing across the surface. This is not the world I come from, and I know it can't go on, but for now it seems strangely right.

Professor Strozzi walked through the gardens as he does each morning. When he saw us, he turned from his usual path and stopped to talk. "Matthew, you must be important." He smiled.

"Okay, I'll bite. What do mean, Professor?"

"The Italian government has quietly contacted me. It seems

someone in your government believes I may have information about a certain fugitive from the United States, sought by the NSEO and FBI. Murder, theft of secret materials. Much intrigue." He raised his eyebrows, feigning surprise and shock. He was enjoying himself, rubbing his hands together as if planning dastardly deeds.

I was alarmed, of course, but not sure what to say or do.

He could see I was speechless. He held up his hand. "Fear not, friend. No one will show up here, at least not for a while. These friends in the Italian government will say nothing. But I'm thinking perhaps it may be time to find you a place you can take your family and stay anonymous for a bit longer. Are you nearing the end of your tale?"

"Actually, sir, I think we have the tapes about finished. I just need a few more days to wrap it up."

He removed a folded map from his back pocket and spread the map on the ground in front of our bench before he kneeled and pointed to a spot. "I have a wonderful place in mind if you are comfortable being the guest of my family. You can stay as long as you like."

I had no plan, but this was unexpected. Kristine and I leaned over to scan the map.

I was speechless again. "It's too much, Professor. You have been so kind and generous. We can't just live off your friendship."

"Nonsense," he said, sounding genuinely offended. "We are friends, and I can do no less than keep you safe."

"But we're not even paying for our food, and we're in no position to repay such hospitality. I left all our money in the safe at La Calcina."

He stood up, easily I thought for someone his age, sat between us on the stone bench and put his arms around both of us. "Please. Let's not talk of this as a problem. Your money will be returned, and you are not a burden in any way. I am having much delight in hearing all of your story and seeing your family together. If anything, I owe you for creating such an interesting time in an old man's life. Now I will hear no more of this."

I looked at Kristine and shrugged. "Thank you, Professor. But as soon as we know things are safer for us, we need to figure out where to go on our own."

"Excellent. You will leave when the time is right, and until then we will speak of this no more." He stood and walked a few steps, paused, then turned around and looked back and forth between us. "It's clear you like horses. The new place we want you to go is the ranch where we breed our wonderful horses that my family so loves. Even better horses and trails than here. You can ride them every day if you like."

Kristine and I looked at each other, speechless.

———

That afternoon I thought about the other big issue I'd been avoiding. Kristine and me. I knew it had to come to a head now, before I moved her to yet another hiding place. As the day passed, I thought about the future. I could imagine no scenario without Kristine and Winter in my life.

Once or twice I had written out passages of John Ruskin books that made me think differently. I had run across one of them earlier that morning as I went through some notes I'd made, and I couldn't get it out of my head. He wrote, "It is advisable that a person know at least three things, where they are, where they are going, and what they had best do under the circumstances."

What should I best do under the circumstances? I sat outside and drank coffee at a table and forced myself to answer his three questions.

After agreeing that we would accept more help from the Professor, I focused entirely on deciding what I wanted, what she wanted, and what Winter needed. I wasn't very accustomed to working out that last issue. During dinner, I asked Kristine if she would again walk the garden path with me after we finished. We loved the worn stone walkway, each stone bordered by a narrow strip of bright green moss that joined them into a path smooth even to bare feet, meandering through flower beds around the inside of a huge stone and metal fence.

Italians love after-dinner drinks. Clear, strong-tasting Grappa, made like brandy from the grape peels left over after wine-making. Not my favorite. Or Sambucca, another strong clear liquid that I had learned to like when flavored with a coffee bean they ignite as it floats on top. Tonight, Professor Strozzi poured us a chilled glass of limoncello, a yellow-colored lemon liqueur that was his favorite. He served Pallini brand this time, though he seemed to have dozens of different brands. I think he favored Pallini because some Strozzi cousin back in the 1800s had married into the Pallini family, and today many Strozzis lived in the village of Antrodoco where limoncello was first made.

Kristine and I excused ourselves after a few sips and carried our glasses with us.

I was nervous, so I didn't want to stall and make it even more awkward. As soon as we entered the first garden, I started talking.

A quarter moon was visible on the horizon.

"Kristine, I've been trying to figure out where this goes. All of this."

"You mean how we get out of this mess?"

"No, more than that. Us. You and me. The future. After the mess is cleaned up."

She turned her head toward me and stopped walking. "Is there a you and me? I don't come as a 'me' Matt, I come as a Winter and me."

I didn't know how to answer exactly, so I just said it as straightforward as I could. "If it's up to me, there is an us. My past failures aside, I have never loved anyone else. And I love Winter. I want to help raise him. I want to call him my son, but I know I haven't earned that yet. I just want that chance."

"So, you love me?" she asked. "Tell me something, Matt. Is this a new love or an old love?" She still hadn't moved. Her question was serious. "Sometimes when people are thrown together in a bad situation, they may think they have feelings that aren't necessarily real."

She let me take her hand, and I stepped closer to her. "I made a mistake eight years ago. I had no plan, no idea about the future. I was a kid. I didn't know how important you were to me then."

"Do you now? I'm not sure."

"I know this much. When this is over, I want to be with you and Winter. I want to be a father and am truly finding I love him. I want to be with you," I told her.

She pulled her hand away and walked on down the path, saying nothing.

At first, I almost panicked. I caught up and walked beside

her, waiting. I realized she was not angry when she looked at me and smiled. We sipped our limoncello and wound our way down the path.

After a few minutes, we came to a stone bench. She sat down and motioned me over to sit. She put her hand on my chest. "Are you sure you want this?"

"I'm sure."

She nodded and looked away, obviously thinking.

I waited.

Minutes went by. I could see her vaguely smiling, not really a big smile, but with a look that seemed contented.

She held my gaze for a few seconds. "Okay, we'll be a family."

"I want to get married," I told her. "Will you marry me?"

Now she laughed. "You're pushing it, aren't you? You're just all in, all the time now, aren't you?"

I shrugged, feeling a tiny bit embarrassed.

"Yes, I'll marry you. But there is one thing."

"Anything."

"I never answered you earlier."

"What?" I didn't know what she meant.

"About what kind of man you would be if you didn't finish this thing. Yes, I know you have to finish it. With tapes or whatever you have to do. Otherwise, you will never be able to live with yourself … and you would not be the father I want for Winter. Just finish it. Do whatever you have to do. Then come get us."

chapter 34

After Kristine said she knew I had to finish the tapes and get closure, I became certain it was time to move on, time to turn the page, to start a new chapter, whatever the hell they say. The tapes had to go out to Peter, to go out into the world so I would know if there was more for me to do. I more or less locked myself away for two days, determined to wrap up the story. Besides, I had made a deal with Peter, and I would have to honor it. Peter thinks this is how I get my life back. I don't know if this is right, but I expect myself to do something, and equally important, I know Kristine expects me to finish this, one way or another.

I chose to work in a tiny study on the second floor at the end of a long hallway. A wooden desk not much bigger than a suitcase with a comfortable straightback chair sat pushed against a window. I could see out over the back garden and watch Winter playing or others walking the pathways or lunching on salads at the long table on the patio, one of the bottomless pitchers of lemonade from Bella on the table.

The walls of my little study had two small paintings of landscapes with distant mountains behind rolling hills and farms and a larger one of a hunting scene, my favorite. A group of men on horseback, dressed in colorful formal hunt clothes carried shotguns over their laps. Men with long sticks walked in front of the hunters through a field of high grass to flush pheasants, which the flushers gathered as the birds were shot, tied leather thongs around their claws, and slung the pheasants over their shoulders. Three small white and brown dogs ran circles around the men beating the tall grass. I stared at that painting for hours as I thought about the events in my own life I was trying to remember accurately.

Mid-morning on the third day, a sunny day, I walked into the garden and knew my task was finished, having worked through the night for the past two nights. Kristine, Eleanor, and Winter were together. Eleanor and Winter were on separate swings. Kristine pushed our son, whose small fists gripped the ropes tightly. He squealed when she pushed him high.

"Is that it?" Eleanor said, seeing the package in my hand. She dragged her feet on the ground to stop her momentum.

Kristine turned around, a look of hope in her eyes.

"It's ready to ship," I said.

Kristine let Winter swing on his own. Mother and daughter looked at me with the same expression on their faces, the reality of knowing a dark phase of our lives had ended.

Eleanor said, "I need to go to town anyway, so I'll ship it for you. Is the film and everything there?"

"Yeah, it's all here. Wrapped and addressed. Ready to go. But I can run it down to the UPS store. You don't need to."

"No, I insist. This is a big day. Why don't you take Kris and Winter for a picnic or something to celebrate?"

Winter hopped out of his swing. "Yeah, a picnic!" he said as he ran up to me and tugged at my arm. "Can we?"

Who can say no to his eight-year old child whose entire life he had missed?

"If you don't' mind, Eleanor, that would be great," I said, handing her the box. "It's already addressed. The tapes and the film are in the box."

She took the box and started toward her room. "I'll change into something more appropriate for town and go now to be certain the shipment gets out today."

Kristine and I stopped by the kitchen to have a picnic prepared. The cook, a fabulous woman everyone called Mama Carmela, though I don't think she could have been more than forty-five or fifty, loved to make us picnic baskets. She always hugged Winter and called him, in her heavily accented English, "Her little Agnello." Baby Lamb, I think it means.

We had the stable master saddle two horses for us. Winter would ride behind me as we ambled the two miles to a high spot above a river that had become my favorite place on the ranch. Our packs stuffed with food and blankets were tied behind Kristine. She had taken quickly to riding and seemed at ease as she mounted the hunter hack, as we learned to call him, a tall, gleaming black horse with white at the bottom of his legs. Her horse, like mine, was retired from the shows where he had apparently won many awards for jumping.

It's hard to describe the feeling I had as we sat on the horses ready to head out for a ride and a picnic on that perfect afternoon that this might be the best day of my life. The past would now stay in the past. An ugly chapter would be closed. And the future was a family life beyond anything I had ever dared dream.

As I sat in the saddle and waited for the gate, I saw Eleanor drive down the winding gravel drive to leave. And something bothered me. I felt I needed to tell her something. Then I realized it. She had not said a word about the box being labeled to David Collier. I had mentioned to no one the plan to send the package to David, as Peter felt that his mail was no longer safe. David was to personally deliver it, but all I had ever talked about was sending the tapes to Peter. No one else knew the plan. I remembered Eleanor staring at the label when I handed it to her, but she said nothing. Why? She should have at least asked about it, but she seemed in such a hurry. Something wasn't right.

"Stay here," I yelled to Kristine, as I turned my horse toward the front. He easily jumped over the low stone wall separating the front and back yards and galloped toward the front gate, but we were not even halfway down the mile-long drive when Eleanor reached the highway and was gone. I stopped and watched the big iron gates close behind her, just as a black Mercedes sped past going her direction.

I rode back to Kristine and told her I had forgotten something on the address and jumped down, handing the reins to the stable boy. I didn't wait to answer the questions she shouted at my back as I ran to the other car parked in front. As I drove to town, I felt something was missing from the picture, but I didn't know what. The knot I felt in my stomach let me know I was right, even if my brain couldn't catch up.

The highway was virtually free of cars, so I made good time. I couldn't have been more than two or three miles behind Eleanor. In ten minutes, I reached the edge of the city and dodged between cars as I made my way to the Mail Boxes Etc. store where we received mail and had shipped things a couple of times already.

I was a block away when I saw Eleanor on the sidewalk, arguing with a broad-shouldered gray-haired man I instantly recognized as

Mark Pugh, my Suit. Here of all places. It didn't make sense. They were standing almost nose to nose. I heard a pop and saw Mark fall backward and grab his shoulder. Eleanor had a pistol in her hand. She turned to walk away. Although he was on the ground and I could see blood spreading over the front of his shirt, Mark raised his gun and fired. Eleanor dropped to her knees and leaned into the building. The box was in her hand.

In that moment, I realized Mark had been the other person who kept showing up. It may have been him who killed Jim and maybe Bugs. But why? I had thought he was one of the good guys.

Without thinking much about it, I drove straight at Mark and slammed on brakes right beside him. I opened my door into him to knock him backward and stepped out almost on top of him. He was on his back as I kicked the gun away from his hand and stood on his wrist. His eyes were open, but he was not resisting in any way. He lay back and just stared up, blinking. He didn't look like he could resist or run away.

I walked over to Eleanor to see if I could help her. Her eyes were closed.

I heard Mark behind me, wheezing, but speaking loud enough to hear, "It was her."

I ignored him and kneeled on the warm sidewalk. Eleanor was bleeding high on both the front and back of the right side of her chest where the bullet passed through. I pressed my hands against the wounds. I could already hear the sound of sirens and knew she would get help soon, but it looked bad.

People gathered around, and a young woman pressed a handkerchief against Eleanor's wounds. I eased her backward to the sidewalk and saw her eyes open, but she said nothing.

Over my shoulder, I watched Mark try to stand up. "Press very hard on both of these places," I said to the girl. "Do you understand me?"

She nodded yes.

I walked back to Mark and pushed him down with my foot. "You're not going anywhere."

He smiled, though the grimace from pain was there in the background. "It was her all along, Matt."

"Yeah right, so you shot her to keep her from helping me?"

"Read the address. I had followed her and confronted her once I realized nothing else made sense but for her to be at the center of all of this mess. I got a glimpse at the label. That's when I knew it was her. Don't believe me? Just go read the address on the box. I'm betting that's the film."

I walked over and picked up the box. My label had been covered over with another.

It read C.R. Leopold, at a D.C. post office box.

chapter 35

Mark Pugh sat upright with his arm in a sling, his Marine posture a lifelong habit he couldn't break even in a hospital bed.

I dropped into the empty chair in the corner, and we just looked at each other. Finally, he spoke, "How is Eleanor?"

"Not good. Fifty-fifty maybe."

"I'm sorry about her. Honestly. It's not the way I wanted it to go down."

"Funny from the man who shot her."

"We were friends once."

I didn't respond. I was trying not to judge, but I didn't know how to put these pieces together. Friends turning on friends. Lies. Everyone with a hidden agenda. And there might still have been details I didn't know.

"Tell me what you know," he said.

I pulled the chair up near his bed.

"I was able to get into Eleanor's phone," I told him. "She had several texts from right before you caught up to her that I guess she didn't have time to delete."

"And?" he said.

"They were all to Leopold. Cryptic but clear. Her plan was to save Kristine and Winter, and she was squeezed in the middle. She told him that day that she had a way to get the film and my audio tapes. She'd send them, but Leopold had to call off anyone after her daughter and grandson."

"Nothing about you?"

"No, but he guaranteed the two of them would be fine. I think they still cared for each other in an odd way."

"I guess she knew she couldn't get you saved by the deal since you could still prove it all. Understandable under the circumstances."

I sat there not speaking, thinking about it. I was not used to deals where lives were bargained over like poker chips in a card game.

He leaned in and looked me sharply in the eye. "Leopold's promise to Eleanor wouldn't have worked. They would have been targets anyway, at least Kristine."

I knew he was right.

"What about your Dad? Have you finally figured out who he really was?"

I looked out the window, though all I could see was sky and treetops. "I guess I know more or less he didn't start out as a bad guy."

Pugh laughed. "Your father was a fine man. Never a bad guy. He didn't start out as one and didn't finish as one."

"I only know my father was a lifelong employee of the National Security Enforcement Office. I knew that growing up, but having a father who worked in an office and pushed paper all day wasn't that exciting, so I didn't pay much attention. From bureaucrat to drunk in sixty seconds wasn't impressive."

He chuckled. "He worked for a little-known department of the NSEO, the same one I worked for. One of those many Department of Justice offices we hardly ever hear about."

"Growing up, I just thought it was a joke when Dad and his friends referred to their group as the Bomb Squad."

"That was just our inside joke. Officially we referred to it as C-4, from Section C, Paragraph Four, of a Presidential Executive Order from President Eisenhower in 1960, authorizing the formation of the NSEO. This unit handled special security assignments for DOJ that didn't fit the FBI well," he explained. "There is so much more you will be surprised to learn about C4 and your dad. He did some important things."

"I keep hearing that," I said, remembering the funeral comments.

"What you didn't hear was who was running the show."

"What do you mean? And what was Jim talking about when he said the shooter was the key. Elvis wasn't shot."

"For someone who seems pretty sharp, you refuse to see what is right in front of you."

I was getting a little frustrated. "Just say it."

"Eleanor. It was Eleanor. It was all Eleanor. She wasn't the secretary. She was the boss, the direct line to Leopold. She was there that night and shot the film herself. *The shooter* was the term we always used."

I didn't know what to say.

He saw I was confused. "The plan was hers, Matt. She and Leopold cooked up the whole damn thing to take out Elvis. She wasn't just trying to get the film just for Leopold. She knew that the secret had to be buried for her, too, especially if she would have her family back, at least her daughter and grandson."

Two days later, Eleanor died. It took me another three days after the funeral to get up the nerve to tell Kristine the whole story, but she didn't doubt the details and said they made everything make sense. She took it hard, but perhaps better than I expected. She said to leave her alone.

After a week she came to me and said we have to move on, as a family. So we did.

———

I often wonder if the C-4 unit is even now in operation. The NSEO officially denied that such a unit has ever existed other than to manage support staff background checks for people working in the White House or the NSEO. They claimed its purpose was to relieve the FBI of the burden of handling this type of work for all of the DOJ.

chapter 36

Several weeks ago, about ten days after Eleanor died, we came here to a ranch where we can stay until things settle down a bit. We arrived by private air and were driven another forty-five minutes from the small-town airstrip. But that's all I'll say for now. The Professor's family owns the place, and he insisted on helping, as usual. He says we'll be safe, and his family has a few hundred years of practice at keeping the family away from bad guys. I don't doubt him.

The events in this story are told as I remember them, or the way they were told to me by people I trust. I filled hours and hours of audiocassettes trying to record the story, which I did eventually send to Peter Clay Thomas (through David Collier as I said earlier) hoping Peter would do his own research and then write a news story about what happened. He says you'll probably see this in a book.

Peter is a former investigative reporter well-known for revealing corruption in government in both Washington, D.C., and New York City. Kristine got it right when she said, "He reports the ugly truth about abuse of power in government as if he's just a weatherman reading off the highs and the lows."

Along with the audiotapes, I sent Peter the original of an 8mm home movie that was retrieved from the street after Eleanor was shot. I asked him to get film experts to verify what we now know depicts an attack and apparent murder of the world's most admired entertainer. I believe the actions of certain men and women of this unit represent the disturbing result of government agents doing the wrong thing in the name of doing good.

Peter turned over the audiotapes and original film to a Congressional subcommittee, but he says after one long interview no one has contacted him. An official investigation has begun, but for some reason no public reports have been filed. Who knows if we will ever hear from them again. The final decision of the truth of the events that I believe happened may be left to you. I know what happened to my family, but I'm sure I'll never know the whole story.

For reasons that are obvious, I plan to remain with my family in seclusion until I'm sure the right officials have had time to respond and make sure the people who did this are caught or dead. I have no idea what that really means in actual time. Or what I'll have to do if they fail.

———

We have plenty of cash from Dad's money, though most everything we need is provided, and the local town is so small, there's not much to buy, so we're fine without working for a while. I'm talking with Kristine about where she might like to live and jobs I think I would like to try. In a few weeks, we'll be getting out of here and on our own. I've told Professor Strozzi a couple of times that I'm not comfortable freeloading off him, but he just laughs and says to let a rich old man have some fun. That's the only time he's ever mentioned money, and most of the time he seems like a regular guy.

Kristine and I told Winter about getting married, but we're not setting a date just yet. Winter has a tutor for his home schooling. He's learning Italian, too. Kristine says he's picking up my mannerisms and sometimes sounds just like me. He certainly looks like me, now that my hair is dark again and longer. While he's very polite, well-mannered, and quiet, he's quick with a smile and loves to play jokes on people. I can tell he's still a little uncertain how he feels about me and how it works to share his mother's time with me, but I think we'll work it out. I'm teaching him to play pool. Kristine isn't so hot about that, but she tolerates it. For now, I'll just have to be patient and enjoy being with him. We laugh a lot, and that's a start.

I could not have been more wrong about my parents or the typical, dull middle-class lives I thought they led. Kristine can say the same thing about her mom. I can remember how as teens I just thought they didn't get it. They were such a drag, and Dad was just an abusive drunk I couldn't live around anymore.

All of my early tapes have already been delivered and made public. I decided to make one more tape and I'm winding it up now. Today, the last tape will be shipped to David and then to Peter to edit and get rid of the stuff that doesn't matter. After that, we'll just wait on the fireworks.

Right now, I'm watching Kristine as she looks out from a balcony that faces an incredible mountain vista. Or maybe it's a lake at the edge of a desert, but you'll understand if I don't actually describe it too closely, won't you? I will tell you horses run free here. And after seeing them every day, they never seem to visit me in my sleep any more.

The news over the months has been interesting. Recently, Agent Harvey Sullivan was honored posthumously for his service, after being killed in Venice several months ago. The official NSEO statement and news release on his death states that Agent Sullivan was killed at the hands of an unknown assailant while vacationing in Italy, with robbery as the motive. I also read that Agent Robert Hansen of the FBI was arrested for spying for the Soviet Union. I bet folks at the DOJ are hard to live with right now with all their children misbehaving.

Hearings on NSEO management have been scheduled and then postponed by Congress for some reason. The Department of Justice has announced an official inquiry after news reports surfaced claiming that certain members of the NSEO had executed covert operations never sanctioned by the agency, including what they called an "outrageous claim" that the agency was involved in the death of Elvis Presley. They say the report may take years. I can wait.

The NSEO denies that the little-known department in question ever conducted secret operations, as reported in an article by Peter Clay Thomas, and they continue to describe the group as responsible only for recruitment and screening of support staff. I'm sure their story will change when Peter starts releasing the meat of his story in the newspaper.

Coincidently, the NSEO head Leopold and several high-level agents from the department have recently resigned or retired. Investigations are ongoing by Special Prosecutors appointed by Congress, which doesn't seem to trust the DOJ to probe one of its own agencies. But the DOJ has refused to provide documents or emails.

Kristine and I talk often as she tries to sort out her emotions about her mom. While Eleanor may have done something that put me at risk, she did save my life once, and whatever she did was to protect my wife and son. I can forgive a lot for that. Kristine says she could not have faced Eleanor going to prison and that Eleanor would have chosen what happened if given the choice.

———

Just as I was starting to think my life would finally begin to move on from the strange events of the past several months, it all changed once again.

Mark Pugh had contacted me a week ago to say someone wanted to meet me. He said it was someone that felt he owed me and that it would be worth my time. Another part of Dad's team I figured. I knew Mark had very high-level government connections, but he wouldn't say who it was. All he would say is that this is the person who can help put the final pieces together for me. That I would know why my father and Jim and he did the things they each had done.

Around four in the afternoon, I was in the study, at the window, using binoculars to watch half a dozen horses at the far edge of a field. I'd seen them there a lot lately, romping and kicking and running. But today was different. They were not moving, just standing still and facing me. If I hadn't known better, I would have thought they were looking back at me. I felt a chill, and the hair on my arms stood up as the horses turned as a group and walked slowly toward the scrub trees lining the field, disappearing into the brush like early morning mist fading in sunlight.

I was still staring at the empty field when I heard gravel crunching under car tires. I looked up the driveway and saw a long white limo coming down the drive. The car stopped in front, and the rear door swung open before the small dust clouds around each tire had settled.

A leg with a glossy black cowboy boot slid from the back seat, and a man stepped out of the limo. He wore a light blue western-style suit with wide lapels sporting swirling white embroidery and a black cowboy hat that matched the boots. His face was covered by his hat as he stood there straight, hands on hips as he surveyed the front of the house.

Suddenly he reached up and pulled off the hat, running his other hand through his shoulder-length silver hair shining in the bright sunlight. When he looked up, he saw me staring down from my window. He smiled and shuffled his feet in a quick little dance. He struck a pose I'd seen before in film clips with his knees slightly bent. He turned sideways and pulled an imaginary pistol from his holster. He pointed his finger gun at me and fired the make-believe round, and then held his finger up and blew away the imaginary smoke. And with that smoke, all of my doubts.

Acknowledgments

I will always be grateful to Jeanie Thompson for reading the manuscript in its first iteration as an expose-style book of experimental fiction, convincing me the story was better told as a straightforward first-person narrative. Many thanks also to publisher Edward Garner of MindBridge Press for his keen insights into making a book that readers can enjoy and his thoughtful guidance once again. And special thanks to Anita Garner of MindBridge Press for her work as fiction editor, reading multiple drafts and providing her patient support despite my failure to understand that I can't insert a comma just because I took a breath in the middle of a sentence.

I feel very indebted to Rachele Rebughini of Personal Media in Milan, Italy, for her translations of Professor Strozzi and suggestions that transformed my literal translations into more realistic conversation. She had great patience with my efforts to use her native tongue. Any mistakes that made it through are all mine; the good stuff is hers.

Michael Coates read an early manuscript and provided encouragement to bring out the book. Merrijane Yerger also read an advance copy and provided helpful suggestions about where the reader might disconnect and told me to be more careful about where bullet wounds are placed. My sister Nan Shirley Auston supplied me with piles of Elvis clippings, books, and magazines that provided helpful background.

None of my writing would ever see the light of day without the support of my wife Virginia Shirley, who patiently suggested hundreds of times as the clock neared midnight that perhaps I should go to bed. Her reading and proofing of the manuscript offered valuable insights.

Of the many books I have been associated in some way or another with producing, the design of this one is my favorite by far. Books are like a favorite cocktail glass; the look and feel in a hand both of a tumbler and a book makes a difference in how we savor and experience the contents. My most heartfelt thanks go to James "Jimbo" Harwell for his fun and enticing cover design, to Felicia Kahn for an inviting interior book design, and to Virginia Shirley for the author photo.

To all the readers out there and to the booksellers who serve them well, I'll never for a moment forget that it is you folks who make this job possible and fun. Thanks especially to you indie booksellers who make a place for new voices to be discovered.

Philip

About the Author

Philip Shirley has published six books, including two novels and a collection of short fiction that was a finalist for the Jefferson Prize. He grew up in Alabama, living for six years in Monroeville, officially designated as the Literary Capital of Alabama. He presently splits time between Dauphin Island, Alabama, and The Town of Lost Rabbit in Mississippi.

Philipshirley.com
INSTAGRAM philipshirley
TWITTER @philipshirley
FACEBOOK @philipshirleybooks

The Graceland Conspiracy
Book Club Discussion Guide

The following overview, questions, and topics contain many spoilers for the plot. It would be best to avoid reading them until you have read the book.

The story begins in Birmingham, Alabama, as young Matthew Boykin stumbles across evidence that perhaps his parents were murdered. He had believed his father died from car wreck injuries and his mother from suicide a few days later. The author has described the novel as a coming-of-age story wrapped in a thriller. A series of murders by the rogue leadership of a government agency —all supposedly in the best interests of the country—provides a backdrop for the story. We find certain agents were somehow involved with the death of the King of Rock and Roll years before. Matt's father may have known the truth. Young Matt's search for answers puts him in jeopardy as he begins to put pieces together. What he learns becomes a threat to powerful people in high places. He reconnects with his old girlfriend, and they both become targets because they know too much. The young couple flees from unknown attackers, traveling through Texas to Mexico, then to Belgium and ultimately to a showdown in Italy as the puzzling truth comes together piece by piece.

1. Matthew Boykin is twenty seven when he "comes of age" in this story, having fled from home to get away from an alcoholic father years before. Have you experienced seeing anyone who has run from becoming an adult until their late twenties when circumstances force them to accept responsibility and finally grow up?

2. If you read the author's last novel *The White Lie*, you may have observed a common theme. Did you notice how he writes about people who are put into an unexpected and dangerous situation and their choices are to either flee or confront it head on? Doing nothing is never a choice for the characters. How does this reflect real life?

3. The author's style includes detailed, close observation of the surroundings, weather, gestures of people and other tiny details in most scenes. How did this establish a mood for the individual scenes? In this first-person narrative, which of the little things Matt observes helps you understand his character?

4. What was your initial response to the cover? How did it set your expectations for what you would find in the novel?

5. Matt gradually learns he has new responsibilities well beyond finding out who murdered his parents. How does his evolving character and efforts to rebuild his relationship with Kristine offer him redemption from his actions as a freshman in college when he abruptly left his family and friends behind?

6. Matthew and Kristine have a shared history. Do Matthew and Kristine share any traits?

7. Kristine certainly had to grow up faster than Matthew when she had their child. Did she do the right thing in fleeing with Matt as a way to minimize the danger for Winter? Is Kristine smart, brave, and capable? What actions/decisions show this? Describe any times in the novel when you questioned Kristine's decisions?

8. What did you learn from this book? Was the author's historical research important to the story? How did facts about the World War II history of Italy, the writings of Ruskin, Elvis' involvement with President Nixon's cabinet, and the underground crime economy add to the way you engaged with the story as a reader? Was the research done properly and did it provide proper setting for the story?

9. Why do you think the author was interested in writing this book? If you could ask him one thing about it, what would that be?

10. Did the book maintain the right amount of suspense to keep you interested? Which aspects of the suspense in this novel appeal to you as a reader?

11. The word 'conspiracy' is used often in the public and private dialogues of Americans. Does this fictional novel help explain how a small number of people in government agencies could use their positions to perform acts that have political motivations or acts which are outside the bounds of what we would want our public servants to do?

12. If this novel were made into a movie, who would you like to see play the roles of Kristine and Matthew? Who would you like to see play the role of Mark Pugh, who is important but only appears at the beginning and the end?

13. Did the ending leave you satisfied or hoping for something else? Was anything left unanswered? Should there be a follow-up book and, if so, what should it address?

14. Did you have a favorite scene? Or favorite quote?

15. Was Matt reliable in telling the story? Were there times you thought he didn't understand the situation well?

16. Matt changed throughout the story. Did you like the way his character evolved? Was it believable to see those changes?

17. There were numerous books about Elvis mentioned in *The Graceland Conspiracy.* Were you aware that these were actual published books? How did the way these were incorporated into the story help the plot move forward?

18. Have you seen photos of Elvis and President Nixon together? Did you know about this visit by Elvis to the White House?

Praise for other books by Philip Shirley

The White Lie

"Crime fiction of the highest order."

Marlin Barton, author of *The Cross Garden*

"Worthy of the late Elmore Leonard ... it's arresting and unforgettable."

Dayne Sherman, Author of *Welcome to the Fallen Paradise*

"Can stand by Grisham on any bookshelf."

Charles McNair, author of *Pickett's Charge*

"So enthralling that it can't be put down ..."

Mississippi Libraries

"A wild Southern ride of exciting twists and turns ..."

First Draft Magazine

Oh Don't You Cry For Me

"A memorable debut in the world of fiction."

Mark Childress, Author of *Georgia Bottoms*
And 2014 Winner of the Harper Lee Award

"Tales that can hold their own ... in the proud tradition of Southern Storytelling."

Sonny Brewer, Author and Editor of
Stories from the Blue Moon Café series

"Consistently great stories ..."

POP Matters

"A master story teller ..."

Portico

"Immensely enjoyable."

First Draft Magazine

"A superb collection."

Enter the Octopus